☑ W9-AZJ-200

NO MORE HEROES

A CAL INNES BOOK

NO
MORE
HEROES
Ray Banks

 HOUGHTON MIFFLIN HARCOURT   Boston / New York / 2010

First U.S. edition
Copyright © Ray Banks, 2008

ALL RIGHTS RESERVED

www.hmhbooks.com

First published in Great Britain in 2008
by Polygon, an imprint of Birlinn Ltd

Library of Congress Cataloging-in-Publication Data
Banks, Ray.
    No more heroes / Ray Banks. — 1st U.S. ed.
        p. cm.
    Originally published: Edinburgh : Polygon, 2008.
    "A Cal Innes Book."
    ISBN 978-0-15-101459-0
    1. Private investigators — Fiction. 2. Manchester
(England) — Fiction. I. Title.
PR6102.A65N6 2010
823'.92 — dc22   2009026621

Printed in the United States of America

DOC   10   9   8   7   6   5   4   3   2   1

Tom Waits interview quote courtesy of *NME*
(19 October 1985)

TO ANASTASIA,

all the stars make their wishes on her eyes . . .

'A hero ain't nothing but a sandwich. It's tough on the heroes, all they really want to do is strip you of your name, rank and serial number. It's like a hanging, a burlesque. It's spooky. They have you all dressed up with a hat on, make-up and a stick that goes up the back of your neck. Then they take a 12-gauge shotgun and blow your head off.'

TOM WAITS

PART ONE

✕✕✕✕✕✕✕✕✕✕✕✕

THIS TRAIN IS BOUND FOR GLORY

ONE

I've been staring at Daft Frank for the last five minutes, wondering why he hasn't turned into a puddle of sweat.

We're both sitting in the car with the windows rolled up, it's hot as fuck, and the air-conditioning in my Micra might as well be someone blowing on your face. But there's Frank, North Face jacket zipped to the throat.

It's annoying. Either he has ice for blood, or he's too simple to notice that he's burning up. Maybe he's just got big old pit stains on his shirt and he's too embarrassed to show me. Still, it won't get any better if he doesn't do something about it.

'Francis,' I say.

He doesn't say anything.

'You alright in that coat, mate?'

He turns his massive head towards me and blinks like a cow.

'Y'alright?' I say.

He returns his gaze to the street.

Hardly a satisfactory answer, that. So I keep watching him. He keeps trying to ignore me.

'I'm just asking, Francis, y'know, if you're a hundred per cent set on wearing that coat.'

Nothing.

'If you're warm,' I say. 'Are you warm?'

'I'm fine,' he says.

'It's just that you won't feel the benefit when you get outside.'

Frank's face puckers, but he still doesn't look at me. I can hear him moving in his jacket, though. Tensing up. Getting just that wee bit narked at having to share the car with me.

I start drumming on the dashboard, but I can't maintain the rhythm I've started. Keep trying, but I can go about thirty seconds before the beat goes wrong. Fuck it, I was never meant to be a drummer.

So I look at Frank again. He can feel me staring at him, I know it. And that irritates the fuck out of him, but he's such a Quaker, he won't do anything about it.

'Francis,' I say.

Silence.

'Francis, did you bring your colouring book?'

Frank shifts around again, his jacket making a swishing noise. A hurt look on his face. 'Okay, what's the problem?'

I stare straight ahead, watch the street. 'I don't know what you mean, Francis.'

'That,' he says. 'That Francis stuff. Everything.'

'I don't have a problem. Anyone round here's acting like they've forgotten their crayons, Francis, it's you.'

'See? That nipping at us. Don't think I haven't noticed, Cal. I'm not daft, y'know.'

Contrary to popular belief.

'No, Francis. You're not daft.'

There's a return to silence. I hear Frank turn back in his seat. And before long, I'm back to chewing the inside of my mouth again, so I stop. Shift around in my seat to get into my jeans pocket, pull out some gum.

It won't stop the cravings for long, but it'll have to do. I can't smoke in the car – *my* car, by the fucking way – because Frank's lungs can't take it, and he's now declared the motor a work environment. So the way Daft Frank tells it, if I choose to smoke in my own fucking car, I'm breaking the law and am liable to be fined up to fifty quid a cigarette. Sounds like a joke, but the man's serious. He brought a pamphlet in and everything.

So, it's a fucking sweatbox in here. And I can't smoke. If that wasn't enough, I have to put up with my back roaring at me.

Normally, I'd take a pill and let that work its magic, but every time I reach for the bottle, Frank gives me the old bovine eyes again, all disapproving.

I hate that look. Next time he does it, I'm going to tell him he looks like a special needs case.

Which he kind of is.

But Frank Collier wasn't Daft Frank until him and a couple of his wannabe gangster mates tried to knock off a Securicor van with a half-brick and a rounders bat. Reckoned they had it all worked out, knew when this particular van picked up from the new casino by Ordsall, had an escape route all planned, the lot.

So, not so daft, really. And fair play to him, Frank was one of the few who managed to grab a cash box and sprint up Regent Road with it. Course, he wasn't too fit back then. A diet of pints and bacon barms caught up with him – he'd hardly made it halfway up the road before his heart kicked at the inside of his chest and his lungs screamed for oxygen.

He sat the box down on a wall, leaned on his knees to get his breath back, and caught the exploding dye pack right in the face.

When the police found Frank, he was coughing his guts up, his face day-glo pink. Since then his sense of smell's gone for a Burton and he has the lungs of a life-long smoker. Some say the dye got into his brain, made him a bit tapped, which is where the Daft Frank thing came from.

And sometimes, Frank does nothing to prove those people wrong.

Like now, fiddling with the radio because he's bored.

'You can't blame me for being restless,' I tell him.

'Still no reason to take it out on me.'

I sniff some sweat up my nose. Mash my nostrils with the heel of my hand and sniff again. 'Fine. Fair enough.'

A pause as Frank processes that. 'Did you just apologise?'

'Whatever you need.'

Frank goes back to yipping through the stations and I concentrate on staring out of the window.

Someone starts singing, and I know the voice.

Saying that money talks, but it don't sing or dance, and it don't walk.

I look across at Frank. His lips are moving, but it isn't his voice. Frank nods his head, his eyes closed. His jacket rustles in time to the music coming from the radio, his arms moving like he's milking a really big cow.

It's too much for one man to take. So I kill the song and look out of the window.

'Whoa,' he says, 'what you doing turning off The Diamond?'

'The Diamond?'

'Yeah.'

I tap the side of my head and pull a face. 'You're not right in the fuckin' head, Frank.'

'What?'

'The *Diamond*. Jesus wept.'

'I get you,' he says. 'You've just got no taste.'

'I've got taste, mate. But we're on a job here. Say our boys turn up and see you fuckin' *dancing* in the car. Hardly going to shite it, are they?'

'Then I won't dance.'

'That's not the point, Francis.' I grab my cigarettes from the dashboard and Franks starts coughing.

One of those non-smoker, I-really-wish-you-wouldn't, hacking fits. False as you like.

'Relax,' I tell him. 'I won't light up till I'm out of the car, alright?'

Frank nods, and his cough winds down to a cleared throat. He rubs his mouth and says, 'I don't know that you should get out of the car, like. They might see you.'

'Then they see me. But I'm telling you, I can't stand it in here anymore – I need some fresh air.' I put the Embassy in my mouth.

He starts coughing again, louder this time.

'Illegal,' he says. 'I'm telling you –'

'Is it lit?' I say. 'Really, Francis, did I light the fuckin' thing?'

'No.'

'Then stow the theatrics, alright?'

A fist to his mouth, he says, 'Just making sure. I don't need you aggravating my condition.'

'Yeah, okay.'

I peel myself from the seat, get out of the car. It's cooler outside, but not by much. I light the cigarette, away from Frank's delicate lungs. Look across at the house we're supposed to be watching.

Two weeks on what Donald Plummer calls an 'accelerated procedure', and if this is accelerated, I'd hate to see slow. But then I don't know the first thing about evictions, I just do them for a living. All I know is how to slap a piece of paper into someone's hand and leg it back to the car.

Tag, you're it. No backsies.

Difficult when there's never anybody home, though. Which is the case with this student house. If it was up to me, I'd slip the eviction notice through the letterbox and be done with it, but Plummer's a people person. He prefers the personal touch. I know that because he tells me every time I whinge about the job.

I said to him: 'You want these people out of the property, Don, you take it to court like a human being.'

Make it the law's problem, right?

Wrong.

Plummer's got this jaded view of the legal system. He reckons Frank and I should share that view, seeing as we've both done time. It was the legal system that put us away, so we should be bitter. We're not, really, but that doesn't stop Plummer from banging on about it. He doesn't trust the law, and the reason he doesn't trust the law is because he's bent it enough times himself. The man's a smooth-talker, all mouth and expensive trousers. He doesn't like courts because every time he's appeared, it's as the defendant.

Someone's singing again. I glance inside the Micra. Frank is mouthing along to whatever's playing on the radio, but that's not where the singing is coming from.

Up the road. One loud, strangled song. Other voices joining in now. I check my watch: past kicking-out time.

Rap one knuckle on the window. 'You hear that, Frank?'

He sticks his head out, catches my cigarette smoke in the face. Starts waving his hands in front of his mouth, coughing and whooping like he took a chest full of mustard gas.

'You want to keep a lower profile?'

'You want to stop killing us with your smoke?'

'Shut up.' I jerk my head towards the noise, coming closer. 'You hear that?'

Stupid question, because the noise is impossible to miss now. Blokes, young, rowdy, singing at the top of their lungs. A chant more than a song, but there's a melody in there somewhere.

I flick the cigarette away, give the air a quick waft and get back into the car.

Coming round the corner now. Students. Definitely. Not so strange around here, but these lads are special.

I turn off the radio. Frank opens his mouth to moan at me, shuts it when I point through the windscreen at the new arrivals.

'D'you think –'

'Looks like we're on, Francis.'

TWO

It's definitely them. Three blokes, off their faces. Veering towards that very same house we've been watching for the past two weeks. Plummer told us it was a student property, but that it shouldn't be any trouble. From what Plummer could tell us, they're studying artsy subjects. It's the wannabe lawyers we need to watch out for.

'Don't let them give you any guff,' I say.

'Don already told us that.'

'Just making sure it stuck.'

'I'm not a spaz.'

'Never said you were.'

'You treat us like one.'

One of the students stops in front of the house. The other two crash into him. Laughter, mock martial arts, a couple of swaying poses. Looks like one of them actually knows how to fight, even if he is pissed.

I feel sick for a second. Hope he's not a guy I'll have to deal with.

Reckon the chief tenant is the student at the front door. The one holding his keys up to the other two.

He shouts, 'Tea and toast!'

The students head up the path, the front gate left swinging. Once the door's open, the three of them bottleneck in the doorway. A few seconds of shoving and swearing, and they spill into the house.

I wait for the front door to slam shut and a window to light up before I say, 'You got the paper?'

Frank looks at me, puzzled. 'No.'

'I gave it to you.'

Frank's face creases. He rustles around in his coat pocket.

'I gave it to you, because you wanted to hold onto it.'

'I didn't –'

'If you've lost it, Frank, just tell me. And then me and you can have some words about responsibility.'

Frank waves me off with one hand. Pulls out the official eviction notice with the other. The paper's all mangled. Frank reads it, still frowning.

'Give it here.'

'Could've sworn you had it.'

'See, that's why I treat you like a spaz, Francis.' I grab the paper, push open the driver door. ''Cause sometimes, mate, you fuckin' act like one.'

'Don't call us Francis.' Frank gets out of the car. Glares at me over the roof as he slams the door. 'You had the paper. You're the one Don gave it to. Just gave it back to me to mess with my head.'

'Okay, Frank. Whatever you say.'

'I'm just –'

'How's about we stop bickering and do the fuckin' job?'

Frank opens his mouth, then decides against saying anything. He nods.

'Now stay behind me and try to look like a hard bastard. Remember, no dancing.'

He laughs, and I reckon that's me and him mates again. Which is good, because appearances are everything, and if Frank doesn't look a hundred per cent hard, then we're both fucked. But if he's in character, it's a brave or shit-stupid bloke who'll mess with the big lad.

I lean on the doorbell until I hear movement from inside. The student who had the keys opens up. He's wearing a Dangermouse T-shirt, hipster jeans. Longish hair, tousled like a thousand bad guitar bands, and a three-day growth on his face and neck. Friendship band on his wrist. Right now he's shoving toast into his mouth and looking at me through half-lidded eyes.

'Y'alright?' I say.

He doesn't say anything. He's noticed Frank.

'You Simon' – I have to check the notice – 'Standish?'

He chews with his mouth open, looking at me. 'You what?'

Frank shuffles behind me. The student looks over my shoulder again, pushes the rest of his toast into his mouth, holds his fingers splayed and glistening.

'You renting this place?'

His eyes narrow. 'What's it about, like?'

Fuck it, that's good enough for me.

I slap the notice into his butter-drenched hand. 'Notice of eviction, Si. You have thirty days.'

Simon frowns, opens the piece of paper in his hand. 'You what?'

'Sorry.' I nod at Frank, turn away from the door.

The student puts his hand on my arm. I shake it off. Look down, and he's left a stain.

'We paid up,' he says.

'Doesn't make any difference to me.' I brush at my arm, then start walking again. I can hear Simon huffing behind me. Then he breaks into a short run, his voice trembling with the effort. 'Hold on, wait a second.'

'Take it up with Mr Plummer.'

Simon nips in front of us, his hands out. I back out of the way. That lad touches me again, I'll touch him right back. Or else get Frank to.

Simon thrusts the eviction notice at me like it's on fire.

'I don't want it back,' I tell him. 'You've got butter all over it.'

'No, we've been through this with Mr Plummer already, we've –'

'I don't make the rules, son.'

A flash of disgust. 'Who the fuck d'you think you're calling son?'

'I don't decide who to evict, do I? You want to complain about it, you take it up with Mr Plummer like I said.'

Simon mutters something, but I don't catch it. I try to dodge around him, but Simon hangs on, gets right in my face. The smell of booze on his breath means we're going to have a problem. This lad's had a long night in the pub and it's made him more than a little ballsy.

'We sort this out now,' he says.

'No, *we* don't, mate. *We* fuckin' leave it.'

His voice harder now. 'You're not going anywhere.'

'Here, don't get any ideas, mate. Don't make this difficult.'

'You alright, Si?'

A new voice. I turn, see someone in the doorway to the house. His silhouette, at least. From where I'm standing, it looks like he has one long arm.

I'm about to point that out to Frank when Simon blindsides me with a short, stinging punch to the ear. I duck and twist to one side. Frank lurches into Simon, grabs him in a hug that slams the wind out of him and keeps the lad's fists from swinging at anything but his sides.

'The fuck was that, Simon?' Rubbing my ear, trying to get the sting away, hissing in air, but the pain won't shift. 'Jesus, I'm just doing my fuckin' job here, man.'

Simon's face is twisted, his neck showing cords as he screams, 'Gaz, fucking do him!'

And then I realise as I turn towards the house, that lad, he doesn't have one long arm, he has a fucking baseball bat in his hand.

Gaz comes roaring out of the house, slams through the gate like a berserker, the bat raised high above his head. Obviously never swung in anger his entire life, but it won't take much practice. One lucky shot to a bloke's head is more than enough to put him down. But this guy's all over the place, the booze still in his system. Means he's way off-balance, but it also means he won't know when to stop swinging.

'Frank. Bat.'

He's still wrapped around Simon, can't see me. 'What?'

'Drop him and run.'

Gaz swings wild, slicing the air over my head as I drop to a crouch that spikes my back. I dig in, put my palms to the tarmac for balance and scramble out of the way as Gaz chops the bat once off the road. The vibration must've kicked a shock up his arms because he pauses. Shakes his hand out, adjusts his grip.

It's all the time I need to run to the car. I pull open the driver's door.

I shout at him, 'Frank, I'm telling you –'

Frank's broken the hug, and I see Simon stagger a few steps off to one side.

Turn back, and there's Gaz coming for me again.

I put up a warning hand. 'Hang fire a fuckin' second –'

Have to whip my hand out of the way as he swings at it. Then again, aiming for my head this time, but I shove the open driver's door at him and the bat goes through the side window.

He kicks the door shut and I back off, break into a run as Gaz slices at me with the bat, connecting this time, the end of the bat switching my hip out. I twist painfully and fall against the boot.

He backs up, prepares another swing. Looks like the fucker's all set on killing me. Eyes like a purebred mental case.

Then Frank's in front of me. Gaz swings with the bat, but he's way off the mark. Frank launches himself at Gaz before the lad has a chance to swing it like he means it. The two of them hit the tarmac, the bat jolting out of Gaz's hand and rolling across the road.

'Frank,' I say.

There's a liquid thump as Frank puts his fist in the student's face. He draws his hand back, pauses for a second as if he's hefting the weight of his own knuckles for the first time, then lands another blow.

I grab my hip, my other hand wrapped around the empty window frame. Sucking air to kill the throb and stifle some of the fear. I'm just waiting for the martial arts expert to come out of the house now.

'Frank. Leave him. Get in the fuckin' car.'

Frank pulls himself to his feet. As he does so, Gaz rolls out onto his side, his hands up over his face, fingers caging the mess that used to be his nose. He lets out a low guttural moan as Frank backs off across the road towards me. I slap the big lad on the shoulder and get into the Micra. He slams the passenger door as I struggle with the ignition. I'm twisting the key, but the engine won't catch.

'Cal,' he says.

'C'mon, you fuckin' –'

'*Cal.*'

A bang against the windscreen throws me back in my seat. 'The *fuck* was that?'

And I see him out of the corner of my eye. Simon. He's picked up the baseball bat, glaring at us through his guitar band hair, his mouth open. Then his lips slap shut and he takes another pass, swinging at the windscreen. The glass rattles in the frame.

Frank panics. 'You want to start the engine, Cal?'

I wrench the key in the ignition again. 'No, I thought I'd fuckin' leave it and see if he can get through the windscreen, you *Deacon.*'

Simon backs off a few steps, the soles of his trainers scraping against the road. Still breathing through his mouth. He's saying something to himself, but while he's moving his mouth, there's no sound coming from him. Then, when he's far enough away for a decent run-up, he kicks into the tarmac and charges us, bat raised.

Another twist, the engine catches.

The radio blares at us, but at least it's not The fucking Diamond.

I stamp the accelerator, feel the car grind and stall, the gears crunching, and pull hard on the steering wheel. The Micra lurches forward and up onto the pavement as Simon swings. There's a loud crack, and the wing mirror on my side whips into the air.

'You fuckin' *bastard.*'

'Keep your foot on the pedal,' says Frank.

I do. Simon throws the bat at the car. It bounces off the bodywork, forcing me to flinch. In the rear view I can see it roll onto the road again.

Simon makes a move to pick up the bat. Then he straightens up, watching us roar out of there.

I watch him in the rear view. I only slow down to take the corner at the end of the street.

Thinking, next time, we keep the engine running.

THREE

Fifteen minutes of silent driving, give or take. But I can tell, the big lad's sitting there next to me just *itching* to talk about what just happened. Couple of times, I hear the sharp breath of him about to say something, but then he bottles it. Probably thinks I'm going to chuck him out of the car if he tries it on.

So he waits until we're closer to his flat.

'Alright,' he says, 'I've got to ask –'

'Don't bother.'

'Where's your head?'

'Still on my shoulders, Frank. Just about.'

'Nah, I mean it. You can tell us.'

'I mean it an' all.' I shift in my seat. Switch on the radio. Some song about truckin' right, and I try to do the same. But it's difficult when it feels like my hip's been fractured. 'There's nothing the matter with me a little quiet won't fix.'

'We've been quiet,' says Frank, pushing his seat back a few notches. He's stopped shaking out his hand now, content to cradle it palm-up in his good hand like a wounded bird. A pained look on his boat and blood spattered across his North Face – lucky for him it's washable.

He sighs to himself and stares out of the window.

'Normally,' he says, 'you're fine. Normally, you'd be able to see a bloke with a baseball bat.'

'I did see him.'

'Before he started swinging it at us.'

'I told you. I said, *Frank. Bat.* How much more specific do you want it?'

He shakes his head. 'You ask me, it's them pills –'

'No, not now, don't start on the fuckin' pills, Frank.'

'You ask me, they're making you slow.'

'You ask *me*, you keep it shut, Francis, 'cause I'm sick of fuckin' hearing it.' I chew the inside of my cheek, keep my eyes on the road.

A pause.

Then: 'You want to talk about the pills, it's not the fuckin' pills, alright? I'm fine on them.'

'Okay,' he says. But he's still pouting.

'Frank, when I don't take the pills, I'm in pain. How's that for slow? Can't *move*, reckon that's pretty fuckin' slow. What d'you think, eh?'

'I only know what I see, Cal. You don't look well –'

'You don't look like an arsehole, but you sure as fuck *sound* like one.'

'Yeah, see? Tetchy.' Frank sucks his teeth. 'That's what I'm talking about right there. Slow and tetchy. There's me, I got my hand broke –'

'You just bruised your knuckles, you queen.'

'Nah, reckon it's broke, the way I hit him. Hit him hard, y'know?'

'You'll heal.'

He breathes out through his nose. 'I don't want to go back to prison for this.'

'You won't.'

'Something that I've been very careful about, you know that.'

'You still on licence?'

Frank doesn't say anything. I glance across at him. He's looking at his hand.

'Are you?' I say.

He shakes his head.

'Well then, you want to look at the bigger picture, mate. That bastard was brandishing a baseball bat, right?'

'Right.'

'It comes down to it, you were in fear for your life, so you struck out. It was defensive, what you did. Anyone who says the odds were in your favour, they're just as tapped as you.'

'I don't know that he's alright though, do I?'

'If he was moaning, Frank, he was breathing. Believe me, I've been there, fuckin' done that. You thank your lucky stars it was just your hand.' I point around the car, checking it off: 'New windscreen, new side window, new wing mirror –'

'Don'll pay for it.'

'Oh, you think so? Because what I think is, he'll laugh at me if I ask him for compensation. You know yourself what Plummer's like for fuckin' money. Get him to put his hand in his pocket for our wages, it's like we're stealing bread from his kids' mouths. Might as well forget about the incidentals.'

'Well,' says Frank, 'maybe if you'd been a bit more on the ball –'

'What'd I tell you?'

'I'm just saying –'

'Well, don't.'

Frank doesn't carry on. His lips bunch as he turns his face to the window. Sulking.

'You want dropped at your mum's or yours?'

Frank grunts. 'Mine. Please.'

He's quiet for the rest of the journey. I think I hear a 'thanks' and a 'night' out of him, but I might be wrong. I don't hold it against him. The lad's in pain.

Which is probably why he slams the passenger door too hard.

I watch him head to his block, then reach for my pills. Swallow two with some bottled water, shake out the stiffness in my neck and take a deep breath. Finally. A little fucking relief. Then I throw the car into gear and head home.

FOUR

I'm well into the bottle when the phone rings. Takes some concentration to pick up the receiver. A deep breath before I answer, because I think I know who this is going to be. Only one person I know who disregards the ten o'clock cut-off.

'Tell me why Frank's just tried to phone in sick for tomorrow,' says Plummer.

'Alright, Don? How are you?' I take a drink. 'You almost get your head kicked in tonight?'

'I asked you a question.'

'And I fuckin' answered it, didn't I? Look, you want to send us round to a place where they keep a weapon by the front door, it'd be nice to have a wee bit of warning, eh?'

'Did you serve the notice?'

'Is Frank alright? What about Callum? Is he okay?'

'Sorry?'

'Those are the questions you *should* be asking, Don. Should've enquired as to the wellbeing of your favourite employees.'

Plummer sighs. 'Did you get the job done or not?'

'Well, you'll know that Frank's tried to call in sick, 'cause he's talked to you, but I reckon he'll show up tomorrow anyway. See, thing is, he's a bit scared because he thinks he did a lad more damage than he was supposed to. Fucked his knuckles on the lad's face. But I reckon once he gets over the shock, has a good night's kip, he should be fine. Me, I'll tell you, I took a *serious* fuckin' whack to the side. I'm having trouble walking right, actually. Lot of lingering pain. I *think* I should be alright, but I need you to understand that I'll be putting myself on the sick if I'm not.'

I drain the vodka in my glass.

'And yes,' I say, 'we got the fuckin' job done.'

A pause. Then, 'Good.'

'But see if I have to go into battle on your behalf again, you can stick that job up your arse.'

'Right.'

'I mean it, Don. Circumstantial inflation, know what I mean? The money's not worth the kickings anymore. And the bastards messed up my car.'

'Tomorrow's an easy job, Cal,' he says, stringing out the 'easy' like the Caramel bunny.

'Tonight was supposed to be an easy job, Donald. Students aren't supposed to put up a fight, are they?'

'No, they're not. But how was I supposed to know –'

'I'm just saying. You never know. But if I get hurt tomorrow, that's it. Call it a fuckin' night, because life's too short to take this many knocks. I don't heal as fast as I used to.'

'You say that,' says Plummer. Sounds like he's smiling. Picture him now: he's sat back in his large chair, that all-too-familiar self-satisfied grin on his shiny fucking face. 'You say that, but you'll come back, because what else are you going to do, Callum? Go back to private work? Yeah, because *that* worked out wonderfully for you, didn't it?'

I don't answer.

'Whatever happened tonight, it's nothing to worry about. You have yourself a couple more drinks and forget about it. I'll see you tomorrow.'

'Fuck off. Call me a fuckin' drunk, you wanker –'

'Don't do that.' The smile's gone from his voice now. 'Don't think you can talk to me like that. You want to walk, Callum, by all means walk. And if you want me to take this as something other than the drink talking, you'll be out on your arse anyway. Loads of people on licence right now who'd kill to have your job. So treat me with some respect, okay?'

I don't say anything. Can't think of anything but swear words.

The pause translates to Plummer as if I've conceded defeat. When he starts talking again, I hang up on him. Takes a few slams to get the receiver back where it's supposed to be, but I manage it in the end. Then I take the phone off the hook.

Wait a few seconds, and my mobile starts ringing.

Mithering bastard.

I turn off the mobile, drop it onto the couch and pour another vodka.

Fuck him. *Fuck* him. Reckons just because he's paying me, he can talk to me like I'm his fucking slave?

He wants to talk respect, about time he paid some to me, isn't it? Fucking hell, I'm the one doing all the donkey work. Me and Frank. Even when I did menial shit at Paulo's club, the man treated me like a human being. Still looked at me and talked to me like I was a fucking person.

But Plummer. Pays a man's wages, thinks he's got the bastard *owned*. He wants to have a word with himself.

Put him on tonight's job, see how he'd handle it. Bet he'd shit his pants.

Too right.

I fetch my Pot Noodle and slurp it sitting on the couch. Grab the remote and turn on the telly. I need a distraction, so I stab the remote until I find something to watch, something loud and obnoxious to smother my mood.

Finish the Pot Noodle, none the better for it. I light an Embassy, stop surfing when I catch a black-and-white film on ITV.

Vincent Price is in it, looking like a stretched-out bulldog. He's goggle-eyed and chewing the scenery like he hasn't eaten in a month, talking about a mute woman who's in the room with him. Except he's talking about her like she's some kind of specimen or he's conducting some sort of experiment on her. A touch of the weird to the situation, so I keep watching, even though the film looks familiar. I put it down to the actors and the sets – they re-used everything in the glory days of schlock.

After a while, Price's voice becomes narcotic. I settle back on the couch. The vodka, the pills, the nicotine, the fatigue and now Whispering Vince, they're all delivering blows to knock me out. It's not long before the television becomes radio, and then the lot drops away.

Then I don't know how long it is before the pain starts again.

FIVE

'Christ Almighty, what happened to you?'

'Bad night.' Slouched out on the walkway, hands dug deep into jacket pockets. It's warm out here, but there's still that chill against my skin. 'Can I come in?'

Greg nods, leaves the front door open for me as he walks back up the narrow hall. I can make out Cat Stevens singing, 'I'm Gonna Get Me A Gun' from the living room. I lean back against the front door until it closes, take a moment to breathe some stillness into my churning gut, then follow him on unsteady legs.

It's taken all my energy to get to my feet, and Greg's the only person I know who can keep me upright and alive.

As I head into Greg's living room, I see the two massive lava lamps he keeps by the windows. The glow's supposed to soothe his customers, provide a languid lightshow to take the edge off a Jones, but I can't bring myself to look at them right now. The lava movement matches the way my stomach's lurching around. And Cat Stevens is doing fuck all to help the situation.

'Surprised to see you back so soon.'

Greg drops into a worn-out wingback, leans forward and snorts a chunky line of coke from a CD case. Looks like Cat on the cover – the white shoes and cocky position. It's the disc that's in right now: *Matthew And Son*. Not what I would've expected from Greg – certainly not music to get coked up to – but then he's an odd bloke.

'I didn't expect to be back,' I say.

Gregs sniffs, pulls at his nose. 'Difficult to factor in those really bad nights, huh?'

'That's right.'

A bad night, that's a mild way of putting it. Nightmares of a blood-soaked arm reaching out of a scarlet bath and grabbing at me, fingers streaking red across my wrist, digging into flesh, nails tearing at skin. And the cloying smell of the blood, like the inside of a fucking abattoir. That forced me awake. The TV screen was black, but the telly was still on.

I thought it was, anyway.

White shapes flashed, nothing I could make out.

And then there was Vince again, no more whispering, *shouting*: 'Ladies and gentlemen, please do not panic! But *scream! Scream for your lives!*'

They did. Women screeching in terror, men doing their version. I was twisted to one side on the couch, the bottle of vodka knocked over on the coffee table.

A bloke shouted, 'It's over here!'

Felt like a dream, but then I realised that dreams weren't this painful. My hip felt swollen and infected, a low pulse beneath the skin. Panic drained the booze out of my system and I found that I couldn't move my legs. I wanted to scream right along with everyone else, but I couldn't find my voice, the breath torn out of me, my chest burning. I grabbed at one side of the couch, tried to get up. My leg twitched, jerked a shadow across the carpet, flickering in the dull light from the television.

So I wasn't paralysed. That was something. Small comfort with the pain burrowing its way through my back, my hip flared.

I pulled myself to the edge of the couch as my gut flipped. It kicked me into a heave. I convulsed, belched, splattered the carpet with puke. I hung on there for a while, spit abseiling from my open mouth, more wind following. My eyes closed as the movie played on without me.

This wasn't good.

I'd been sick before, had pain before, but it was Blue Square Premier compared to this. So I hung on, waited for it to pass, and when I thought it was safe to move, I turned and fumbled for the prescription bottle.

And found it empty.

Greg laughs now, which is about the usual level of sympathy I can expect from him.

'Fuck me,' he says, gesturing towards the widescreen telly in the corner of the room. 'Talk about coincidence, I was just watching that, man.'

'Not a lot on, this time of night.'

'*The Tingler*,' he says, playing it out like Price. Gives me the wide eyes and spooky expression to go along with it, but he can keep them. I'm not in the mood for fucking impressions.

I nod slowly, run my tongue along the inside of my mouth. Still that vomit taste. I should've brushed my teeth before I came over here, but there wasn't the time or the inclination. And this bastard's never been in a hurry his entire life.

'Thought I'd seen it before,' I say.

'Fuckin' classic, but a hell of a thing to watch when your back's playing you up. That fuckin' beast on the spine? Jesus, no thanks.' Greg ducks to the CD case, rattles off another line from Cat's leg. Comes up, thumbs one nostril. 'Shit, sorry, I forgot to ask – you want a line or something?'

'No, y'alright,' I say. 'Just the usual.'

'Right. I get you. You need to ease down. I'll see what I can dig up.'

I look at him.

'Codeine,' he says. 'It's a pain in the fuckin' rear to get.'

A spike of panic. 'You don't have any?'

He jerks his chin at me. 'You got a ciggie?'

I give him an Embassy. Greg pulls some gum from his combats pocket, starts chewing, then lights the cigarette. When he catches me watching him, he says, 'Just smoked my last menthol.'

'You got any codeine or not, Greg?'

'Did I say I didn't have any? I didn't say that, Cal. Supposed to be an investigator –'

'You know I don't do that anymore.'

'You should be listening to people when they say things.

Otherwise you won't be too good at your fuckin' job. I mean, I know you got a trick ear an' that, but, shit, open the other one, eh? All I said was that it's a pain in the fuckin' rear to get. I mean, fuckin' *codeine*. You're talking specifics there, man. You want painkillers, I can do you painkillers.'

'No,' I say, but it doesn't matter. The coke's kicked in. Too much chatter, the white stuff bringing out the bullshit and the barker.

'You sure? Diazepam – blues and yellows. I don't do the whites 'cause they're fuckin' bobbins. But I got the blues and yellows, you want them. Valium. If you need Valium. Take a couple of them, they kick in nice, gets your muscles relaxed, that's fuckin' *medical.* Methadone –'

'Do I look like a smackhead to you, Greg?'

He grins, the Embassy twitching towards the ceiling. 'You want an honest answer?'

'No. And I don't want you slipping me methadone, either. I came here for codeine. I've got a medical *condition.* That's what was prescribed, so that's what I need. You keep the rest, sell it on to someone who isn't so fuckin' *specific.*'

'Alright, Mardy. I wouldn't slip you nowt anyway. I don't work like that. Shocked and stunned you'd ever say that to me, truth be fuckin' told.' Greg gets out of his chair, smacks the gum. 'Tell you what, I'll have a butcher's, see what I've got. See if I have anything close to what you're after.'

'No,' I say. 'Fuck's sake, Greg, nothing *close.* Codeine or nothing.'

'Yeah, alright, okay. Codeine or nowt. No need to suck your pants about it.' He waves at me as he leaves the room. 'Make yourself comfortable.'

I hear him thump about in another room. I look around. Make myself comfortable. That's a joke and a half right there.

I sit on the arm of his threadbare couch. Probably an antique, could be worth something if it wasn't for the fact that the stuffing's been knocked out of it and it smells vaguely of wet dog. A long strip of wood threatens to split my arse in two. I shift position, but there's no relief. Still feeling the itch and the burn. Better than the pain, but only just.

I promised myself I wouldn't act like a junkie in front of Greg, but it's getting harder with each visit. Because each time I'm leaving it longer – or it *feels* like it – so I'm normally a wreck by the time I get round to his flat.

Up until recently, I've been able to rely on overworked and stressed hospital staff for my painkillers. Got myself a repeat script when I fucked my hand on Mo Tiernan's skull and they weren't too bothered when I kept coming back – a hospital has more important people to worry about than a bloke with a bandaged hand.

But I could only push it so far without questions, and I wasn't about to start messing myself up on purpose just to get a prescription. So I came to Greg. And talk about right under your nose – he lives just across the way.

Greg's not a proper dealer, though. I mean, it's not his only job. He's also a croupier on George Street. Legitimate, yeah, but his job's turned him snowblind. The constant rattle of Mah Jong tiles and heavy roulette games took its toll on Greg a while back, but seeing as he's a clever lad, he reckoned he could deal pills as well as the games. The money keeps him in his habit, and he never sells from his own stash.

Because Greg's small-time. I made sure of that. He isn't about to play Tony Montana, despite all the white powder. Working in the city centre, he knows who's who, knows better than to tread on anyone's toes. As long as he stays like that, remembers his place, everybody's happy. Most of all, me.

Now all I need to do is pop out onto the walkway, see if there's the glow of sixties' kitsch in his window. Like the old song, Greg's is the light that never goes out. He keep cokehead croup hours – 24/7.

The CD pauses, then kicks in again from the beginning. The title track, and the rhythm of Cat's ode to the working man is too fast to keep me seated. I get off the arm of the couch, grab the hi-fi remote and fiddle with it until the volume drops. A whiff of ash and kebabs as I replace the remote by the CD case. Turn around and look at the posters of Johnny Cash flipping the bird and *Hot Fuzz* on the walls. A couple of consoles on the floor by the telly, a load of ex-rental DVDs.

I'm about to go through the movies – anything to keep my mind off the itch – when Greg comes back into the room. I try not to snap to attention. Take it slow, act like I don't need what he's carrying.

He frowns, a bag of pills in his hand, the cigarette hanging from his bottom lip. Smoke rising into narrowed eyes, he says, 'What happened to the tunes?'

'It was doing my head in.'

'That's Yusuf's best work you're fucking around with there.'

'Cat,' I say. 'He wasn't –'

'Man's a genius, I don't care what name he's using or who he's praying to.' Greg picks up the remote, changes the track to 'Hummingbird', which throws my mind for a loop.

'Greg –'

He puts a finger to his lips. 'Say the man's a terrorist, I'll slap you. Listen to the music. It'll calm you down.'

It doesn't. 'Can we get on with this?'

'Fine.' He sits down, flicks ash into a mug. 'Getting harder to come by this stuff, y'know.'

'Yeah, you told me.'

'No, I mean it's *really* hard. Nobody's dealing this.' Greg moves the CD case out of the way, starts counting out the pills.

'What? That your subtle way of jacking the price on me, is it?'

Greg frowns. 'Fuck me, you're in a mood.'

'You want to charge more, Greg, just come out and say it.'

'Would I do that to you, man?'

'No, Greg, you're salt of the earth.'

I turn my back on him. Can't stand to watch him take his time with the pills, and I wish I didn't have to keep this conversation going, but I'm supposed to be all cool about this. I'm sure the fucker does it on purpose, just to see if one night I'll crack. But I can't afford to look too needy. Part of the reason Greg's so willing to have me come round is that I don't look like the rest of them.

I'm not bringing any attention his way. So I try not to look too desperate. Besides, salt of the earth or not, a needy punter is a punter about to be fucked over.

'You working much?' I say.

'At the club?' Greg sniffs. 'Yeah, still got some shifts. Not doing doubles anymore, like. Don't need to.' Another sniff, I don't think he realises he's doing it half the time. 'Couple lads from *Corrie* came in the other night.'

'Which ones?'

Greg looks up, surprised. 'You watch it, do you?'

'No.'

'Then it won't make a difference, will it? Anyway, they come in, ask where they can score. Like they're all set for a long night out and reckon of course I'm going to know where they can get something to keep their eyes open. Don't know me from Adam, like, so I could get offended. Anyway, these two might be as discreet as pillheads get, but they've got cash, so you know how it is. Way I see it, if they get fuckin' stupid about the situation, it's their jobs down the drain.'

'Or going great guns as soon as they're out of rehab.'

'They're not Pete Doherty, these lads. They fuck up, they're not going to get the column inches.'

'Right. And how d'you class me, Greg? Pillhead?'

He doesn't look at me. 'I sell you pills.'

'Oh, right. Cheers.'

'But you, Cal, you've got a *medical condition*, right?'

I don't like his tone, but I'm willing to let it go. 'We doing the same price or what?'

'This one time, I don't see why not. Next time, I might have to hike it all to fuck, mind.'

'Cash good for you?'

'Always good,' he says, bagging and twisting. 'Never took a cheque in my life and I'm not going to start now.'

'Thought you'd have gone chip-and-pin.' I dig out my wallet, hand over the cash, take the bag.

'Chip-and-pin's fuckin' insecure, you didn't hear about that? And the people I deal with – present company excepted – I'm sure they'd find some way to fuck me over.' Greg slips the cash under the CD case so he can get a good look at it as he goes down on the next line. 'Anything else I can do you for?'

'Nah, I'll let you have the rest of your night.'

He nods, then asks, 'You're alright, though?'

'I'll be good.'

But as I leave Greg's flat, hand in my jacket pocket, fingers in a tight claw around the pill bag, I reconsider.

And reckon I'm pretty fucking far from being good.

SIX

Air from outside has wafted the puke smell all through the flat, but these pills need transferred sharpish. Greg might have been taking the piss with the whole 'medical condition' thing, but I'm the one still on the codeine so for all intents and purposes it *is* a medical condition.

Technically.

It's not my fault my GP's a vindictive prick and he can't get his head round one stolen prescription. Never darken my doors again, be fucked. It was desperate measures and, Christ, it's not like I'm popping them like sweets. I only take what I'm supposed to take. I might up the dosage in proportion to the pain, but it's not like I've graduated to heavy-duty opiates or anything.

I could've taken the harder stuff. Easily. Before I hooked up with Greg, there were a couple of seriously bad nights, thought I was well on the way to shaking hands with St Peter. But edging into methadone territory, that's a line I'm not willing to cross. As soon as my back gets better, as soon as it stops crippling me, I'll kick the pills into touch. Methadone – that's another beast entirely, and I know how hard it is to pin the fucker. My brother'll tell me all the gory details of his long, slow trek to recovery in between the protracted silences of his monthly catch-up call.

Which reminds me, there should be one of those due soon. There's something to actively avoid. Not that I don't like my brother, I just don't like feeling I have to talk to him. And he's on a forgiveness kick at the moment, must be one of the steps they taught him when they were urging him to kick the habit. He keeps telling me to come up to Edinburgh, the pair of us can go over to Shotts to talk to my dad.

Spend quality time in prison with my father, and not just any prison but fucking Shotts? That place is home to Scotland's nastiest: the coat-hanger pimps, the paedos, the killers, the serial rapists. Whatever my dad did to deserve a cell there, I don't want to go through it with him. Mind you, knowing him, the bastard probably requested Shotts. He wouldn't be seen dead in an Edinburgh nick.

So somehow I don't see that happening, but Declan can't understand why I wouldn't want to go into the type of place that used to give me nightmares to see a guy who did the same.

Declan left home earlier than me. He doesn't know how bad it got after he was gone.

So, fuck forgiveness and healing old wounds, whatever the fuck he has to do as part of the rehab he's doing.

Last month, he said, 'How's your back these days?'

'Fine,' I told him.

'Still on the painkillers?'

'They're still being prescribed.'

'Right.'

And I told him right then: 'Settle down, Dec. Not everyone in this family has to have a fuckin' addiction.'

He didn't say much after that.

One day at a time. That's the mantra. Except right now it's one pill at a time, because I can't trust myself with more than one, not with my hands shaking this much. My knee twitches as I pick pills.

One of them slips out of my fingers. I panic, slap it against my leg.

Cold sweat on the back of my neck.

Concentrate.

I don't want to drop one and have to go scrabbling on the carpet to get it back, especially if it goes into the puke. Drop a codeine in there, talk about a dilemma.

So I keep the ritual going, don't think about the vomit on the floor or my brother or my father, just the slow transfer from bag to bottle. The label's started to wear off the plastic, the prescription's barely legible, but this little brown bottle represents a legitimacy that Greg's plastic baggies don't. It makes me feel better, too. This way, the stuff I'm taking, it's still prescription medicine. I just don't get it on prescription.

I save the last two pills, hold them in the middle of a sweaty palm. Slap myself in the mouth and wash the pills with some water before I swallow. I lean against the kitchen counter, take deep breaths, wait to see if my stomach's going to be a good boy and let the codeine digest. A small gurgle just above my belt, and I think I'm going to be okay.

I give it to the count of ten to be on the safe side, then grab a cloth and the washing-up bowl, get to work on the puke.

SEVEN

The sound of progress also happens to be the sound of Galaxy FM, and the summer morning brings out the best in the Lads' Club renovations.

I get out of the car, walk to the double doors. Someone's propped them open with a couple of fire extinguishers. Sunlight glitters across new paint and a slight breeze pushes plaster dust out onto the street, crap dance music thumping hard after it. The smell of the paint hits me as soon as I step inside the place, gets right up into my sinuses. Paulo's painters are hard at work, which is weird, because I haven't seen them do anything in the last month.

Paulo's standing in the middle of the club, the calm eye of the storm. He sips from a Starbucks cup in his hand. Things must be looking up if he's gone to the coffee shop for his morning brew. That, or the kettle's still packed.

'You look busy.'

He turns and grins when he sees me. 'Callum.'

'You want to move those fire extinguishers, mind. Inspector'll have a fit if he sees that.'

'Health and Safety'll have one if I don't. We'd have this lot passing out from the fumes. Besides, inspector's been around already.'

'And?'

'Right little wanker.'

'The whole "smoke kills in seconds" bit?'

'Had pictures of burnt-up dollies, Cal. Made me sick.'

'Apart from that, how's it going?'

'It's going,' he says. 'And that's all that counts.'

'How long till you open?'

'Way it's going, Friday. That's what we're aiming for, anyway.'

'Thought there was more work to do.'

'Nah, it's mostly smoke damage, so it's a lick of paint – primer, another coat, whatever that bloke said to me before – and then we just need to move the new equipment in.'

I look at him. 'You're replacing everything?'

'All the stuff that was in here, it's black, Cal. Had to junk it or punt it on. Even if I could bring it back, I wouldn't want all that old shite making the place look untidy.' Paulo moves away from me, opening his arms, a kid about to show off his imaginary new toys. 'Let me give you the guided tour.'

'If you feel you have to.'

'You don't have a choice,' he says, and gestures towards the middle of the gym with his coffee. 'Ready?'

'As I'll ever be.'

'Right, two new rings over here – a nineteen-foot championship AIBA one and a sixteen-footer. Can't be big enough. You've seen the lads coming in here, they're fuckin' monsters. Must be something in the water. We're also going to have another floor ring, like fourteen foot, for training purposes.'

'Hang on a second, should I be taking notes?'

'Yeah, there'll be a test later, so pay attention. A line of speedballs down the right side there, then the heavy bags and super heavy bags next to them. I'm talking all the good stuff too, Callum. Brand name stuff, no expense spared.' He turns to the back of the club, and now he's a stewardess pointing out the emergency exits. 'Custom-built fuck-off huge locker where we'll put the hook and jab pads, headgear, ropes, all that. And the changing rooms, all new lockers in there, new benches –'

'This is all coming straight out of the catalogue?'

'Thought I might as well start fresh.'

'Sounds pricey.'

Paulo's smile stays on his face, but he lets out a long breath. 'You would not *believe*.'

'And you can afford this?'

He walks back to me, swirls his coffee around the bottom of his cup, then takes another drink. 'Mostly. Sold a bit of gear second-hand, got some grant applications sorted, a few more pending. Looking to turn this place into more what Shapiro's got in the States, like a place we can hold local amateur smokers, all that.'

'So it's on tick.'

'Hey, the press get interested, I was hoping to raise a little more cash at the opening.'

'You're a registered charity now, are you?'

He pulls a flyer from his arse pocket, hands it to me. Looks like one of the lads who used to come into the club did it – Sean. Kid's an art geek, doing a foundation course at college, got a thing about a bloke called Richard Hamilton. And Sean's taken a liberty with The Smiths, plastered them in pieces across the flyer. I don't know that it's going to get many people round, but it's eye-catching, I'll give him that.

'You had any bites yet?'

'Nah,' says Paulo. 'The *Evening News* are a bunch of bastards.'

'The ENS thing.'

Paulo pulls a face. 'Try to do a bit of good, inject a little pride back into the community and who gets his picture in the paper? Jeffrey fuckin' Briggs.'

'He's a local personality.'

Paulo stares at me. I smile.

'Good,' he says. 'For a second there, I thought you were serious. Now you're going to turn up, aren't you?'

'If there's a hedgehog, I'm there.'

'I think we can do better than a hedgehog, Cal.'

'A wine box?'

'Maybe.'

'Red or white?'

'Push the boat out, we'll have *both*.'

I push the flyer into my back pocket. 'Then I might pop by.'

'You better. I don't want to be standing around here on my lonesome.'

I slap Paulo's shoulder. 'I'm sure everything'll work out fine.'

'I hope so.'

There's a pause. Paulo seems to be watching his feet. The bloke looks funny, like he's got something to say, but he hasn't worked out what it is yet. There's tension in his face, so much I think he's going to have a heart attack if he doesn't spit it out soon enough. I'm about to tell him that when he beats me to it.

'Look,' he says, 'when we're open again, d'you think you'll come back?'

'To work?'

He looks up, regards me. 'Yeah. Why, do you need the work now?'

I think about Plummer, what I told him last night. I did promise to chuck the job if I got hurt again. And it's really only a matter of time before that happens. 'I might soon. But it's no big deal.'

'You don't like Don Plummer,' he says.

'It's not that I don't like him. I mean, he's a prick, but that's not the reason I'm thinking about it. I'd rather get paid less and not have to knock heads, to be honest. Why, what d'you need sweeping?'

Paulo laughs. 'I'm not saying come back as a fuckin' *caretaker*, Cal. Your licence is up, isn't it? You don't need to do that anymore. I'll put you on the listed staff, dole you out a steady wage for the lean times, but if you wanted to do the PI thing, you could work out the back office. When you're doing well, I'd expect a little back as rent, something like that –'

I shake my head, smile. 'You going to get me a frosted-glass door with my name on it, Paulo?'

'I can arrange it if you want.'

'I'm joking, mate.'

'I'm not. Here, c'mon.' Paulo jerks his head towards the back of the club. 'I want to show you something.'

EIGHT

'Well, what do you think?'

Like the rest of the club, the back office is empty but freshly painted. The window overlooking the bins is open, and the breeze swirls dust and lint across the floor. I never realised how much space there was back here until now.

When I look at Paulo, he's grinning.

'I reckon, if you wanted to go back at it, a PI should have a proper office,' he says. 'Somewhere to meet clients and that.'

I rub my nose. That new paint smell's starting to get to me; I can taste emulsion on the back of my tongue. But I'm still looking around my brand new office, or the ghost of it. 'Paulo, you know I'm not serious about the PI stuff.'

'I thought you were.'

'I was at the time, but I don't think so now. You have some time away from something, it gives you a chance to see it for what it is. And I honestly don't think I want to go back there, mate.'

'Right.' He looks serious. 'What's stopping you?'

'What, you mean apart from the fact that I'm no good at it?'

Paulo narrows his eyes and points at me. 'It's the fuckin' Liam thing, isn't it?'

'No.' Shake my head. 'Not *just* that –'

'What happened in Los Angeles wasn't your fault, Callum.'

'I know.'

'You did the best you could. Couldn't have foreseen any of that shite.'

'I could've rolled with it better.'

Paulo moves closer. 'Here, sometimes you kick, sometimes you get a kicking. Doesn't stop it from hurting, but there you go. Liam's a tough kid and he's not daft. He came round here, told me his side of things –'

'You saw him?'

'Course I did. He's coming back to the club when it opens.'

I nod. 'How is he?'

'He's good. Helping me out with this lad who could be a decent little fighter if he manages to keep his hands off the fucking wraps and his head on straight. I mean, I know you don't like working with them, especially the newer lads, and that's cool. Not everyone's cup of tea, is it?' He takes a deep breath, holds up his hands. 'But I'm saying, look, you want to come back, work legit, get yourself licensed and everything, you can come back to a new office. I'm not saying I'm going to stretch to an antique desk and a busty secretary, but at least you won't be working out of a broom cupboard.'

'I don't know, man.'

'All I'm asking is you give it a proper think before you make your decision, okay?'

I smile at Paulo. He's still got his serious face on.

'What?' he says.

'Admit it.'

'Admit what?'

'You miss having me around, you soppy old get.'

Paulo snorts and moves out of the office. 'Yeah, that'd be right. I'm just offering you the job because I know you'll think about it and turn it down. Your type, Cal, you'll always say no to a good thing. Rather crawl through shite and broken glass than take a fuckin' favour.'

'Plus, you'll be able to get someone prettier in here.'

'Too right.'

'Let me think about it, mate.'

I follow him out into the gym. Paulo stops in the middle of the room. He appears to be watching a fat bloke on top of a stepladder. The fat bloke's busy slapping a brush full of white paint against the wall.

'You know what?' says Paulo. 'I never thought I'd say this, but the best thing that ever happened to this place was Mo Tiernan.'

'Don't say that too loud, eh?'

Paulo shrugs. 'He's gone, Cal. Haven't seen hide nor hair of that little knobhead for ages.'

'Doesn't mean anything. He's probably just laying low.'

'And he doesn't have any buyers here, so there's no reason for him to come back. Besides, I reckon that beating you gave him finally sorted his head out.'

'You're sure you haven't heard anything?'

'He's long gone, Callum. Trust us on this.' Paulo turns and stares at me. 'Don't go looking for trouble when there's nowt to find, alright? Some things you need to take at face value.'

I nod. He's right. I need to stop chasing Mo Tiernan. Christ, if he's managed to forgive the bastard for what he did to this place, then I should too.

'Give it a couple of weeks,' he says. 'We'll be bigger and better than ever.'

And even though I can't quite see what he's seeing, I can't disagree with him either. There's the infinite potential of a blank slate with the Lads' Club, and Paulo's forever the kind of optimist who'll more than likely get it done. I have to admit, it's kind of contagious. I look around these bare walls, this empty space, and I can almost see it filled with all the crap Paulo was raving about, just about see the place become everything he wants it to be. But I can't picture myself here for some reason.

Maybe because this place is a nice dream, but it's not mine.

'I've got to go, mate. Look, give me a ring when you get the opening sorted.'

'You've got the flyer. It's all on there.'

'Give me a ring anyway. As a reminder. You know what I'm like. Too many knocks to the head made me stupid.'

Paulo walks me to the door and squints at my car. He whistles. 'What happened there, then?'

'Bad job. Someone took a baseball bat to it.'

'You want to get that looked at. Police get you on that, you're fucked.'

'I know.'

'Well,' he says, still looking at the Micra. 'You be careful, eh?'

I nod and walk to the car. Paulo watches me pull away from the entrance to the club. I don't need to see his face to know the same old expression. The guy's a mother hen at times. Which is what makes him so good with the lads, I suppose.

I dig out my mobile, call Frank. Takes him five rings before he picks up. 'You want me to come and get you tonight, or are you chucking a sickie?'

Frank coughs down the phone.

'It's your hand, mate. Your hand's the sick thing, remember?'

'I know,' he says.

'So, how is it?'

'Swollen. I taped my fingers together.'

'You break anything?'

'How do I know? You wouldn't let me go to the hospital, would you?'

'C'mon, mate, don't try to make me feel guilty. Are you coming to work, or do I get kicked to shit by myself tonight?'

'I don't know, Cal.' He sighs. 'You got your work head on?'

'Yeah.'

Frank makes a sound as if he's thinking. It's unlikely, but I let him make the noises until they become irritating.

'Well? I've only got so much charge on this phone, Frank.'

'You're sure you're not going to be on the pills all night?'

'I'll be lucid.'

'And no more of that Francis rubbish.'

'Best behaviour, I promise.'

'Fine,' he says. 'But I'm going to see my mum this afternoon. Is it alright to pick me up from there tonight?'

'Not a problem.'

NINE

There are new houses being built all over Longsight, but the ramshackle terrace across the street from us isn't one of them. Plummer doesn't believe in new unless it's a crisp orange fifty. As landlord, he does the minimum to make the place habitable, then lets a hundred revolving-door tenants wear it down to this: patchy, yellowing grass out the front, paint blistering from the sash window frames. I'd say it was just cosmetic, but I've been inside these properties before. The sickness runs right through the whole house.

'Looks alright,' says Frank from inside the car.

Yeah, it *looks* alright. But you never know.

I blow smoke, look up the road; a couple of adverts look back. There's a Tory billboard left over from the last election: *It's not racist to impose limits on immigration – ARE YOU THINKING WHAT WE'RE THINKING?*

Some wag's spray-painted a red cross through the *not* and written *NO YOU CUNTS* underneath the question. I'm guessing it's the same bloke going on about climate change on the advert for the Mitsubishi Warrior on other billboard. And right enough, while I don't see global warming being a hot button issue round here, I don't think any of Longsight's residents are diehard blue-bloods either.

Check the eviction notice. The Rashid family: mother, father, one kid and a grandmother. Seems like a shitty thing to do, evict a whole family, but I've done worse for cash. And the way Plummer justifies it: they should've paid their rent. If they hadn't messed us around on that, I wouldn't be here, and they wouldn't be out of there about ten minutes from now.

I look at the house. No lights in the windows, but that doesn't necessarily mean anything. They could've seen us coming.

Dump the cigarette, slap the roof of the car and Frank gets out.

He waves non-existent smoke away. 'Doesn't look like anyone's home, mind. What d'you think?'

'I think we should get it over with. If there's nobody in, we sack it.'

'You sure?'

'If there's definitely nobody at home, yeah, fuck it.'

As we reach the front door, there's the sound of breaking glass. Frank starts and looks around. Neither of us can make out where the noise came from, but it's too close for comfort. Thing is, something like that, it's not worth investigating, isn't in our remit. If someone wanted that window dead, good for them. Hope they're happy.

I ring the doorbell, then take a step back. Upstairs, a curtain twitches closed, swings a little.

'You see that?'

'What?'

'Someone's in.'

'You think?'

'That curtain just moved, Frank.'

'Could be a breeze. Open window.'

'You feel any breezes tonight?'

He moves one shoulder. Could be a half-shrug, could be a knot he's trying to work out.

'That's what I thought,' I say, turning back to the house. 'I'm going to give it a knock, so pull up behind me. We walk away because it's a dangerous situation, that's one thing. I don't want Don giving us shit because we didn't knock long enough.'

'How's he going to know?'

'He'll ask you, Frank. And you're not the lying type.'

Frank thinks about that, his eyes closing to slits. Then he says, 'Right enough.'

I press on the doorbell again, lean on it. Can't hear anything inside, so it's probably knackered. I bang the letterbox a couple of times. Frank's started to shuffle behind me. 'That doesn't sound very mean, mate.'

'I'll be alright on the night,' he says.

Nothing from inside.

'Do me a favour, have a look up at that bedroom window again, see if there's anything moving up there.'

Frank steps back. 'I dunno. Maybe. Ah, hang on.'

'What is it?'

He huffs. 'Yeah, okay, I think I saw someone.'

'Right.' I rattle the letterbox again. The noise echoes inside the house. I crouch down, push the flap through.

And get a belt of hot air to the face.

'Whoa, ya fucker.'

'What?'

I straighten up, wipe my nose on the back of my hand. 'You smell smoke?'

'Cal, I don't smell nowt, mate.'

'Right, your *condition*.' Never stopped him from being a bitch about smoke before, and I'll say something about that later, but right now there's more important stuff going on. I crouch down again, flap open the letterbox and catch another belt. I wipe my eyes, squint down the hallway.

'Oh shit.'

'What?'

I tell Frank. 'The fuckin' place is on fire.'

'Oh dear,' he says.

'That's the PG version, yeah.'

'You sure?'

'I know a fuckin' fire when I see it, Frank.' I stand up, look at him. 'Do me another favour, would you?'

'What?'

'Kick the door in.'

Frank smiles, then laughs a little. It doesn't last long before his face creases. 'You're joking.'

'There's someone in there, mate.'

He shakes his head. 'You don't know that.'

'I saw someone. *You* saw someone, that's your second opinion. Enough for you to kick down this door.'

'I didn't see anyone, I saw *movement.*'

'Frank, fuck's sake, grow some balls, man.'

He points at me. 'You do it.'

'I can't do it. I've got a back problem. I even look like I'm going to try, I'll end up in the fuckin' hospital, you know that.'

'What about me?' he says, unzipping his jacket. 'I got a condition too, y'know.'

'I'm not debating your condition, Wheezy. I'm not asking you to run in there and blow the fuckin' fire out yourself, either. I'm just telling you to put your foot on the door, man.'

'Nah, they'll be fine. I'll just call the fire brigade.'

'Don't be a twat about this, alright?'

'Nah, hang on.' He fumbles with the buttons on his mobile, the phone tiny in his massive paw. 'Stupid thing's built for kids.'

His hand's shaking. He's scared. I don't know why.

I turn, aim at the handle and connect awkwardly, stumble back, my arse almost meeting ground. Trainers aren't made for kicking. I steady myself, the sole of my foot throbbing, making me hop. 'I'm not joking, Francis. Put your fuckin' shoulder to that door right now.'

'I'm *dealing* with it, Callum.' Frank keeps prodding at his mobile. 'I just can't dial the right number with you screaming at us like that.'

I slap the phone out of his hand, send it jumping onto the grass. Frank stares at me like the ice cream just fell out of his cone, but I haven't got time to feel sorry for him. I hobble off down the road, looking for an alley that'll take me round the back of the terrace.

'What'd you do that for, you daft sod?' Frank shouts after me.

'Nine-nine-nine!' I shout back. 'Easy enough fuckin' number, Frank.'

I shake my head, reckon I shouldn't expect anything from a bloke with a fluorescent pink brain. He's supposed to be the muscle, but when push comes to kick, where the fuck is he? Messing with his mobile like a scally in a bus shelter. Fine for fighting – you want a student pummelled, he's your man – but watch him shite it when it comes to tangling with inanimate objects.

I glance back at him, and Frank's on his hands and knees in the yellow grass and dog shit, looking for his precious phone.

Can't get the staff these days.

Round the corner, and I count houses on the other side, picking up the pace now the ache in my foot's subsided.

The door to the back yard swings open. Footsteps somewhere in the back alley that don't belong to me. I stop, listen. Whoever it is that's running around out here, they're running *away* from me. I think.

Fuck it. Doesn't matter.

I push the back door open, head into the yard. The smell of smoke is strong out here, and there's already a flickering light in the kitchen window, a spot-on sign the place is already burning hard.

My first idea was to put a brick through the back window, but it looks like someone's beaten me to it. Light reflects off the broken glass in the back door, grey smoke billowing out into the night air.

I don't want to go in there, not if I can help it. But this isn't a normal fire, and Frank saw someone in there.

I pull my sleeve over my hand, knock some of the glass from the frame. Feel around for a deadbolt and the door swings open.

The smoke makes me squint, brings tears to my eyes, just as the heat brings fresh sweat to my forehead. And there's that smell, unmistakeable – burning petrol, and a lot of it. A pool of fire stretches out into the hall. This might be amateur arson hour, but even amateur arson burns.

I'm about to turn back – sack it, I'll wait for the professionals – when I hear movement upstairs like my conscience thumping in my ears.

Shit.

Frank was right. I'm not alone in here.

TEN

'Anyone home?'

Knowing I'm not going to get an answer.

Another thump from upstairs. Could be human. My luck, it'll be a fucking dog. Risk my life to save the family mutt.

I pull off my jacket, run it under the cold-water tap, soak the material right through. Should give me a fighting chance. Pull the jacket back over my head and push through the heat, the water evaporating with a hiss. Out into the hallway, and the walls have caught. I pull my jacket further, drop low and take the stairs as fast as I can.

Stumble halfway up, a drop of cold water breaks against the bridge of my nose. My heart beats double-time as I scrabble up the carpet, crawling up to the landing.

There's a blur in front of me, a sudden breeze. From under the jacket, I can see legs, running left to right. Small feet, uncoordinated steps. I throw out a hand, try to grab but miss. The door on the far right slams shut.

So it's not a dog. Which isn't as comforting as it should be, given the circumstances.

Smoke keeps me at a crawl, trying not to breathe too hard, trying to keep the panic from welling up and dropping me to the floor. I make it down the landing, start battering the door. Shouts, high-pitched and frightened come from inside. A language I don't understand. I ease myself up to the door and batter a little higher. The door doesn't budge. Fucking kid must've wedged something against it.

When I look around, I realise that whatever started this fire caught fast, now spreading like a dirty joke.

I hammer the door until my fist throbs. More shouts. Sounds like a warning now. This kid definitely isn't speaking English – I haven't made out a single word so far – but maybe he understands it.

Worth a try.

'Let me in, you little bastard.'

Press my ear to the door. The kid's still at it, screaming terrified gibberish. I try putting my shoulder where my ear was at high speed. The jolt puts screws in my spine, nerves whipping tight around vertebrae. I curl like a slapped kitten, drop to the carpet.

Jesus. Fucking. Christ.

That hurt.

This isn't the way it's supposed to go. This daft kid's supposed to have the basic nous to open the door and let me rescue him. What the fuck does he think this is, a home invasion?

Tears streaking down my face, but I don't know whether it's from the smoke or the pain in my back. Probably both, because when I speak, my voice comes out cracked. 'C'mon, son, open the door, eh? Do your Uncle Callum a fuckin' favour, just so's he doesn't crisp up out here . . .'

Nothing.

I look down the landing, see the first flicker of flame against wallpaper. Soon the place'll be crackling from floor to ceiling and we'll both be screaming. I try to swallow, but my throat's already parched, my sinuses clogged and painful. Pull the prescription bottle out of one damp jacket pocket and shake it. No fucking chance these pills are going to kick in any time soon. So I sack the meds, stick the bottle back in my jacket.

'Open the fuckin' door.'

Keep saying it. More to myself than the kid, knowing I might as well be throwing shadow puppets out here, all the good it does.

'Open the fuckin' door . . . Open the fuck –'

The door moves, shifting my support away. I slip against the wall, see the kid peering through the gap, brown eyes wide and shining, dirty tear-tracks down both cheeks. I smile at him. He flinches, makes a move to slam the door on me.

No fucking way, mate.

I throw my arm through the gap, catch the door in the crook of my elbow. The boy bolts out of reach. I ease myself up, using the doorframe as a guide. Cough up something thick and spit black at the carpet.

Open the door and the kid's standing on a mattress by the far window. I wipe the water from my eyes, see pictures from magazines – dinosaurs, mostly – scattered across the wall, stuck with tape that's already curling in the heat. The boy steps further back, turns towards the window and peers over the sill.

Must be what, six? Seven? He's small – that's about the limit of my kid expertise. Probably small enough to carry. *Hopefully* small enough to carry.

I hold up my hand. 'It's alright, son. We'll get you out of here, okay?'

The kid stares at me. He's shaking.

'It's okay,' I say. 'It's alright.'

He glances at the window, like he's seriously considering doing a bunk from the first floor. Weighing it up in that tiny brain of his, already considering suicide as a viable alternative to letting me pick him up. Be a real kick to the balls for me if he pitches out that window.

'Wait a sec –'

The boy moves and I'm there. I grab him by the throat. One hand clamped tight, shifting to move into a headlock. He lets out a scream that sets my ears ringing; I tighten my grip on him. Fuck it, I'm not going to get any awards from the NSPCC, but I'm not used to handling kids. I just hope the lad doesn't break my hold, and that I don't accidentally break his neck. He keeps on wriggling until I give him a swift backhand to the arse.

The boy goes limp for a second, starts kicking again as soon as I pull him out of the room.

'*Naaaaaaaani!*'

I think about belting the kid again.

'*Naaaaaaaani!*'

A thick layer of smoke at shoulder level now. It's enough to choke the lad, let me get my hearing back. Through the ocean in my eyes, I can make out flashes bouncing against the wall of smoke, strobing blue. And somewhere beyond my heart beating in my ears, I can hear sirens.

Looks like Daft Frank got his mobile working.

I take the stairs, and my back spasms hard. I drop to my knees halfway down, reach out and grab at the banister, manage to correct myself before I take the rest of the flight on my head. I catch the stench of what I reckon is burning furniture. And there's that stabbing fear that Plummer fills his properties with all manner of cheap shit just to say they're furnished, so that stench is probably toxic. I turn to look at the kid; he's got the right idea, his hands up over his nose and mouth.

'You okay?' I say.

The kid doesn't say anything. He's too scared.

He's not the only one.

Back to my feet, the kid weighing me down. He's tensed right up, gone rigor-mortis rigid. I hope to fuck he hasn't died of fright. A quick glance in the kitchen once I drop into the hall, and I realise my exit's blocked, the fire raging out of control back there.

So I head for the front door. My senses gone, packed up with snot and fear, can't think. I pull down on the door handle. Yank it hard, but it won't go all the way.

The bastard's locked.

I scream for help. The boy joins in.

Nice to know he's still with us. More volume.

I bang on the door with my fist, risk messing up knuckles that have only just managed to heal.

There's a flash in the kitchen. Just once, blinding white in the corner of my eye. Then a mule kick of heat to the back.

A crack against the front door. At first I think it's my head, then that it's the entire fucking house coming down on top of me.

Another crack. Pounding the door off its hinges. I duck down as the door flies open. There's a hand on me. I look up. A fireman, full uniform, oxygen mask, looks like a cross between those blokes at the end of *ET* and Jesus, this halo of flashing light behind his helmet. A blast of fresh air grates through me, brings up the shite in my lungs, and the fireman drags me out of the house.

I hit the grass, coughing up lumps of lung and blackened phlegm. Then I throw up. Sit back on my knees, taking deep gulps of air with my eyes closed, my cheeks wet and stinging with tears.

When I open my eyes, the street's heaving with people. A two-engine alarm, this one. People from neighbouring houses out to see the show, hugging themselves, suddenly chilly with the idea that this fire could spread.

A paramedic comes over to me, tries to help me up.

'Fuck off.' I push his hands away, feel my knees start to give, then grab onto him.

He leads the way. Feels like my head's packed with fibreglass. The flashing lights blur into one dull strobe. Someone drapes a blanket over my shoulders – like I need warming up, someone's taking the piss there – and sits me down near the ambulance. Something is pulled over my face. I hear someone telling me to breathe. I do what I'm told, too weak to fight.

Frank's sitting on the ground next to me, his arms stretched out over his knees. When I look at him, he grins at me.

'Nine-nine-nine,' he says. 'Easy enough number.'

I nod, put one hand on the mask covering my nose and mouth, and concentrate on taking deep breaths.

ELEVEN

This doctor's a piece of work. Looks like he's just finished his GCSEs and he has a trio of tiny scabs on his neck that shows he's yet to master the art of shaving. He's also patronised the fuck out of me for around the last fifteen minutes. He'd know the exact length of time, because he's looked at his watch more than he's looked at me.

So, I'm not entirely convinced when he says, 'No harm done.'

I squint up at him, the strip light burning my eyes. I bring up one fist to meet a rattling cough. 'You think so?'

'Some smoke inhalation,' he says. 'We can do more tests, but I don't think they're necessary. You'll be fine.'

'I don't feel fine.' I attempt a disgruntled sigh, hear the crackle in my chest. 'That sound fine to you?'

'Like I said, you took in some smoke. But you should bring that up in a couple of days.' He looks at his watch again.

I don't say anything for a moment, just stare at him until he actually looks at me. Then: 'You late for something?'

'Sorry?'

'Yoy keep checking your watch, makes me think there's somewhere you need to be.'

'No,' he says. 'Look, what I suggest you do, if you have any lingering concerns, you should see your GP.'

I pull myself from the bench, taking the tissue paper with me. 'Well, thanks for your time, anyway.'

Leave the room, fumble for my cigarettes, just to make sure I've still got them. I head down corridors full of coughers, bleeders, sniffers and moaners with one hand over my nose and mouth. Like

I haven't got enough problems with my health, I need to pick up something nasty from this bunch of invalids.

Head for the exit, push out the double doors and let my eyes adjust to the rapidly fading light. Must be knocking on ten-thirty, but the sun's refusing to go down without a tussle. Dim enough to let my headache drop in intensity, though. Just as soon as I can open my eyes properly.

I pull my cigarettes from my pocket, shove an Embassy between my lips and look around the car park. Can't see my Micra anywhere, so it's probably back in Longsight. Which is a major pain in the arse. Still, that taxi fare's going to Plummer, and I don't want to hear any complaints out of the bugger.

Daft Frank turns up just as I'm lighting the cigarette. I frown at him. 'What you doing here?'

He holds up one bandaged hand and grins. He stands well out of my smoking range.

'Right. You break it?'

'One of my knuckles went out of whack,' he says, touching the bandage. 'Slight dislocation, the doctor said.'

'You get anything for it?'

He frowns. 'How d'you mean?'

'Painkillers.'

'Nah.' Frank pulls a face. 'Got no use for painkillers, man. They make you loopy. I don't want to take any chances.'

'So, you did that student some damage, then.'

'Don't, Cal.'

'I'm not trying to wind you up, mate. Just saying, thanks for stepping in.' I exhale, breaking into a cough that I have to quell with one hand.

'You shouldn't be smoking,' he says.

'Frank, don't –'

He waves his bandaged hand through the cloud of smoke. Making a point.

'Don't start that shit again, mate. We were getting along for a moment there.'

'You're killing yourself.'

'You fuckin' drama queen. I think I'm entitled to a smoke, Frank. Had a bit of a rough night tonight.'

'And that's making it better, is it?' He reaches forward, plucks the Embassy out of my mouth and tosses it to the ground. Then he makes a show of grinding it into a mess of paper and tobacco.

I look at the carnage, then up at him. Can't quite believe he had the balls to do that. 'Very mature. I've got more, y'know. And we can go on all night.'

I take out another Embassy. Frank steps back. Shakes his head as I light the cigarette. He works his mouth.

Whatever he has to say, I don't want to hear it. So I cut him off. 'How's the kid?'

'He's fine. Family's here.'

'Good.'

'Should've seen the dad, Cal. Bloke was crying, like *weeping*.'

'What's he crying for?'

Frank shuffles his feet. 'I don't know. Relief, maybe. People get emotional, times like this. Can't really blame him.'

'Probably a fuckin' stamp collection or something. People are pigs.' I press my lips together, a cough threatening to break out of my mouth. Buggered if I'll give Frank the satisfaction.

'Someone looking for you an' all,' he says. 'Lanky bloke, says he's with the press. I thought he wanted to talk to me, like, but it's you he's after. Wanted a quick chat.'

'He mention my name, did he?'

'Called you a PI.'

'Fuck that. Can't be arsed talking to a fuckin' reporter. I've got to get back, get my car, man. Can't leave it in Longsight.'

Frank grins. I look at him.

'What's so funny?'

He points to the car park. 'Right at the back there.'

'You nick my car keys, Frank?' I pat my jacket. The prescription bottle rattles. 'The fuck you doing going through my pockets, man?'

'You gave them to us.' Frank looks hurt. 'Remember, before they put you in the ambulance and you conked out.'

I shake my head. 'Frank, no offence, but I wouldn't trust you to wipe straight, let alone drive my car.'

'Well, you did. You told us to bring it back to the hospital.'

'I said that?' I look at the car park. Sure enough, right at the back, I can see the Micra's white roof. Can't really miss it – my car's the only one that looks fit to be scrapped. 'I don't remember.'

'Yeah, you told us. Mind you, if you're going to be all weird about it, I'll take it back to Longsight.'

'No need to be a fuckin' child, Frank.' I start walking towards the car.

'It's in one piece. Just so you know, you *can* trust us to drive your car.'

'Right.' I put the cigarette in my mouth.

Wrong move. I cough and the Embassy goes flying out onto the ground.

'Fuck.'

Frank takes the opportunity to use his foot on the cigarette. He's quick about it, but there's no need for the obvious fucking relish. 'See, you shouldn't be smoking.'

I stare at him. 'I appreciate your concern.'

'C'mon, least you can do is give us a lift home.'

No, the *least* I can do is leave him here, but I jerk my head towards the car anyway. Frank walks out in front and starts telling me about the press attention at the fire, the number of fire engines, all the people out front. Some of it I remember, most of it I don't, and I'm interested in none of it. I'm about to tell Frank that when I hear someone shout my name. I turn round. There's a lanky bloke running towards us, and the movement of his long limbs is strangely hypnotic, like a slow-motion John Cleese. He's wearing a cheap suit that probably looked good three days ago.

'That the bloke who was looking for me?'

Frank nods.

'Thought as much. Get in the car.'

'Callum Innes,' says the bloke, stuttering to a walk, reaching into his pocket.

I think about lying, but I've already stopped, and I can't think of anything convincing to fob this bloke off with. It's been a long night. 'What d'you say this bloke's name was, Frank?'

'Andy Beeston,' says Beeston. '*Evening News.*'

'Yeah, my mate told me about you. What d'you want?'

Beeston brings out a small tape recorder, clicks a button on the side, and holds it up to me. I step back.

'Just wondered if you had a second,' he says, 'maybe you could give me a quote or two about tonight?'

'Okay, how's this: nice tape recorder.'

'Not long enough.'

'Look, I'm knackered, Andy, alright? I just want to get to bed.'

'I understand that. Absolutely. But just one question. You can do one –'

'Okay.'

'How does it feel to be a local hero?'

I look at him. 'I'm not a local hero, Andy. I was just in the wrong fuckin' place at the wrong fuckin' time.'

Reckon he'll have a job using that. Media savvy, that's me.

'And how come you were there?' he says.

I shake my head and start walking. 'I told you, *one* question.'

'You work for Donald Plummer, don't you?' There's laughter in his voice that sets me on edge.

'You're making this a piece about Plummer?'

We stop walking. Beeston rolls his shoulders, but he looks more uncomfortable than confident. Still, there's something going on he doesn't want to tell me about. 'I'd appreciate your thoughts on the matter.'

'What matter?'

'The recent allegations surrounding Donald Plummer.'

'I'd appreciate you fucking off out of my sight, you keep that shit up. Got something to say, say it straight.'

Beeston looks off at something behind me, still got that thin smile on his face. 'Alright, that was a stretch.' Back to me, and talking like we're old mates: 'But do me a solid here, Callum, and I won't disappoint. Plummer's not the story if you give me something else instead.'

'The fuck do I care about Don Plummer?'

'I'll make you look good.'

'I already look good.'

Frank laughs in the car. I shoot him a glare.

'But you've got to give me something here, mate. All this bad news recently, the public need someone to look up to, know what I mean?' Beeston opens his free hand, the other still holding the tape recorder within range. 'All I'm asking, you give me a couple of quotes that I can actually use, we'll get a bloke round tomorrow to take your photo and that'll be it. Way I hear it, you could probably use the publicity, right?'

'I don't get you.'

'For your PI business.'

I stare at him. 'I'm not a PI.'

'That's what I heard.'

'I used to be. Kind of.'

'Even so —'

'Andy, I'm tired. I just got out of a burning building, doctor says I've got smoke inhalation. Now all I want to do is go home and get some sleep. You want to make up a story, you go right ahead, go fuckin' nuts. Make it about me, make it about Plummer, whatever you want, because right now, I couldn't give a shit.'

I move back to the car, get in. Start the engine as Beeston appears at my side. If I had a window, I'd roll it up on him and go. He makes a show of turning off his tape recorder. Puts it back in his pocket and holds his hands up, his expression approximating sincere.

'Before you go,' he says, 'there's just one thing you probably need to know.'

'Okay.'

'The kid's fine —'

'I know. I was told. But thanks, anyway.'

'His granny isn't.'

Beeston's fucking smiling at me. Like he's enjoying this.

'What granny?'

The smile disappears from his mouth, but it's still apparent in his eyes. 'I can focus on one or the other, Callum. Your choice.'

'What fuckin' granny are you talking about? There wasn't a granny in the house.'

'You checked, did you?' he says.

Looking at him, trying to see beyond the cocky expression on his face, and I've got the word *Naani* in my head, thinking it's not that big a leap from 'granny'.

There's me, I thought the kid was just frightened. I glance across at Frank. He's staring straight ahead, doesn't want to be involved. It's obvious from that pitiful look he's wearing that he knew about it, but he didn't want to tell me. Feel like reaching across and slapping the guilt off his face.

But I don't. I sit there. Stare at the steering wheel.

The dad was crying. Wasn't relief. Wasn't some fucking stamp collection. He'd just lost his mother.

'You okay?' says Beeston.

Like he gives a fuck. It's a story.

'Tomorrow morning,' I say.

'Great stuff. What's your home address?'

'The Lads' Club in Salford.'

'You live there?'

'No, but you're not coming round my flat. You want to do some good, you mention that place a lot. And tell your photographer I'm not pulling any daft fuckin' poses.'

I put the Micra into gear and pull away. Frank stares out of the passenger window.

'When were you going to tell me, Francis?'

He doesn't say anything. Just as well. Otherwise I'd be dropping him off at the nearest fucking bus stop.

TWELVE

'Couple more, Callum. Just so's we've got a choice.'

This from the bastard with the Nikon. The sun shines off his head, making him look balder than he actually is. He's already had me standing in front of the club, throwing hero poses for what seemed like ages. If he'd had a cape and a wind machine to hand, I wouldn't put it past him to force both on me.

'Wanker.'

'Fuck. In. Wank. Ah.'

Now there's a gang of kids on bikes heckling me, I reckon it's time to call it a day.

'That's it, that's your lot, mate. I've got work to do.'

There's a chorus of catcalls as I head towards the club. When I make a move at the kids, they scatter, the fattest one almost hits a note only dogs can hear as he slips onto his crossbar and separates his balls. He waddles off, straddling his bike. I could catch him, but I don't know what I'd do to the little bastard if I did. So I leave him, reckon his bruised nads are enough punishment.

Paulo grins at me as I walk in. 'Local fuckin' hero, eh?'

I shake my head. 'Not you too, man.'

'You want me to get you a special cake, Callum?'

'I've just had the most humiliating experience of my life, and you're giving me shit. That's nice, Paulo. 'Preciate it, man. Really.'

The interview with Andy Beeston wasn't too bad, just mind-boggling. Felt like as soon as I'd said something, I forgot all about it. Heard myself talking about stuff I didn't want to talk about, saw myself digress all over the fucking shop. Kind of like having an out-of-body experience, except the body's acting like a twat and you desperately want to shut it up.

Paulo grabs my arm. 'You loved it, you little tart. Wait until that story comes out, they'll be offering you the key to the city.'

'I don't want the key to the city, I want a drink. You got the kettle fixed yet?'

'Nope,' he says. 'But I can offer you something cold.'

'You got beer?'

He shakes his head and gestures to a vending machine in the corner of the club. I blink at it. It's huge. And it's new.

'You didn't mention that yesterday,' I say.

'I had a brainwave while you were out rescuing children. You'd be surprised how quick they can drop these things off. I thought I'd have to wait ages.'

I walk to the machine, rifle in my pocket. Look up and Paulo's holding a pound coin. I take it from him, drop the coin in the slot and press the button. A can of Coke clatters into the trough. At a pound a fucking can, I can understand why the company were so keen to get it round – once Paulo gets some kids in here, they won't be able to fill it fast enough. I pop the lid and take a swig, the bubbles tearing the back of my throat out.

'Listen, thanks, man,' says Paulo.

I swallow. 'What for?'

'Bringing the press round.'

'I didn't want them round my flat, did I? It's a fuckin' tip.'

'Still.'

'It's not a problem. You wanted the *Evening News*, you got 'em, for what it's worth. Not like you couldn't do with the exposure now you've got a brand new rip-off vending machine to pay for.'

'Pays for itself.' Paulo leans against the machine and looks at me. 'Done any thinking on what we talked about yesterday?'

'Nothing but, man.' Another drink from the can and I can feel the wind building in my gut. I give it a second, burp a quiet one before I continue. 'And yeah, I'm jacking in Plummer's job. Told him the other night if I got hurt, I was going to walk. I got hurt, so

I'm walking. Simple as. Whether I'll come back and do the PI thing, I don't know yet.'

'You told that reporter you were a PI.'

'Did I?'

'Yeah.'

I should really watch what I tell people. Or at least try to *remember*.

'I didn't mean to tell him that,' I say.

'Doesn't matter. You told him. You're committed now.'

I shake my head. 'Fuck that.'

'Hey, people see that in print, they're going to want you to work for them.'

'I really doubt it, Paulo.'

'Never underestimate the power of the press,' he says. 'Look, people read about you saving a kid, that's going to reflect well on you.'

'Suppose so.'

'They hear you're a private investigator, they're going to think, I'll have to remember that name. That boy's got balls and he's got integrity. You can't fake that, y'know.'

'The balls or the integrity?'

'Both.'

I guzzle the rest of the Coke and drop the can in the bin. 'Either way, it doesn't matter. I've finished working for Plummer, so if the offer still stands, I'd be glad to come back.'

'Yeah, I'll put you on the staff list.' He pauses. Grins, his eyes shining. For a second, I think he's about to start crying. 'I'm *proud* of you, man.'

'It was nothing.'

'It was nothing, bollocks.' Paulo makes a fist with one hand, shakes it. 'I ought to knock some fuckin' confidence into you.'

'Enough. You'll be hugging me next.'

My own fault for mentioning it.

Paulo grabs me before I get a chance to move out of the way. He hugs me so tight, the breath rushes from my lungs and my arms get pinned to my sides. For someone so affectionate, it feels like he's about to break my fucking spine. I try to struggle, but it's no good. This old bugger's still got some muscle on him.

'Easy,' I say. 'C'mon. My back, man. I've got a bad back.'

He lets me go. 'You asked for it.'

'No, I fuckin' didn't.' I brush myself off, punch him in the shoulder. 'I'm off before you try to get more familiar.'

Paulo keeps grinning at me as I turn back towards the double doors.

'Later, *Mr Incredible!*'

That smart arse always has to have the last word.

THIRTEEN

HERO PI SAVES CHILD FROM INFERNO

There you go, there's the best ad I could hope for. Fuck Paulo's 'balls and integrity' stuff, the early evening edition says I'm a *hero*. And I'm making sure that everyone in the pub knows it, holding it up so anyone who wants to can see the headline over my shoulder. If they're going to be nosey, they might as well be impressed at the same time.

Unfortunately, the headline's about the only decent thing about the story. One picture makes me look like a puffy, drunk version of my dad. I try not to look at that one if I can help it. And after a quick scan of the interview, it sounds like even though Beeston had a tape recorder with him, he hadn't switched it on. That, or I wasn't entertaining enough for him, because he obviously decided to make up the whole fucking thing.

'I did what anyone would do,' said private investigator Callum Innes. 'You don't think about yourself in those situations.'

And what does Innes think about his new status as Salford's very own local hero?

'You do what you have to do,' he said. 'I'm just an average guy who happened to be in the right place at the right time.'

I didn't say any of that, I'm positive. Doesn't sound like me. Far too cool and optimistic. No, what I said to Beeston was I was sorry to be anywhere near the place, that I didn't do anything particularly special and if Daft Frank had bothered his arse to kick down the door when I told him, I wouldn't be suffering from black lungs right now.

Except that didn't meet with Beeston's approval, obviously. Not the way a 'hero' should talk, so he's gone and made it all up. And I sound like some square-jawed smug bastard who reckons his shit doesn't stink. But then that's what the public need, according to Beeston. They need someone to look up to. And it's easier to believe in a cliché, because they're familiar with them. They're comfortable, and God help us if we make anyone uncomfortable.

Which explains why my brother isn't mentioned, even though I was asked about how I came down to Manchester. Smackhead family doesn't reflect well on a bloke. Neither does prison time, which excuses my dad – not that I'd mention him anyway – as well as my own experience.

It also explains why Granny Rashid made half a sentence, a glance of death buried deep in the text of the story. She was old, going to die soon anyway – that's the implication. Doesn't matter that she burned to death, went out screaming.

No, look at the pictures instead, people of Manchester. Look at Innes standing in front of the Lads' Club, looking for all the world like he's just staggered to the end of a week-long binge drink. Those half-lidded eyes, a touch of the early morning nausea, his tongue pressed to the roof of his mouth because the photographer told him that would hide the double chin he never knew he had.

Across the page, the Lads' Club again, this time with The Smiths in front of it. Bring up Paulo's place, they have to trot out Morrissey and Marr. One of the commandments of Manchester journalism – tie it to the music, might make people read the fucking thing.

Same deal with the flats that used to be the Hacienda. A mass murder in there, and they'd have a picture of Bez and Shaun to accompany it.

Still, I never thought I'd ever be in that close proximity to Moz.

I take a drink from my pint. I want a cigarette, but I'd have to go outside to have one. Still haven't quite got my head round that yet.

I keep going through the newspaper. There's a small, but perfectly libellous story about Donald Plummer, calling him the 'Slumlord of Manchester'. And for all Beeston's promises, it's his name on the byline and most of the story's pure hearsay. Next, some local spokesbastard for the English National Socialists harping on about the rise in racial assaults against whites in the city centre. Got himself a right cob on about it. Reckons these cases have been overlooked by a liberal constabulary 'more concerned with policy than policing', whatever that means.

Then there's the gang of rude boys with baseball bats who took apart a grandmother of six, robbed her of the money she'd stashed in the biscuit tin.

And the nine-year-old Asian lad who's been stabbed to death in Moss Side over his mobile.

Vox pops in small boxes, the average person on the street asked, should kids of nine have mobiles in the first place?

The general consensus: yes, they need 'em. Too many paedo kidnappers about.

So there it is. The good stuff engulfed by the bad. Hero news doesn't survive when there's tub-thumping and hand-wringing to do.

Still, it was nice while it lasted. I knock back the rest of my pint and get up from my table. I leave the paper behind, open at the story about me. One of the regulars, a fat, oldish bloke who I think is called Terry, waddles over to the table and points one chipolata finger at the newspaper. I notice he's missing a nail on the pointing finger.

'You finished with that, son?'

I glance at the paper. 'Yeah, you go ahead.'

'Ta.' He grabs the newspaper, looks at the story, then up at me. 'Here, is this you, then?'

'Yeah.'

His mouth parts in a gummy smile. 'Christ. Well done.'

'Thanks,' I say as I'm heading to the door, one hand on my cigarettes.

'Here,' he says, just as I'm about to leave, 'you've not half put on the beef since they took this, eh?'

I don't say anything. Just push outside and shove an Embassy into my mouth. Turns out celebrity means politeness goes out of the fucking window. I'll have to get used to that. Or else develop selective deafness. Either way, I can only hope that with celebrity comes paying work.

Once I get home, I find it does. It just happens to be the last person I want as a client.

FOURTEEN

Plummer's read the same paper I have. I know that because he's been leaving me messages all afternoon.

'Callum, it's Don. Give me a ring back.'

'Callum, Don. Call me.'

'Hey, come on, I know you're there, alright? Ring me, will you?'

Variations on a theme. Now I've turned the ringer off, all I need to hear is the click of the machine every hour on the hour. I don't need to hear the message to know it's Plummer, and I don't need to listen to it in order to know he's no longer the suave Cary Grant wannabe. The early messages showed the strain in his voice. The last one I heard, he was beginning to sound more like Jimmy Stewart.

'Callum, this . . . This is important. You better – I'm warning you right now – you *better* call me back, okay? It's really urgent that you call me. Right? Call. Me.'

Desperation will do that to a bloke. And this kind of mithering's enough to drive someone like me to the bottle. Course, my local offy just had its shutters pulled because of rats and green lager, so I have to make do with the rest of the Vladivar.

So by the time Plummer calls back, I've had enough booze to feel like I've got something to say to him.

I blow smoke as I answer: 'Good evening, Callum Innes, private investigator, speaking. How can I help you?'

'Oh, you're a PI again, are you, Callum?' says Plummer.

'Maybe.'

'Where've you been?'

'About. You know me.'

'I know you're not picking up your phone.'

'What's this, then? ESP?'

A sigh. 'You were supposed to come by the office and pick up work today. I've got a backlog for you and Frank.'

'Ah, I thought we talked last night, Donald.'

'Right –'

'And I thought I told you then that if I got hurt one more time, I'd walk.' I clear my throat. 'So guess what fuckin' happened.'

'You didn't get hurt. I've got the paper in front of me right now. You look fine.'

'The pain's internal, Don.'

I cough dramatically. Reckon if it's good enough for Frank, it's good enough for me.

'Don't be cheeky about this, Callum. My office, tomorrow morning.'

That's supposed to be the end of it, a direct order. No ifs, buts or questions. I have been told.

Except I catch him before he hangs up. 'No, I don't think so.'

'You what?'

'I'd love to be able to help you out, Donald, but I'm afraid I think my cup runneth over.'

'What're you talking about?'

'Let me just check my availability for the thing you just mentioned. One moment, please.'

'Your *availability?*'

I put the phone in the crook of my neck, choke back a giggle with some more vodka and pour another glass. Leave Plummer hanging for a slow count of fifteen before I put the phone to my ear and clear my throat. 'Donald. Hi. Thanks for holding there. I appreciate it. Thing is, though, I checked my diary, and what d'you know, I'm all booked up for the foreseeable. Maybe some other time, eh?'

'You're pissed,' he says.

'You're quick.'

'And you're not serious.'

'As fuckin' cancer, Donald.' I tap ash, talk with the cigarette in my mouth. 'I've had enough of this shit to last me a lifetime.'

'Come round, see me tomorrow morning, we'll talk about it.'

'Nothing to talk about. I'm through. I'm finished. I've decided, the decision has been made, I'm no longer going to be responsible for chucking people out of their homes.'

Plummer exhales loud and long into the phone. There's the rustle of the newspaper at the other end. 'You've read what they're saying, have you?'

'About you? I saw something.'

'So you know what they're doing to me,' says Plummer. 'Hounding me.'

'It's not that bad.'

'I can't do business like a human being. I'm being *written* about.'

'That's very sad, Donald. But, I'll tell you, if you want to put your tenants in firetraps, that's your problem. Can't expect to get away with it forever. And it's hardly my fuckin' fault the place caught alight, is it?'

'It didn't just *catch alight* and you know it.'

'Whatever. Not my problem.'

He must think I'm going to hang up on him, because he suddenly speaks quick and high. 'I need your help on this, Callum.'

'You remember who you're talking to, right?'

'Seriously, I need to know who did this to me.'

'I'm sure you do. I suggest you hire a private investigator. Yellow Pages is a good start.'

'I'll pay good money.'

'You don't have good money.' I sit on the couch, stretch. Try to relax, because there's an edge to my voice that I need to control. No sense in getting upset here. I'm the one in control. 'I've done your jobs before, Donald. All the showers I had to take, my skin's puckered to fuck. And, hey, I lost count of all the beatings I took on your behalf. Which is, I believe, what prompted this in the first place, am I right?'

'Callum –'

'I've walked, Donald. This is me, having *walked away.*'

There's a pause. Plummer sounds like he's growling, but it's probably interference on the line.

'This is your fault. You know that.'

'I don't think so.'

'If you hadn't been such a bloody hero about all this, it would've blown over. Just would've been a tragic accident, local landlord gets slap on wrist. But no, you had to go mouthing off, get your picture in the paper.'

'To take away from the fact that someone fuckin' *died,* Don.'

'And who's paying for that? I'm the one they're calling –'

'The Slumlord of Manchester.'

'Because you can't let go of your fifteen fucking minutes. I'm the *victim* here, Callum.'

'Oh, *you're* the victim? See, I must've been confused, because I thought the *dead woman* was the victim. Maybe her family, who, just in case you hadn't noticed, are now homeless. Not that they would've had a place to live for very long anyway.'

'You self-righteous –'

'You finished?'

'No.'

'Yeah, you are. And you know what? You *are* a slumlord. And a prize cunt into the bargain.'

I put the phone down on him. Look at it and finish my drink. Light another cigarette and get off the couch. Keep staring at the phone.

Fifteen minutes. Fuck him.

I pour another drink. Suck the smoke out of my Embassy and grind it out. Sparks and ash fly onto the coffee table. I batter the sparks into the table.

I *did* something. Paulo's proud of me, which is a minor fucking miracle, the way things have been going since I got out of prison. And I'm a hero PI, I'm a *name,* I am known. People actually *know* me now. And that's not going to last, I know that, but there's no reason I can't enjoy it while it's happening, is there? Fuck it, if nothing else, it'll be a story to drink on for a while.

I grab the newspaper again, realise I can't focus on anything because my vision's gone double, triple, all over the fucking shop. Doesn't matter. I think I know most of it off by heart anyway. So I stare at the picture of myself looking all shitty and drink the vodka.

When the phone rings again, I pick up the receiver, slam it down once, then leave it off the hook. He can shove his fifteen minutes up his arse, right along with his job. Top up my drink and propose a toast to myself.

Here's to living the fucking dream.

FIFTEEN

Donald Plummer doesn't think a slam-down hang up is a strong enough response. Say no till you're blue in the gills, Plummer's never been one to cut his losses when he can just pester someone into an affirmative. But I still don't expect to see him hanging around outside my block car park first thing in the morning. I also don't expect to see Daft Frank in tow. He's dressed in a suit, which makes me wonder who died.

When I reach the gate, Frank raises one bandaged hand in greeting. I nod to him, then tell Plummer: 'I thought we talked last night.'

He does not look good. Like he's been hanging around here all night waiting for me to show up. Plummer's cheeks show the greyish stubble of a man suddenly grown old and tired. It's been a while since I've actually seen him in the flesh, but I'd swear that he wore the same suit, except then it looked clean. Now it's crumpled, sweat stains on his shirt collar, darker patches under the arms. Frank's a daisy by comparison.

'You going to let me in, Cal?' Plummer wraps one hand around a bar in the gate. 'We need to talk.'

'No, we don't.'

'I think you should hear him out,' says Frank. 'It's only polite.'

I look at the big lad. Wonder when exactly he became a full-on company man. Thinking Plummer must've given him a hike in salary and told him he was promoted. 'You still doing evictions, Frank?'

'Driving,' he says.

'He's a good driver, Don. You lucked out there.'

'Wait in the car,' says Plummer, staring at me, but talking to Frank.

'Sorry?'

Plummer snaps his head around. 'Wait in the fucking car, Frank.'

Frank hesitates, his face starting to screw up. Then he turns and walks towards Plummer's silver Merc which is parked across the street. I watch him duck and heave himself into the driver's seat. He slams the door, sits with his hands on the steering wheel, and stares through the windscreen. Vague look on his face, like he doesn't know what he did wrong.

'You shouldn't talk to him like that,' I say. 'He might be touched, but he's a good bloke.'

'He's cheeky.'

'What do you want, Don?'

'I already told you, we need to talk.'

'You want to offer me the job again.'

'I can't talk about it here.'

'I already told you –'

'Please,' he says, 'I just need you to hear me out. That's all. I wouldn't ask if I wasn't desperate, Cal.'

I look at him. And he does look desperate.

Swipe my card, pull open the gate. Plummer pushes through the gap as if he's scared I'll slam the gate on him. I turn, head for my car. 'We talk and that's it.'

'Right, of course, that's all I want.'

'If I say no, I want this clear, there's no more negotiation, right? I don't need you pecking my head when I've got real work to do.'

Plummer nods as he catches up with me. 'Absolutely.'

I unlock the driver door, get in the Micra and open the passenger side. Start the engine. Plummer doesn't move.

'Are we going somewhere?' he says.

'Yeah. You can't talk about it here, and as much as you want to keep this just between you and me, I *really* don't want to be seen with you. So get in.'

Plummer nods, drops into the passenger seat. Slams the door a little too hard for my liking. He fumbles with his seat belt, manages to click it on his third try. Once we're moving and he can feel the breeze coming through my window frame at him, Plummer looks as if he has second thoughts about being in the car with me. I swipe the gate again as I pull out of the car park. As we pass Frank, the big man's face crumples in confusion.

'Should I tell Frank to follow us?' says Plummer.

'No.'

Plummer pulls out his mobile, the size and shape of a credit card and probably cost enough to max one out. I watch him in glances. A couple of fiddly button presses, then he tells Frank to stay put. He slaps the mobile off and returns it to his jacket pocket.

I head out towards Salford Quays. A weekday morning, the Lowry Outlet mall should be dead. And right enough, the Outlet car park has only a couple of spaces filled. I take us right to the back of the car park and kill the engine. Outside, the sun's beating down so hard, I expect to see bubbles in the tarmac. A woman wearing a smart dress suit heel-clicks her way to the entrance of the mall. She checks her watch, turns and glances my way. For a second, I think I recognise her and my heart throws itself against my rib cage.

'Callum,' says Plummer. 'Are you listening to me?'

'Not at all. What were you saying?'

'I said, you know why we're here, right?'

'Yeah,' I say. 'You want me to find out who torched the house in Longsight.'

'No.'

I turn and look at him. He's shaking his head. 'No?'

'I already know who torched the house,' he says.

'Who?'

'The same people who threatened me before. Over that Moss Side eviction with the asylum seekers, you remember that one?'

'No.'

'Couple of months back. Think it was your first one after you came back to work for me.'

Yeah, I remember it now. I wasn't going to do it. And then all that shit in Los Angeles, so I came back to Plummer and this job. Came back to a Moss Side community group, pissed off with having asylum seekers as neighbours, even though these people were there legitimately and, as far as I could tell, were keeping themselves to themselves. But somehow they'd rubbed these people up the wrong way, and even though I felt kind of bad for them, I ended up serving the notice. It was a steady wage when I needed it.

'A community group,' I say.

'No.' He's shaking his head again. Reaching into his jacket pocket. 'Not *just* the community group.'

'I thought you said –'

'This came sometime yesterday night,' he says, holding a piece of paper, folded in half. 'Shoved under the door to the office. I mean, I was there all night, I didn't see a thing.'

He hands me the paper. I open the sheet to reveal a typed list of what I assume are Plummer's properties. And there's a cigarette burn in the middle of the Longsight address.

'Okay,' I say. 'I give up. Who's threatening you, Don?'

Plummer pauses. When he looks at me, his face is stone.

Then he says, 'Neo-Nazis, Callum.'

SIXTEEN

I watch Plummer for a long time, waiting for him to burst out laughing. But he's serious.

'Don't look at me like that, Cal. I know what I'm talking about. The Neo-Nazis, the Jeffrey Briggs brigade.'

'I think they prefer to be called National Socialists, Don.'

'They can prefer to be called Susan, I don't give a shit. This is the ENS, Callum, I know it.' He points at me. 'If it was about money, I would've received demands already. Everyone in this city knows I can't exactly go to the police, not when they're thinking about pressing criminal charges over this stupid bloody fire. Who else do I go to, the press? No. So if they're not demanding money, then there's an ideology in place, am I right?'

I put my arm out through the windowless frame, tap my side of the car. 'So what do you want me to do about it? Go break some heads, tell 'em you're not a man to be fucked with? Because I don't know if you noticed, but I'm hardly in the best physical condition.'

Plummer frowns. 'If I wanted heads broken, I would've sent Frank.'

'So what is it?'

'I need concrete proof of who's doing this. Who sent me that note.'

'You just told me who sent you the note.'

'I need it confirmed.'

'And then what?'

'And then I need you to arrange a meeting.'

Silence as I study him. Waiting for the smile, something to tell me that this is a joke. It doesn't happen.

'Don, you need a good night's sleep. Your brain's not working right.'

'I need to know, Callum.' He opens his hands. 'I mean, the way it's being played at the moment, I don't have a fighting chance, do I? I'm being persecuted –'

'That's a bit harsh –'

'*Persecuted* by someone who's either jealous I'm making money, or pissed off because of who I rent to. Whatever it is, they've got an infantile way of showing it. So – hang on a second and listen to me – if I can find out who this person is, I can sit them down, talk to them, work something out . . .'

'You wouldn't want them charged with arson. Or manslaughter. You just want a shot at charming the pants off them.'

He snatches the note back from me. 'I want the opportunity, Callum, to arrange a situation that could be mutually beneficial.'

'Jesus, Don, ever the fuckin' businessman, eh?'

'Look, these people are obviously *connected*.' He holds up the list. 'If they can pull a stunt like this and get away with it, *plus* have the whole thing reflect badly on me, then they've got friends in important places. Man like me, it'd do me good to make those same friends.'

I stare at Plummer. He tries to stare back, but his eyes turn glassy as his focus hits somewhere in the middle distance. I wonder how long he's been awake, and at what jittery point of the night he thought that this was a solid idea. Sure enough, it looks like a good night's sleep would turn into a week-long coma, and the more he leans towards me, the more I can smell the fear on him, struggling to overpower the odours of sweat and stale coffee coming from him. He's clutching at straws, because for the first time in his life he's not the one in control. And he's been kicked silly with guilt because he's just spent an entire night trapped in his own head.

For a moment, I almost feel sorry for him.

But moments pass quick enough.

'I don't work for you,' I say.

'I know that.' He sniffs. 'I'm talking about hiring you in an investigative capacity.'

I look out of the window. Think about it some more. The bloke's fucking nuts and it's never a sure sign of success if your client's a mental case. But as much as I don't want to work for Plummer again, the idea of someone getting away with torching that house makes me a little sick. Call it the Polyanna side-effect of that newspaper story yesterday. Starting to believe I should live up to my own press.

Besides, this'll be on my terms or not at all.

'It'll cost you,' I say.

Plummer nods. 'I expected that. I'm not about to call in any favours.'

'That's good, 'cause you haven't got any to call in. Three hundred a day plus expenses.'

He laughs, but the sound wrestles with the inside of his throat, emerging from his mouth like a sob. He takes a moment to collect himself, says, 'You're kidding.'

'Am I smiling, Don?'

'Callum, be reasonable, that's –'

'Something you can afford.' I shift position, don't look at him as I speak. 'I'll take a week up front as a non-refundable retainer. And that's a seven-day week before you get any ideas. A grand in cash, the rest in a cheque made out to Paul Gray.'

'You think I have that kind of cash spare?'

I pause, look at him. Make sure he gets the full stare before I carry on. 'That's Paul Gray, like the American colour. And I might call him Paulo, but I don't think his bank manager's that familiar.'

'Wait a second –'

'And I don't give a fuck if you don't have that kind of cash spare, Donald. That happens to be the price. If you honestly can't afford it, then that's a pity, and I'll thank you to get your cheap arse out of my car.'

'No, you're being completely unreasonable,' he says, his voice hitting a higher register. 'If you'll just hear me out –'

'Non-refundable, non-negotiable. Which means you can't hag-gle me down or blag your way out of paying. That cheque's got to be as good as cash, you get me? You do not want to bounce on Paulo; he's liable to bounce on you.'

'I'm not trying to . . . *blag* anything, Callum.' He's attempting liquid-smooth with his tone now, but he's too tired to maintain it and he's failing miserably. 'You just have to understand, I can't *magic* that kind of cash out of thin air. Not at such short notice.'

'Okay, Don.'

Plummer smiles. Relief sets in. 'Good. So what price d'you think –'

'You've got until one o'clock. Actually, no, let's be dramatic and make it noon.' I check my watch. 'That gives you just over two hours to get the money together. Now, I'll be in my local around twelve, so you just come in with the cheque and the cash and we'll talk about what happens next, okay?'

'Christ.' Wide-eyed, looks like I've just kicked him in the balls. 'Jesus, I don't believe you, the fucking *gall* on you.'

'That's the deal. Take it or leave it.'

A long pause as Plummer weighs up his options. Then he starts nodding so hard I could stick him on the back shelf. 'Right, okay, you just drive me back to the office and I'll see what I can scare up.'

'Your legs broken, are they?'

Plummer stops nodding. 'Excuse me?'

'There's a tram station up the road there, should take you right into town. And until I get fuckin' paid, I'm not working for you.'

He stares at me. Shows his bottom teeth in a grimace that could pass for a pained smile. My guess is he's too tired to notice the faces he's pulling, or the smell coming from him. He's still waiting for me to turn the key in the ignition, tell him it's all a joke, what the hell, I'll even halve my fee for an old mate like him.

'You shouldn't have to wait too long,' I tell him.

Plummer laughs once, harsh. Points at me and says, 'You turned out to be a piece of work, you know that? I always thought you had it in you.'

'You could always call Frank, mind. Tell you, though, the man might be an excellent driver, but I get the feeling he couldn't find his own arse if he didn't whistle.'

Plummer undoes his seatbelt, shakes that finger at me and gets out of the car, slamming the door too hard again. Then he crosses round to the driver's side.

'Noon,' he says.

'That's right. And don't be late. I won't hang around more than one pint.'

'You've never had just one pint your entire life,' says Plummer.

'Keep talking like that, Don, I might just order a fuckin' half.'

I start the engine. A brief wave goodbye and a smile that doesn't feel right on my face, then I pull away. Glance at Plummer in the rear-view mirror, and he's standing there, face pinched as he pulls out his mobile.

Probably calling Frank. Good luck to him with the directions. To be honest, I never expected Plummer to hike it up to the tram station – the man takes public transport the day the Devil wears thermals – but it was such a nice image, I couldn't pass up the hope of it happening.

Another glance, and even at this distance, it's obvious from the way Plummer's carrying himself that he's pissed off.

Good. Let him be pissed off. Let him be forced into an uncomfortable situation. Be a pleasant irony for the bastard. Because if he thinks that I'm going to play go-between for him and the biggest bunch of arseholes in the North West, he's mistaken.

If he pays up – and that's a big if, given the amount and time limit – I'll do what I said and find out who torched his property. I'll do the necessary legwork, talk to the necessary people, act like the private investigator I'll be paid to be. But any proof I get won't be minutes in a fucking meeting, it'll be taken to the police or the press, whichever I find more effective. Get them banged up or ruin them.

After all, I've got a reputation to maintain.

SEVENTEEN

Twelve o'clock on the dot, and I look up from my pint to see Plummer clattering into the pub. He looks full of hell and even more tired than when I saw him two hours ago. Then I realise, he's probably had a splendid time trying to find out which pub in Salford's my local.

He doesn't wait for me to acknowledge him, digs into his jacket and sits opposite. I'm expecting a torrent of excuses, but an envelope appears instead. He drops it to the table with a disgusted flourish. 'That's the right kind of envelope, isn't it?'

'You what?'

He prods the envelope. There's dirt under his fingernail. 'That's the kind you're supposed to use for extortion, right?'

'Oh, I get you.' I smile politely. 'But I wouldn't know.'

'You've got the knack for it.'

'Listen, you want a pint, Don? Getting to be a warm one, today. You look like you could use a drink.'

'Yeah, why not?'

He sits there, waiting. I stare at him.

Then it clicks. 'You not had enough out of me yet?'

'Expenses, Don. Mine's a Kronenburg.'

Plummer pulls himself out of his chair and shambles to the bar with a proper face on. I finish the rest of my current pint. Reach for the envelope, open it. There's a grand in tatty twenties, a cheque made out for the rest slapped against the cash. Fair play to the bastard, he's come up with the money. Didn't think he would, and kind of wish he hadn't. Then I could tell him to shove his job up his arse twice in one week. Which I should do anyway, but now the money's too much of a temptation.

'There's been a slight change of plan,' he says as he returns with the beers.

'And what's that?'

'I'm not paying you any more money.' He sits down, pushes my pint across the table at me. Beer slops over the sides, makes a right mess. He prods the envelope again, looking at me with wide, bloodshot eyes. 'That envelope there, that represents the sum bloody total of what you're going to get out of me.'

'That's a week's worth.'

'And that's all the time you have.'

'What if I can't get the job done in a week?'

'Then you're a fuck-up, aren't you?'

'Don –'

'You don't find anything out, I want that money back.'

'Then take it back now.' My turn to prod the envelope. 'This cash, Don, is non-refundable. I already told you that.'

'You have one week,' he says.

'Or maybe I don't, how about that?' I sit back, spin the envelope back towards him. I want to raise my voice, but I can't do that and keep the upper hand. He's the one upset here, I'm the one in control. Got to remember that. 'How about I give you your hard-stolen money back and we forget the whole thing? Because I'll tell you, I'm only doing this job to stop your mouth from going, and because I kind of feel a bit sorry for you. But if you think you can mither me every step of the way, you can take your money and your job and fuck off.'

Plummer tenses. He shuffles his chair back. He's been at the top of his game too long; he's not used to being spoken to like this and it shows. I should've expected some resistance, right enough. Normally you'd have to break Plummer's fingers to get a penny out of his hand, and there's me wiping out what looks like his petty cash in one fell swoop.

Still, he's got to know who's in charge here.

I'm about to ask Plummer if we're clear, when I feel a presence to one side. I turn in my seat, see one of the regulars, don't know him to talk to, but he's smiling at me. Blonde hair, turning a nicotine-tainted grey at the edges, tousled like he's just woken up, and a red roadmap across his nose and cheeks.

'Sorry,' he says.

'Help you with something, mate?'

'You're Callum Innes, right?'

I glance across at Plummer, then grin at the regular. 'That'd be me, yeah.'

He nods, puts out his hand. 'Joseph Carr. You can call me Joe.'

'What can I do for you, Joe?'

'Uh, right, it's kind of . . .' He holds up a beer mat. 'Daft, I know, not having owt on me, but I wondered if you'd sign this for us.'

I blink. 'You taking the piss?'

'No,' he says. 'Not at all. I told me kids when I was reading the paper last night, I said, I drink in the same pub as you, like. But they didn't believe us. Reckoned I was just spinning 'em summat. So I told 'em, next time I see you in, I'd get your autograph to prove it.'

I jerk my head at Plummer. 'You got a pen, Don?'

He's shaken out of his stupor, looks flustered as he realises the situation, watching Joe to see if the guy recognises him, too. He waits for a few seconds without comment from Joe, then reaches into his jacket and pulls out a silver ballpoint. He's wary about giving it to me, but once my hand's out, he doesn't have much choice in the matter. Plummer starts to say something, but I cut him off, asking Joe, 'You want me to make this out to anyone?'

'Yeah,' he says. Then, as if he's embarrassed about it: 'Could you make it out to me? Just, y'know, so the kids believe us and I didn't buy it off eBay or summat.'

Plummer laughs. I glare at him. He shuts up, but he still smiles at me, his arms folded. Like he's enjoying the show.

I write: *To Joe, the next round's on me! Callum Innes.*

Not great, but it'll have to do.

Joe takes the beer mat, reads it, a smile spreading across his face. 'Cheers, Mr Innes.'

'Not a problem.'

'Look, just so you know, what you did, there's a lot of people round here think it was a bloody good job you was there.' He glances at Plummer, who's staring at him. 'All the rubbish you read in the paper, it's good to know there's people out there who'll do the right thing when the time comes.'

'It was nothing, Joe.'

'You're supposed to say that. But you saved that lad and that's good enough for me.' He nods, smiles at the beer mat again, tapping the edge. Then he holds out his hand. I give him the two-hand shake, one clamped on top, proper politician-style. He glances at Plummer again, then back at me. 'Anyway, I'll let you get back to it. Sorry for interrupting.'

'No worries, Joe. Thanks, mate. You take care.'

Joe heads back to the bar, pulls himself onto his stool. I see him talking to the landlord, showing him the beer mat. Then he goes back to his pint.

'Nice,' says Plummer.

I turn back to him, drop his pen on the envelope. He reaches for the pen.

'About the money. This job. We clear?' I say.

He's smiling to himself as he puts his pen back in his pocket. 'Don.'

'You set that up, did you?' Plummer picks up the envelope and hefts it in one hand, then pushes it across the table to me. 'I wouldn't put it past you.'

'Believe me, Don, I'm not that desperate to impress you.' I nod at the cash. 'I take it this is a sign that we're agreed on the terms of employment?'

'If you want to put it like that.'

'I do. And I don't want any confusion about this.'

'You have the money,' he says. 'A week's all I can afford. I'd appreciate it if you could get this done in that time.'

'Okay.' I sit back in my chair. 'So why do you think you're getting pressure from the White Brotherhood?'

Plummer's mouth parts in a vinegar smile. 'Phil Collins.'

I nod. 'Phil Collins. Right. I didn't know. Kind of puts all that charity work into perspective, doesn't it?'

'Not that Phil Collins.'

'I wondered.'

'He's the one who called me about Moss Side. He's the one that told me to get the tenants out.'

'You got a number?'

Plummer nods, hands me one of his business cards.

'*His* number, Don.'

He twirls a finger. 'It's on the back.'

I flip the card over. *COLLINS MOTORS*, handwritten. A phone number next to it. 'This a garage?'

'I don't know,' he says. 'You'd think so with a name like Collins Motors, wouldn't you?'

I ignore the tone. 'You talk to him about the burn?'

'Why?'

'Because if I mention it to him, I don't want rolled eyes and a fuckin' shrug. If you talked to him about it already, I want to know what he said.'

'I haven't accused him of burning the place down, if that's what you mean.'

'Very tactful of you. You talked to him at all recently?'

'Not since he called me about the Moss Side tenants.'

'Okay.' I put the card in my pocket. 'Anything else you'd like to share, maybe give me a leg-up seeing as I've only got seven days to get this done?'

Plummer thinks about it. He's slumped in his chair, and I can almost see cohesive thought draining right out of him. I've taken the job, he doesn't need to think anymore. He can get some sleep. That's the way he's looking at it. Plummer shakes his head, moves his shoulders at the same time – very Gallic.

'I'll keep you updated, then.' I get up, down the rest of my pint –

nobody's leaving unfinished drinks on my watch – and head for the door. Plummer doesn't say anything. Before I push out onto the street, I look over at him. If I didn't know better, I'd swear he was dead – he's completely motionless, half hunched over the table.

I step through the pub doors, see Frank across the street. Relegated to driver, or maybe promoted. I don't know how Plummer's employment hierarchy works. He's sitting in the Merc right now, waiting for Plummer to come out. I saunter over to the driver's side. Frank buzzes down the window. Neil Diamond sings 'America'.

'Y'alright, Frank?'

He gives me a thumbs-up, singing along to The Diamond.

'Good to hear it. You're busy, I can tell. See you later, mate.'

I tap the roof of the car, cross the road to mine.

I'm glad it seems to be working out for Frank. He still doesn't deserve Donald Plummer as his boss, but at least he's not waiting to get chinned anymore.

I get into the Micra, flick a cube of glass from the frame. I go to check the wing mirror before I remember it's gone, too.

I reach into my pocket, pull out the card Plummer gave me.

Reckon I should really get the car fixed, especially now I've got the money to do it. I reach for my mobile, call the number on the back of Plummer's card.

'Collins Motors.'

'Yeah, got a bit of a job for you.'

'Then just bring her round. Sooner the better.'

EIGHTEEN

Collins Motors is near where the Maine Road ground used to be. Now Man City's moved to Sportscity, all that's left round here is a massive swathe of bulldozed land, as if something reached out of the sky, grabbed the stadium and then patted the ground level. A green fence surrounds the wasteland, but the traffic cones and empty Lambrini bottles show that it's not much of a deterrent. Signs proclaiming that the land is to be used for luxury flats have been defaced.

I'm not surprised. People are getting sick of houses being built that they can't possibly afford.

I pull in outside Collins Motors, get out of the car. Two blokes are busy working on a Punto, the front bumper of the car mangled beyond repair. The mechanics know it, instead concentrating on whatever seems to be fucked under the bonnet. A third bloke, shaved head to disguise a receding hairline, comes out of the back when he sees the Micra. He's a big guy, or was before he realised the joys of takeaway food. Now he's just fat. His gut hangs over his suit trousers as he approaches. Shirtsleeves rolled up, but he's wearing a tie, which throws a lot of preconceptions about mechanics out the window. More follow when he grins at me.

'Mr Innes,' he says.

'Yeah.'

'I didn't know it was you on the phone. Eddie told us it was a Mr Innes like it was nowt special. I didn't clock on till I saw you just now.' He extends his hand. 'I'm Phil.'

I shake. 'Nice to meet you, Phil. What d'you think?'

He looks behind me at the Micra, then grins at me some more. 'Who'd you nark?'

'Nobody important.'

'Somebody *armed*, though.'

'Yeah. Anything you can do?'

'The windows shouldn't be a problem. What's that, a '90?'

'I don't know.'

'Doesn't matter. Tell you what, bring her round back and I'll get one of my lads to have a closer look.'

I get back into the Micra, watch Collins jog across the street. He comes to a stop by an alley that looks way too narrow for a motorbike, never mind my car.

'You're joking,' I say.

'Don't worry,' he says. 'It's a lot wider than it looks.'

It really isn't. After a close drive, sheer brick wall on both sides, I turn the Micra into a large back yard. I notice a couple of scrapped cars by an upturned and doorless fridge. Another car that looks like it should be scrapped sits by the back of the garage. I pull up behind it, kill the engine and wipe the sweat from my forehead.

'Doesn't get any cooler, does it?' says Collins. He whistles, shouts, 'Eddie!'

A whippet of a man comes out of the garage, blue tattoos stretching up his arms like swollen veins. He has a roll-up hanging from his bottom lip and one eye that looks lazy.

'That's Eddie,' says Collins. 'He'll look after your motor for you.'

Eddie doesn't look too happy at the prospect. I can't make out the tattoos from here. Might be prison jobs, but I won't know until I get closer.

'I appreciate it, Eddie. How long d'you think it'll take?'

Eddie looks at the Micra, then at Collins. 'Couple days.'

'We'll give you a ring,' says Collins.

'Great. Look, while I'm here, Mr Collins, d'you think I could have a wee word with you in private?'

Eddie runs his hand over the empty window frame, pretending not to be interested in us.

'What about?'

'Just a couple of questions. It won't take long.'

'Right. You'll be alright with that, Eddie?'

Eddie nods, pulls the cigarette out of his mouth and exhales smoke.

'About time I had a brew, anyway,' says Collins. 'Best thing for you, a brew in hot weather. You want to step into the office, Mr Innes, I'll stick the kettle on.'

He does. And it's not long before he's forced an anaemic brew and a Rich Tea into my hands. With a mug in his hand, sitting in his large and comfortable-looking office chair, he resembles his namesake more than a card carrying Neo-Nazi.

Plus, for a guy who I thought was going to be tight-lipped, he seems pretty eager to talk.

'Mr Innes, I'll tell you, I'm getting tired of all the shite I have to put up with. I'm not an idiot or nowt, alright? I didn't go into the job with blinkers on, but the whole bloody enterprise wears you down after a while.'

'How long's it been now?'

'Five year.' Collins dunks his biscuit twice. 'I shouldn't judge, y'know. I mean, it's really not my place, and if you want to get right down to it, I reckon it's a different generational pull, isn't it? But it's got nowt to do with the area. Honest. You look up Castlefield, or the city centre, all them new posh flats, you get them young professional types, they got *exactly* the same ideas.' He bites down on the Rich Tea and shrugs. As he chews he says, 'Course, when it comes down to it, they don't voice their opinions as loud.'

'So you didn't call Mr Plummer? That's what you're telling me?'

Collins looks at me, about to bite into the biscuit again. 'No, I did that.'

'You threatened him.'

Genuinely upset as he chews quickly and swallows. 'Christ, no. I just called the man, explained my situation. What, he said I *threatened* him?'

'Somebody did.'

'Not me. Here, look, I've got to pass on what my community tell me to pass on. So I did. And I talked to him like a businessman, just like the way I'm talking to you now. I'm not one to go chucking threats about, am I? I mean, it's not the way we do things, I'd be out of a job if I did that. And I'm not about to lean on a bloke with stuff I don't believe myself.'

'But if you believed it, you'd lean.'

He points at me, a half-smile and a twinkle in his eye. 'Don't put words in my mouth, son. It's not nice.'

'I know. But I'd appreciate a point in the right direction here. Maybe to someone who's a little more . . . militant than you.'

He nods. 'I know what you're after. People say stuff all the time.' The chair squeaks as he brings his mug to his lips. 'But that's not against the law, the last time I checked.'

'Incitement to racial hatred?'

'An opinion isn't incitement. Unless you agree with it. And there's no one inciting nowt round here, believe me.'

'Okay,' I say, 'but the bottom line is that someone didn't just threaten, they burned a house down. Way I see it, they've got something against the tenant or they've got something against the landlord. Either way, you telling Mr Plummer that you're not happy about asylum seekers moving into your manor –'

'Not my opinion, Mr Innes.' Collins has one hand up. 'And Moss Side's a distance from Longsight.'

'Not that far. And it doesn't matter that it's not your opinion. Someone believes it.'

'Most of the people round here are just like me. Middle of the road, don't want any trouble. So I resent that accusation.'

'I'm not accusing anyone. I'm not saying anyone round here started the fire. All I'm saying is that someone's been mouthing off, and I have to follow up any lead that comes my way. And I'd like to get this sorted before the situation gets out of hand.'

'Who says this is going to get out of hand?' Collins leans in. 'For all we know, it could be one fire. Whoever it was, that tenant, he might've pissed one of his own off.'

'I don't think it's going to stop at one fire, Mr Collins.'

The smile fades. 'So, you've got proof.'

'I've got enough.'

'You're just pissing around with these questions, then.'

'No. I don't want to take any chances.'

Collins sips his tea, watches me over the lip of the mug. He replaces his brew, breathes out. 'I appreciate you coming to see me. And I appreciate your situation – you got a job to do, got some attention 'cause of what you did, you don't want to cock it all up. But I'm not going to stir the shit on your behalf, Mr Innes. You know what it's like round here, you read the papers. That poor lad, got himself stabbed over his bloody phone, you got the papers saying it's racial now . . .' He shakes his head. 'This whole thing's too raw for me to start naming names and getting people into trouble when the only problem they have is a big mouth.'

'Right,' I say. 'You're not a grass. I get it.'

'It's not about *grassing.*' Collins leans forward so fast, I flinch. 'It's about being a trusted member of the community. I get most of my work from the people round here. You want me to start painting 'em like a bunch of bloody bigots, it's not going to happen.'

'That's not what I'm after.' Keep my voice low, keep him calm by example. Make sure he stays in that seat, and those hands stay away from me. Because for someone so passive and friendly a minute ago, I've touched some nerve in him. And this guy obviously had some danger about him back in the day.

'Then what are you after?'

'I just want to see for myself.'

Collins flares his nostrils once, then goes for his tea again. He seems to control himself, easing down as he takes a sip. He reaches for his biscuit. 'You want to come to the next meeting, you can. It's a free country.'

'These people you don't want to name, are they going to be there?'

'Some of them, maybe. They won't talk to you, mind. I hope you know that.'

'I'm just curious. Where and when?'

'St Dominic's. It's a church hall. Tonight. Seven sharp.'

I push out of my chair. 'Thanks for your time, Mr Collins.'

'You coming?'

'We'll see.' I smile at him. 'I don't have a car, do I?'

On the way out, I catch Eddie hanging around with the other mechanics. When he sees me, he breaks away from the group, dumping his cigarette as he trudges across to my car.

'Couple of days, right?' I say. 'And you'll give me a call as soon as it's done?'

He nods. 'Yeah. Soon as.'

I walk away, pull out my mobile, and call a cab. Reckon if I manage to get to this meeting tonight, there'll be nothing to see, drive on. As soon as they clock me arriving at the hall, they'll be on their best behaviour.

So I can't go. But I know a man who'll blend in no bother.

NINETEEN

'No,' says Frank. 'No way.'

'C'mon, man, I bought you a fuckin' ice cream. The least you can do is consider it.'

Frank blinks, stares at his ice cream, then at me. 'I didn't know this was a bribe.'

'Just a sweetener.'

We're in Piccadilly Gardens, watching the people go by. The big wheel's out for the summer and so's the resident Bible-basher. God's Lonely Man has his mike and portable amp with him today, telling people if they just trust in Jesus, if they let go of temptation, of sin, of hatred and of prejudice, they'll be saved, they'll be taken into the arms of the Saviour, and there will be peace on earth.

It's a nice thought, but not one that appeals to the people walking around right now. Lobster Mancs stroll past, all stripped to the waist and burned above the belt. Give it one week of sustained hot weather and all the flabby bastards turn into hardcore sun-worshippers. Bunch of scallies down by the Gardens have two shopping bags full of cheap lager and they're going to chug the lot before the nine-to-fivers hit the streets.

When I turn back to Frank, he's still looking at his cone like it bit him.

'It's not a bribe, Frank. Eat your ice cream.' I rub my nose. You would've thought he'd be up for any paying work. Especially anything that gets him away from Plummer. From what he's told me, it sounds like this burn's put Plummer onto his downward spiral. 'Look, I'm in a tight spot here, Frank. I can't go myself.'

'I know that. But it sounds dangerous.'

'It's a piece of piss, I'm telling you.' I pull out a wee Dictaphone, the same as Andy Beeston's. Cost me a wedge at Dixons, and the sales guy was an annoying bastard – he kept wittering on about the fucking MP3 version like it was the dog's bollocks. But I reckon this little tape recorder's going to be worth it. 'This here's all you need. Stick this in your jacket pocket, go to the meeting and stand there while they're all going off it. You want to take mental notes for me too, that's great, but it's not essential.'

He doesn't say anything. Looks at the tape recorder. It's obvious he doesn't trust the machine, doesn't trust me either. But there's something about the gadget that holds his attention.

'I'm not asking you to do anything I wouldn't do myself.'

Frank looks up at me, licks some melted ice cream off his hand. 'Then why aren't you doing it?'

'I can't go, I told you. There's going to be this bloke there, Phil Collins –'

Frank snorts, half-smiles. 'From *Buster*?'

'Bit like him – shaved head, kind of fat. But he knows me, and he won't be natural if he sees I'm there. Believe me, Frank, he's not a threat, but he's a slippery bastard.'

'Just spy stuff.'

'That's right. Surveillance.'

He nods once, emphatically.

'And while you're there, see if you can spot this skinny fucker called Eddie.'

'Eddie?' That's Frank making a mental note, already caught up in the prospect of a real job.

'You'll know him when you see him. Got tattoos all over, especially his arms. Thinking it's probably prison ink, but I didn't get a decent look.'

'You think he did it?' Frank lowers his voice. 'You think maybe he's our man?'

'I don't think anything at the moment. But I need to get that meeting on tape.' I hand Frank the tape recorder. 'And if we get something juicy, something tying either one of those wankers to the Longsight burn, then we're one step closer to getting Don out of the shit. And I know you actually care about that.'

'I do.' Frank takes another bite of his cone, presses buttons on the tape recorder.

'Here, don't get it gunked up.'

Frank nods, wolfs the rest of his cone, then grabs onto the railing with his free hand. The other hand, tape recorder in his palm, goes up to his temple.

'Ah,' he says.

'What is it?'

'Headache.'

Brainfreeze. Frank's drawing stares. I look at the pavement until it passes. When I look back at Frank, he's nodding. He lowers his hand, looks at the tape recorder. Wipes his other hand on his trousers and continues pressing buttons.

'You okay?' I say.

'I'm alright. I just shouldn't have eaten so quick.'

'You want me to call an ambulance, be on the safe side?'

He sniffs, concentrating on the tape recorder. 'I'm fine.'

'So, are you going to do this for me, or what?'

He's about to say yes, like he's supposed to and like he *wants* to. But something stops him. Probably the idea that he's doing me a favour. And every now and then, Daft Frank has these moments of clarity.

Like right now.

'I don't know,' he says. 'What's the pay?'

I'm already there. 'Two hundred notes.'

Frank grins, as if he's caught me in a lie. 'One night's work, two hundred?'

'That's right.'

'I thought you said this wasn't dangerous.'

'It's not. The price goes up because it's short notice. And it's precision work. I need someone I can trust, who can be calm under pressure. Yeah, it's not dangerous, but chances are you're going to hear a lot of opinions you don't agree with and you're going to have to keep quiet about it.'

Frank clicks a button on the tape recorder. Sounds like he's already broken it. 'I don't get you.'

'This meeting is the ENS out in force, man. Going to be a lot of anger in that room. Lot of bullshit flying around, maybe even a couple of fuckin' *Sieg Heils*, know what I mean? And that's another reason I can't do it. I get wound up when it comes to politics.'

He frowns. 'You don't have any politics.'

'And I get wound up by people who do,' I say. 'Can't maintain my cool exterior, can I?'

Frank thinks about it. Keeps on pressing the buttons on the tape recorder until I think I'll have to take it back just to stop him fucking around with it. It's not a toy, and it's certainly not supposed to relieve stress, which is how Frank seems to be using it. Cost me enough, and he's got the kind of hands that pet puppies to death.

But I try to let it go, breathe it out. Tell myself it's just Frank getting used to the tool he'll be using tonight.

'What're you going to be doing when I'm up at this meeting?' he says.

'I've got other leads to chase up.'

'Them dangerous, are they?'

'Could be,' I say. 'I don't want to put you in that position.'

He chuckles to himself. 'Yeah, 'cause that would cost you too much.'

'Something like that.'

'I knew it.' Frank pauses. 'Listen, you're working for yourself now, right?'

'Yeah.'

He thinks about it some more. As soon as he slides the tape recorder into his trouser pocket, I know I've got him.

'I'm just thinking, Cal. You know if this thing with Don doesn't work out, I wondered –'

'If I get any work where I need a second gun, I'll send it your way.'

He smiles. 'Okay.'

'If you can pull this off.' I dig out ten twenty-pound notes for him, slap the cash into his sticky hand.

Frank counts the money, then tucks it into the back pocket of his jeans

'You know St Dominic's church in Moss Side?' I say.

He nods. 'I drove past it a couple times.'

'Seven sharp. Don't be late.'

'I won't.'

I'm about to turn and leave, when I remember one more thing. 'Here, when you're out of there, give me a ring, okay? At home or on the mobile, you've got both, right?'

'Yeah.'

'Let me know how it goes, Frank.'

'Yeah, yeah. Will do.'

I go back, punch him lightly on the shoulder. 'You're a good man, Francis. Don't let anyone tell you otherwise.'

TWENTY

Back at the Lads' Club, and I'm spreading the wealth. Stroll in there, cheque in hand. Hold it up when I see Paulo: 'Surprise.'

Paulo looks at me weird, his head cocked to one side. 'You had a haircut since this morning?'

'No.' I wave the cheque about. 'Cheque's for you.'

'I see it.' He twirls one finger. 'Still something different about you.'

'Good or bad?'

'Good. You look almost healthy.'

'I'm fuckin' happy.'

'That'll be it.' Paulo takes the cheque off me, reads the amount, then holds it up to the light.

'It's genuine,' I say.

He bites down on the paper as if it's made of gold. Looks at it again, still frowning. He's so fucking dramatic sometimes.

'Look, if you don't want it, just say the word.'

Paulo waves the cheque at me. 'It's very generous. Thank you. Should pay off a couple of things.'

'You're welcome.'

'Is it any good, though?'

'Yeah. Should be. You might want to get it banked as soon as, though. Comes from a bloke who's a touch bipolar financially. Got a habit of promising cash and then acting all innocent when it doesn't turn up.'

'Donald Plummer,' says Paulo. 'He's the name on the cheque.'

'Then that'll be the bloke I'm talking about.'

'I thought you weren't working for him anymore.'

'I'm not. Not really.'

Paulo gestures to the back office. 'And you're coming back to do the PI thing?'

'That's what this is,' I say, smiling. 'Just so happens, Don there's my first client.'

'And what is it you're doing for him?'

'Oh, I can't tell you that, Paulo. Confidential.'

He nods, but he doesn't come close to my smile. I would've thought that cheque would go some way to putting whatever worries he has to rest, but he still looks concerned about something.

'What is it?'

'Nothing,' he says. 'Just, y'know, I read the papers, man.'

'I know you do.'

He flicks the cheque. 'And I just wonder if you're okay with taking money from Donald Plummer.'

'I've done it before.'

'He wasn't in the news before.' Paulo folds the cheque. For one sick second, I think he's going to tear it in half. 'Look, I'm not telling you who you should be taking on as a client, Cal, you know that –'

'Yeah, I do. And I know you're looking out for me, but I've already been through it myself. The reason I left was because I kept getting my arse handed to me, alright? No way I would take on this job if I thought it was going to happen again.'

'Okay,' he says.

'And let's face it, mate, he's hardly Morris Tiernan, is he?'

'Suppose not.' Paulo tucks the cheque into his pocket and heads into the main gym area. The heavy bags have arrived, and Paulo digs out a Stanley knife, starts slicing the plastic from them.

'Hey, I'll be fine,' I tell him.

Behind me, another van turns up. A delivery guy hops out of the cab, electronic clipboard in hand. Another guy gets out the back, unloading boxes. Paulo shouts at one of the workmen to sign for them. The decorator does what he's told – he knows better than to backchat.

'I hope so,' says Paulo, pulling the plastic from one of the bags in one sudden jerk. 'Because it wasn't so long ago, you were the kind of bloke who'd welcome a good kicking.'

'Fuck off.'

'Hey, you never *thought* you did.' Gathering up the plastic and nudging it into the corner of the room. 'But you weren't shy about throwing yourself into situations that could only end in tears. Fetch those boxes across for us, will you?'

As Paulo lifts and hangs the heavy bag, I head to the entrance, grab one of the boxes. It isn't heavy, but it's bulky as hell, so I struggle returning to Paulo. 'I'm still alive, mate.'

'I know,' says Paulo, gesturing for me to put the box down. 'And are you still on the pills?'

I dump the box in front of him, head back for another one. It gives me a chance to think of a decent lie. I hear him taking his Stanley blade to the tape on the box. Grab another box and heft it up, say, 'I've still got problems with my back, if that's what you mean.'

'Yeah, you look it.'

'This isn't heavy.'

Paulo brings out a bag of focus pads, drops it to the floor. 'That's not what I asked anyway.'

'Then what did you ask?' I say, stalling.

'You know.'

I don't say anything. Put the box down. He stares at me for a second, then clicks the blade back into his Stanley.

'Because I'll tell you something,' he says. 'I don't know how daft you think I am, son, but I do know that you don't get prescriptions that often and that large.'

'Paulo –'

'And if I was of a mind to get fuckin' disappointed, I'd check with your GP and find out if he's the one been prescribing them to you.'

He's bluffing. There's no way he'd be able to do that, but there's a part of me that feels like a scared kid around Paulo. I keep quiet.

Don't want to incriminate myself, and I know that if I start blurting out excuses, he'll just get angrier.

Paulo pulls the unopened box towards himself.

'What I think,' he says, 'is that you're getting them from somewhere else.'

I shake my head. Can't bring myself to deny it out loud. There's a pain in my throat.

He tears open the box, then stands up. His voice drops in volume. 'If I find out you're buying from a fuckin' dealer, Cal, we're going to have some problems.'

'I understand that. I have a medical condition.'

'Then let a doctor deal with it.'

'I do.'

His face tenses for a moment. Same face he pulls when some-one's missed a session and come up with a bullshit excuse. 'All I'm saying, do me a favour on this job and don't get fucked up so bad you keep taking those pills. Because when you come back here, that's something I'd rather you didn't bring with you.'

I say, 'You know that's not going to happen, mate.'

Lying through my teeth, already coming up with future excuses, ways I can get around this.

'I won't put up with dealers in here.'

'Paulo.' I smile. 'Don't fuckin' worry about it. I understand what you're saying and it'll be taken care of, believe me.'

He stares at me for a long time. 'Okay.'

'Now stick the cheque in the bank first thing tomorrow, alright?'

I clear my throat; the ache seems to be going. 'Time is of the essence with Plummer. I don't think he's going to be in business much longer, so catch him while he's solvent.'

'You can spare it?' he says.

'It's a cheque, so I'm going to have to, aren't I? No, I'm fine. It's a bit more than half of what I'm on at the moment.'

Paulo pulls out the second bag – looks like more pads. 'You bumped up your prices, didn't you?'

'Well, I'm a celebrity now.'

'Course you are.'

'And this job, I demanded the extra cash.'

'How so?'

'Danger money.'

He turns. And welcome back to that same old worried expression that used to make me want to slap him. Now I just want to hug the old bastard.

'Joking,' I say.

'You better be.'

'It's Donald Plummer, Paulo. Course I'm going to charge him through the nose. The fucker's been underpaying me ever since I started working for him.'

Paulo continues to unload the box. 'Onwards and upwards.'

'Yeah. Look, I better be going, mate. Got stuff to do. Look like you're kind of busy yourself.'

'Listen, you get some time tomorrow, we're getting the rings delivered.'

I head for the front doors. 'Yeah, that should be fun.'

'We could use some help setting them up.'

'I'll see what's happening, mate. Give you a call about it, okay?'

'Of course,' he says. 'You're a working man now.'

'Fuck, yeah. Working for myself. About time, too.'

TWENTY-ONE

It's been a long day, and I keep thinking I've forgotten something.

But no – everything's sorted with this meeting tonight. Whatever Frank digs up – if he manages to get anything – should keep me busy for a while. It's just I can't stop worrying about it, when I really should take the opportunity to relax.

So I pop round Sainsbury's to get a shop in. I'm in the mood for a big meal, something stodgy, followed by a bottle of the posh vodka – the kind you can't spell without using an entirely new alphabet – and then early to bed. Frank can leave a message on the answer machine and I'll pick it up tomorrow morning before I head out to Longsight, see if I can scare up a few more leads.

'Excuse me, you're Callum Innes, aren't you?'

I turn to see the kind of woman who I know has a people carrier parked outside. The scrubbed face of a young, middle-class mother, her apple cheeks and watery blue eyes passed on to the kid who's currently clutching her trouser leg. I can't place his age, but I try to look friendly. 'Yeah.'

'You saved that boy.' She's smiling now. Shifting the massive bag on her shoulder.

'I suppose I did, yeah.'

She blinks. 'Oh, sorry, have I got the wrong person?'

'No,' I say. Shaking my head, telling myself I should enjoy the attention. 'I saved the lad, yeah.'

She bites her bottom lip. Nods as if I'm the first celebrity she's ever met, when I know for a fact that half the regular cast of *Coronation Street* shop in this Sainsbury's. Mostly in the off-licence part of it, but from what I hear, groceries that clink together are still groceries.

'We're *so* proud of you,' she says.

'Thank you. Who's we?'

'I live in Prestwich.'

I nod.

'You're quite the hero round our way.' Her smile flickers again, a brief frown. 'I mean, in our *area.*'

'News travels fast,' I say. 'It was only yesterday I was in the paper.'

'It's a popular paper.' The smile brightens a notch. 'My name's Kelly.'

'Nice to meet you, Kelly.' I make a move to crouch, but my back won't let me. 'What's your name, son?'

'He doesn't speak to strangers.' She lets go of the kid's hand for a second to open her large handbag. 'Actually, I was wondering . . .'

Here we go again. Another autograph. I hope she's got a pen.

Kelly brings out a sheaf of paper. Sheets of A4, tabled and covered with signatures, different-coloured inks scratched all over. She sorts through them, biting her lip again, hefting the pile of papers as she juggles them, the bag, and her kid tugging at her trouser leg.

'Don't be a nuisance,' she says to the kid. Then she finds a sheet with a blank space on it, hands me the lot.

'What's this?' I say, still trying to smile, but buckling a little with the awkwardness of the thing.

'A petition. I'd love you to sign it.'

So it *is* an autograph. Of sorts.

'What's it for?' I wink at the boy. He flinches.

'Well,' she says, 'you know . . .'

I look up. 'Sorry?'

She takes a step forward, pointing out the names. I don't recognise any of them. 'It would be marvellous if we could get you to sign. Someone like you, well, your name may have a little more weight attached to it.'

I try to read the type at the top of the sheet. The lights in the supermarket make it difficult to focus. I knew I shouldn't have tried to crouch for that kid; the pain's spreading up my back to the bottom of my neck now.

'Sorry,' I say. 'I can't read this.'

Kelly holds out a biro. I take it off her.

'You must have heard,' she says.

'I've heard a lot of things the last couple of days, Kelly. You're going to have to refresh my memory.'

'They're trying to move asylum seekers into Prestwich.'

'Right.'

'Nelson Road. The old flats. You know them?'

'And you're . . . *against* this?'

'Have you ever been to Prestwich, Mr Innes?'

I look back at the petition. Name after name, all in delicate cursive script. 'I've passed through a couple of times, yeah. It's a nice area. Bit too posh for me.'

'Exactly.'

'Sorry?'

'It *is* a nice area.' The smile's still on her face, but it's also hardened at the edges, starting to turn into a grimace. 'And we'd very much like to keep it that way.'

'Right,' I say, trying to swallow the urge to sigh. 'You don't want foreigners in your street.'

Kelly blinks. 'I'm not racist, Mr Innes.'

'Course you're not.'

'I don't care what colour they are or where they come from,' she says, grabbing the boy's hand as if he's going to pipe up and corroborate. 'But you must know the way areas go once they've allowed that sort into the community.'

'That sort?' I shake my head, grab a loaf, shove it in my basket. 'No, I don't. Sorry, Kelly.'

I hand her the petition, start moving up the aisle. She follows me, dragging the kid behind her.

'You've been to Longsight. You were in that house, you know how they live.'

'I really have to be going. Thanks, anyway.'

She grabs onto my arm. I resist the urge to put my elbow in her face.

'You're not going to sign?'

'Politics isn't really my thing.'

'This isn't about politics,' she says. 'It's –'

'It's always about politics, Kelly.' I turn to face her. 'Look, I'm knackered, I've had a long day and I just want to get some shopping in, then go home. You'll forgive me if I don't want to exercise my right to screw people I don't know. It was nice to meet you. You too, son.'

I move away up the aisle. Glance over my shoulder and Kelly is staring at the little boy as if he was the one to scare me off. The boy looks my way. I wink at him again; he still flinches.

I'm not surprised now. Not with that as a mother. I move into the booze aisle and sack the posh vodka in favour of a couple of four-packs of beer. Better I stay away from the spirits tonight. Not only do I have to be up in the morning, get the jump on this case, but there's a strong part of me that's scared I'll end up back round Greg's.

So I'll slow down on the pills. It's going to be a bastard trying to get them past Paulo anyway, so might as well drop my dose unless the pain gets really bad. See how well I function. But as I'm heading to my car, I take two codeine anyway.

Pre-emptive measure.

PART TWO

×××××××××××××××

THIS LAND IS YOUR LAND

TWENTY-TWO

Next morning, I'm on a bus to Longsight, thinking about the list that Plummer gave me. It must have come from somewhere, and it can't have been easy to get hold of. Most letting agencies have some sort of landlord confidentiality. Most places bring up the Data Protection Act, doesn't matter how personal the question. After all, it's the only widely known legal excuse for being an unhelpful twat.

But still, someone managed to get the list.

I don't know what security at the smaller agencies is like. And Plummer only goes through the smaller firms. He looks for a quick, constant turnover of tenants. He's not interested in long-term lets because that means he'd actually have to maintain the properties to a certain level, which just isn't economically viable in his world. He also goes local because the national letting agencies won't touch him with a ten-foot fucking pole.

The trouble is, which local agencies does he use?

When I round the corner on Stockport Road, I see the most likely candidate. Can't make out the name of the place, because it's been obscured by a wall of young people, could well be students. A picket, a protest and enough placards to tickle even the most apathetic bloke's curiosity.

If I needed any more evidence, a girl turns to reveal her sign: GOT PLUMMER PROBLEMS?

Apparently so. I head for the door. A girl with ginger dreads, her hands full of bright yellow leaflets, steps in front of me.

'You going in there?'

She has a look on her face like I've just eaten a dog hair sandwich. On white bread.

I try my best smile on her. 'Y'know, I thought I might.'

'You're not thinking of renting from here, are you?'

'I don't think that's any of your business, is it?'

She presses a leaflet into my hand. A badly photocopied picture of Donald Plummer on the front, nicked from the newspaper article, so he's gurning something rotten. I look up at the student. She knows who Plummer is, but she doesn't know me. That's fine; I can live with that.

'Read that,' she says. 'Be prepared.'

'Okay. You going to let me past?'

'You want to cross the picket, you can cross the picket. We won't stop you.'

Like they're a serious threat.

'Thanks ever so much,' I say, and push inside.

A bell rings as the door opens. A stringy lad with a full beard is sitting opposite a severe blonde woman in a beige suit that looks too much like a uniform to be flattering. The lad's wearing a biker jacket – either vintage, or new and fashionably scuffed – and seems to be in the middle of an indignant rant. Two mates with him, one with a rugby shirt and the features to match, chewed ears, coloured cheeks and heavy features. The other is a girl who looks like a dinner wouldn't kill her, a metal stud shining in her nose. Charity and friendship bracelets hang off one wrist, the kind of doe-eyed girl who makes Bono lay awake at night thinking he's just not doing enough.

'Pending a full investigation?' says the stringy lad. 'You're not going to tell him where to go?'

The blonde woman blinks slowly. 'I appreciate your concern, David. And you know, we have discussed this with your student representative.'

'You haven't discussed it with us.'

A smile, tight and condescending. 'We don't deal with you.'

'You know as well as I do that those people don't know their arse from their elbow.'

'That's as maybe,' says the blonde woman, 'but that's who we're dealing with at this moment in time. We have to go through the proper channels, I'm sure you can appreciate that.'

'Do you want more picket lines?' says David, turning to his two mates for support. 'I mean, we *can* arrange a rolling picket if you want.'

'As long as it's peaceful, you can do whatever you think is right. It's a free country.'

'Right you are, it's a free country.' Nods from behind him, the most emphatic from the skinny girl. 'I'm free to speak my mind, and I'm free to organise protest –'

'David, if there's nothing else . . .' The blonde woman nods my way. 'There's a gentleman I should really attend to.'

David stops talking, twists in his seat and looks at me. His lips go thin, then he nods to himself. Pushes his chair back, gets to his feet and holds out his hand to the blonde woman. All business, frosty now. She takes his hand, but only for a moment.

'We'll be back,' he says.

The agency woman smiles at him. 'I'm sure you will.'

I watch the students leave, hear the bell ring again to signal their departure. Then I turn to the woman. The badge on her jacket reads MEG. Can't say the name suits her. With that nose, she looks more like a Diana.

'What can I do for you?' she says.

'I need a little information. About a landlord.'

'Donald Plummer.' A statement.

'Read my mind. I didn't know you were a *mystic*, Meg.'

Not a flicker of a smile at that one. Just a barely suppressed sigh as she says, 'We're not dealing with Mr Plummer at this moment in time, pending a full investigation.'

'Pending a full investigation?' I'm all mock concern. 'You're not going to tell him where to go?'

Her mouth twitches. Could be, the ice is thawing.

'Bet you're sick of saying that,' I say.

'You have no idea.'

I pull up a chair opposite her and Meg clicks into official mode again. 'Are you looking to rent in the area?'

'Nope. I need information about Donald Plummer.'

'I told you, we're not dealing –'

'I know, pending a full investigation. That's not a problem. If you're not dealing with him, you can tell me how many properties he has on your books.'

'I said, at this moment in time,' says Meg. 'We may well deal with Mr Plummer again in the future.'

'I don't think that's going to happen, do you?'

'Well, until that time, I'm afraid we have to keep Mr Plummer's details confidential.'

'The Data Protection Act,' I say.

'If you like. Really, I'm sorry, but there's nothing I can do, Mr –'

'Innes.' I wait for recognition, get a blank look. 'But let's say I'm a prospective tenant, alright? If I came in here wanting to rent, but I didn't want to find myself in a slum –'

'We don't let slum properties, Mr Innes.'

'You know what I mean.'

The smile returns, but it's the same one she gave David. 'We would not be in a position to let one of Mr Plummer's properties at this time.'

'Meg – can I call you Meg?'

'It's on the badge,' she says. 'And I think you already have.'

'So, Meg, do I have to go through every one of your houses and find out which ones you're not allowed to let? Is that the only way of doing this?'

'No.'

'Then how would I go about getting a list of properties from you?'

'You? *You* wouldn't.'

I grin. 'You're enjoying this, aren't you?'

'I don't know what you mean.'

'Meg, I'm working on behalf of a client.' I pull out an old business card, smooth down the edges and place it on the desk between us. 'I'm a private investigator. And, as such, any information you might want to share is entirely confidential.'

Meg doesn't touch the card. She barely looks at it. Just enough to get my name. 'Callum Innes.'

'That's right.'

'You're the one who saved the little boy.'

Finally.

'Yeah.'

'I didn't recognise you.'

'I didn't think you did.'

She waves a hand at me. 'You're heavier in real life.'

'I take a good photo.' Everyone's got an opinion about my fucking weight. 'Now, I'm not after a list of Plummer's houses, but I do need to know if you've prepared a list like that for anyone recently.'

'We wouldn't do that. It'd be a breach of the contract with Mr Plummer.'

'Right.' I sit back in the chair, then lean forward to disguise my gut. 'Nobody else would've done that list?'

'My boss, perhaps. At a push.'

'Is he here?'

'No. And I sincerely doubt he would have done that anyway. It's —'

'Breach of contract, you already told me.' I get out of the chair. 'Look, tell you what, you hang on to that card, okay? Anything turns up, I'd appreciate it if you could let me know. It's very important.'

'Is this anything to do with the fire?' she says.

'Ah, that's confidential.' I nod towards the card. 'But it's worth bearing in mind.'

TWENTY-THREE

'Mr Innes?'

As soon as I'm out of the letting agency, I back up at the sight of an outstretched hand, someone lurching in front of me.

The beardy student, what's his name, *David*. Looks like he's been waiting for me to come out. The rest of the students are milling around, the picket already tired and restless and it's not even mid-morning. Sun beating down on them, only going to get hotter, I'm not really surprised some of them are wilting. The girl with the ginger dreads is still going, though. Made of sterner stuff, obviously.

'David Nunn,' says the student, his hand still out. 'Didn't get a chance in there.'

I give his hand the same touch-shake that Meg did. 'Listen, I'd love to stay and chat, but I've got to be somewhere else.'

He grins, showing even teeth. 'That's cool. I understand. You're a busy man.'

I make a move to go. Feel his hand on my arm and turn a bit too quickly for him. He drops his hand.

'You got something you need to say there, David?'

'You didn't ask how I knew your name,' he says.

'Reckoned you heard us talking in there.'

'No.' He's still smiling. Nobody can smile this much and mean it. 'I read about you in the paper.'

'Ah, right. You want me to sign something for you?'

That confuses him for a second, then he shakes his head and the smile drops from his face. 'No, I'm not interested in your autograph.'

'Right. Well . . .'

'Are you working right now?'

'Yeah. Kind of busy, to be honest, so –'

'I was just thinking . . . Well, I wanted to introduce myself anyway.' He looks around him, then back at me. 'Did someone give you a pamphlet?'

I reach into my pocket, bring out the list of Plummer's properties along with the yellow paper, hold both up and gesture towards the girl with the ginger dreads. David looks at the pamphlet. His eyes flicker to slits for a split-second, then he's all smiles again.

'Listen, make sure you read that, yeah?'

'I will.'

Another move to go, but he catches me again. Getting sick of this fucking hand on me, and I'm about to say something when he interrupts.

'You've got an office, right?'

'Not at the moment, no.'

'I was going to say, if you could do us a favour, you could take a stack –'

'I don't think so.'

'Ben, mate, come over here for a second. You could take some leaflets, give them out to your clients, what d'you think?'

He doesn't wait for an answer, already waving his rugby player mate over.

'I don't think my clients would be interested.' I smile, but my heart's not in it. 'A right selfish bunch of bastards, most of them.'

'It's the Lads' Club, right? The one up in Salford?'

I don't answer him. Thinking he probably got that from the newspaper, asking me questions so I'll have to answer. Stalling me so he can push more of these fucking pamphlets on me.

'What about the lads that go there? Some of them must be students.'

'Not really a student kind of place, David. You'll excuse me.'

The rugby player appears next to him, and David makes another grab for my arm. I slip out from under.

'Ben, could you get some leaflets for Mr Innes? He needs to take some with him.'

'Really, Ben, is it? Ben, there's no need. You'll be wasting them.' To David: 'You give me those leaflets, they'll go straight in the fuckin' bin, I'm telling you.'

'Hey, just spread the word,' says David. 'That's all we need. Seriously, every little helps, y'know? Look, I'm just happy to meet you, Mr Innes. What you did in that house . . . that was something. Not everyone who can just *act* like that, totally without thinking.'

'You'd be surprised. I do it a lot.' I'm watching Ben head for a blue VW Beetle, one of those newer curvy monstrosities. He reaches into the back seat, pulls out an armful of pamphlets and brings them over. I hold my hands up. 'No. Really, I'm not taking them.'

'You're not?' says Ben. The big guy almost looks hurt. 'Okay.'

'I really can't, Ben. I don't have my car with me. I'd be carrying them on the bus.'

'Okay,' says David, suddenly cold. 'Whatever. Thought you'd appreciate the cause. Doesn't matter that you don't. You take care of yourself, okay?'

And he disappears into the picket, slapping people on the shoulder. Every time he touches someone, they seem to get this wee energy boost. They stiffen and straighten up on his approach. Yeah, he's definitely the leader of this picket, and what's weird is that people willingly accept that. When he touched me, all I felt was a bit sick.

I look back, and Ben's still standing there with his arms full of leaflets.

'How's the boy?' he says.

I squint at him. 'What boy?'

'The one in the house. The one you saved. Is he okay?'

'I don't know. Last I heard he was alright. A bit shaken, you know how it is.'

'And the rest of the family? You reckon they'll be alright?'

I start to back away from Ben. 'I'm sure they're fine. Don't worry about it.'

'Okay. Well, you keep up the good work.'

'You too, mate.'

I turn away from the picket, head back up to the bus stop. I stop to light a cigarette, pull the leaflet out of my pocket and I'm about to chuck it into the nearest bin when I change my mind. When I reach the bus stop, I give it a read, see if these guys know anything that I don't, see what my client's up against.

GOT PLUMMER PROBLEMS?

You're fucking right I do. There's a picture of him on the inside, too. Underneath that, a list of accusations:

DONALD PLUMMER does NOT maintain his properties.
DONALD PLUMMER will SUB-LET his properties.
DONALD PLUMMER will THREATEN students
with BOGUS LEGAL ACTION if they complain.
DONALD PLUMMER has ILLEGALLY EVICTED tenants.

What Plummer calls his 'accelerated procedure' is broken down, chewed up and spat out.

The eviction process is something that should be handled in the first instance by a COURT OF LAW. Should any tenant be in the unenviable position of unwittingly renting a Plummer property, they should IGNORE all attempts at eviction and report such instances to either the student representative or David Nunn.

KNOW YOUR RIGHTS!

I crumple the leaflet into a ball, and force it into an overflowing bin by the bus stop. Take a drag on my Embassy, let the smoke drift out through my nostrils. I can feel the nicotine kick in now, reckon I should've chased it with some codeine because I can feel that wee stab of guilt in my gut.

Like I should've known better. Should've had an ounce of sense, used my brain a little bit, but I needed the work too much to admit what I was doing.

Course, it explains why Plummer hired blokes like me and Daft Frank. Reckoned we were ex-cons, so we must've been short on morality. A bloke doesn't go to jail if he isn't corrupted in some way, and if we've been corrupted once, stands to reason we're open to it again, if the price is right. And the price is always right for someone who's desperate for cash. There was us, thinking we were working legit, that here was an employer, yeah, he might've been a bit dodgy at times, but he believed in our rehabilitation. And if that reasoning stuttered, there was always the fact that he paid us more than Starbucks or McDonald's, plus we didn't have to wear a uniform. Those places, they'd depress anyone. Grown men like kids playing dress up, paper hats and gold stars on their pinnies.

All Plummer wanted was a cheap workforce. Stupid bastards who wouldn't ask too many questions when things got hairy. Which they did. All the fucking time. And when we *did* start asking questions – like why the fuck were we getting *hurt* so much? – he got arsey, told us there were plenty of people willing to do the job we didn't want to do.

I didn't deserve that. And the more I think about the way he treated Daft Frank, the more I think the big guy deserved it even less than me.

He always takes things more personally than anyone else. He's fucking sensitive.

And, now I remember, he's late calling me.

I pull out my mobile, check for messages.

Nothing.

I call his mobile, it skips to voice mail.

Try his home number, it rings out.

Maybe he's called the other number. As the bus rounds the end of the street, I dump my cigarette, get the correct change out. Looks like I'll have to wait until I get home to see what the big man says.

TWENTY-FOUR

What the big man says is sweet fuck all.

Nothing on the home answer machine, still nothing on my mobile voice mail, and the same deal as before when I try to call him. That doesn't look good at all. Makes me think he's fucked up and now he's trying to avoid me. So I call Plummer at the office, see if he's come in for work.

'Hang on a second, alright? This might be important . . . Hello?'

'Don?'

'Can't talk right now, Callum. Busy.'

'Did Frank come –'

He hangs up on me. I stand there open-mouthed for a moment before I put the receiver back. He's busy. Which means the only way I'm going to get to talk to him is in person. Sometimes you have to be standing right in front of the man to get his full attention. So I call a cab, head into the city centre.

The taxi drops me off on Princess Street. Office space is pricey round here, but I suppose Plummer thinks it's worth it. The same reason he's got a Merc – a show of success supposedly breeds it.

I buzz up and the door clicks open without the usual interrogation.

Plummer Properties is on the third floor, but I can already hear him shouting about something. Sound carries and echoes in the stairwells of these older buildings, but shouted speech booms into noise. It's only when I hit the second-floor landing that I'm close enough to the source to make out what he's saying.

'I don't know what you expect from me. You want more money, is that it?'

I push on up the stairs. Plummer's out on his landing, and it sounds like he's talking to the guy who sent him that list. Except now he's asking for money? In front of Plummer, his back to me, is a thin guy in a good suit.

'Ah, Christ, this is all I need,' says Plummer when he sees me. 'Didn't I tell you I was busy?'

The thin bloke turns. He's clean-shaven, young. Has the oily skin of a former acne case, and the demeanour of one of those high-powered briefs. He gives me a cursory glance, obviously doesn't reckon me a threat, then turns back to Plummer.

This guy isn't the arsonist.

'We expect you to be reasonable, Mr Plummer,' he says.

'I am reasonable, pal,' says Plummer, pointing at the lawyer. 'You ask anyone you want, they'll tell you I'm reasonable. I'm a good businessman, and I don't deserve to be treated like this.'

'I appreciate that –'

'You appreciate fuck all, Mr Faulkner.'

'There's no need for language like that –'

'You have to get an *official notice*. You get one of those, we'll have something to talk about.'

'That can be arranged.'

'I'm sure it can. Until then, I know my rights.'

Faulkner smiles at that. 'Your rights –'

'You know what your problem is?' Plummer advances on the lawyer; Faulkner doesn't move, doesn't back down in the slightest. 'You read too much into a local rag. There's nothing on me. Nothing official, anyway. And nothing counts in our business unless it's official. Look at the words they're using, think about how they're telling you the news. It's all fucking hearsay dressed up as fact. I'm the victim of a smear campaign conducted to sell a few more papers.'

'There's the University of Manchester student representative, Mr Plummer. They have some claims which –'

'I can't be held responsible for a bunch of uppity fucking students,' says Plummer. 'Give it a week, they'll be boycotting

Nestlé again. "Oh, I can't eat a Kit-Kat, it's made by the baby-killers . . ." Honest to God, they're as bad as the rest of you. See one documentary about a supermarket accidentally dumping fertiliser into a river six thousand miles away and it's fucking boycott time.'

I clear my throat. Both men look my way. 'Am I interrupting something?'

'No,' says Plummer. 'Mr Faulkner here was just leaving, weren't you, Mr Faulkner?'

The lawyer looks across at me, seems to know who I am – there's that wee spark of recognition – then he nods at Plummer. 'We'll be in touch, Mr Plummer.'

'Yeah, I'm sure you will.'

Faulkner moves past me. I give him a sarcastic smile that isn't returned. Plummer doesn't wait for me to approach. Instead, he turns back towards the office, shoves the door open so hard it slams off the inside wall.

'You having a nice morning, Don?'

'Fucking *leeches*.'

I stop in the doorway to the office. It looks like a hurricane has swept through Plummer Properties. Papers all over the place, chairs upturned, filing cabinet and desk drawers hanging out. Either someone's done a number on the place, or Plummer's had a fucking full-on hissy fit in here.

'What happened?'

Plummer twists in the middle of the office, glares at me. The colour's still high at his collar. 'The fuck do you care?'

'Alright, I can see you're in a filthy mood. You've made your point.'

'You come round for any particular reason, Callum, or was it just to piss me off in the comfort of my own office?'

'Looks like that's already happened,' I say. 'And no, I came round to see if you'd heard from Frank –'

'Frank? Frank's a useless piece of shit and I'll be having words with him. Supposed to pick me up this morning, he's nowhere to be found and I couldn't get the lazy bastard on the phone. I had to get a taxi in to work, Cal. You have any idea how demeaning it is when you get recognised by a cab driver? These people don't read, they don't watch the news, they don't even *think*, half of them. But they don't need to, because I'm the most hated man in Manchester right now. I'm part of the local popular culture.'

'No, you're not.'

'So you didn't read it.'

Plummer marches through to his office. I follow him. He grabs a newspaper off his desk and hands it to me. He's made front page this time. The pickets are city-wide.

'He gave me earache all the way to the office,' he says. 'And then I come in to this bollocks, and you're giving me gyp because you're, what, *bored?*'

I fold the paper, drop it onto his desk. 'Right, then. I'll leave you to it.'

'Where d'you think you're going?'

'You haven't heard from Frank, I'm going to see him.'

'That's why you came round?'

'What were you expecting?'

He leans against his desk, folds his arms. 'A progress report.'

'Nothing much to say.'

His eyes narrow. 'You're fucking this up, aren't you?'

'I have a couple of leads,' I say. 'You didn't tell me what happened to the office.'

'What do you think happened? Someone trashed the place.'

'When?'

'Last night.' Plummer gestures to the office behind me. 'Broke in. Of course the building manager knows nothing about it. What am I saying, building manager? The man's a fucking caretaker, bent as the next ex-squaddie. He probably let the little shit in for a couple of twenties.'

'Anything missing?'

'How am I supposed to know? I've got five years' worth of tenants scattered all over the place. I don't *think* anything's missing – I mean, I've checked what's left of petty cash – but I don't have time to file, do I? And I don't have the money to pay anyone else to do it. Whatever they took, they took. Good luck to them. I hope it's what they wanted.'

I look behind me at the carnage. Doesn't look like the work of one person. If it is, it must've taken them some time to wreck the place this much. 'Any idea who might've done it?'

'Oh, what, you think I should let you investigate this too?'

'I didn't say that.'

'Because you're doing such a bang-up job of earning your money so far, aren't you?'

'I'm working on it, Don.'

'That's great news. Well done.' He sighs, and the life seems to drain out of him as he exhales. 'Doesn't matter anyway, does it? I'm pretty much finished here. What with that little prick Beeston trying to make out I'm Satan, the student reps giving me grief every minute of the day and that bastard that just left, I'm done. The rest of you are rats leaving a sinking ship, as far as I'm concerned.'

'Who was that bloke?'

'Craig Faulkner,' he says. 'Come here on behalf of the company that owns the building. He's the weasel they get to do their dirty work.'

'How d'you mean?'

'They want me out, Callum. Said they don't want to do business with someone like me.' He scratches his ear, eyes bugging with suppressed rage. 'Doesn't matter that I've paid my rent in advance, they still want me out. Tell you, they better do it properly. I'm not about to give them one fucking inch. They'll have to take this through the courts. Get an official notice of eviction and I'll think about it. Fight the bastards the rest of the time.'

Plummer breathes out. Then he looks up at me.

'Yeah, and don't think the irony of the situation has escaped me,' he says.

'I didn't say anything.'

'You were going to.'

'I'm still trying to help you, Don.'

'Of course you are. Help me like a hole in my fucking head.' He looks around. 'Which is beginning to sound like a good idea.'

'Don't be daft.'

'Daft?' He pulls out his wallet, flicks through it and extracts a photograph. He holds it up to me. Him, a middle-aged woman who looks like she barely remembers her best years, and a kid who's maybe in his early teens. 'That's my family. My wife and son.'

'Okay,' I say. I didn't know he was married. Always thought of him as a bachelor, definitely always thought of him as someone who lived alone. I didn't honestly think anyone would be able to stand his company long enough to marry him.

'Fourteen years,' he says. 'Wedding anniversary the night that fucking house burned down, did you know that?'

'No, you didn't mention it.'

'No, I don't think I would have.' He looks at the photo, then around at the office. 'Spent the night here. Slept in my chair. It's amazing where you can sleep if you're tired enough. Makes me glad I spent all that money on it. At least it reclines.'

He looks at me now. A red rim around his eyes that I hope is fatigue and not some crying jag waiting to happen.

'Things have been . . . strained,' he says. 'For a while. Really, since the press got their hooks into me. She – Cheryl, my wife – thinks that it's best we separate for a while.'

I don't say anything. Try to look sympathetic when I probably just look uncomfortable. Plummer places the photo back into his wallet and breathes out painfully.

'She says it's for my son's sake. He gets shit at school because of me. My boy's not much of a fighter, I'm afraid.'

He doesn't continue. He hasn't burst into tears yet, but if I don't say something to pull him out of this, I can see it coming. He tugs at his face, showing his bottom teeth. I doubt he knows he's doing it.

'Well, I haven't given up,' I say. 'But I still need to get in touch with Frank.'

Plummer snaps his attention back to me, his mood switched from maudlin to indignant. 'Poach my workforce, why don't you?'

He frowns. 'No, it's good you've got help. Let's see, should take that lot another couple of days to send me totally broke, and then you and Frank will be able to stop those Nazis from burning down a house that I don't own anymore.'

'You had any more notes?'

Plummer shakes his head.

'Then we've still got time, haven't we?'

'Yeah, you do what you want, Callum. I doubt it'll make a lick of difference, old son, but you carry on.' He moves from the desk, goes round the back and pulls out a bottle of Glenfiddich. 'Me, I'm going to get off my face and snooze the rest of the day, but you call me if anything comes up.'

'I will.'

I leave the office, take the stairs as quick as I can, calling for another cab on the way down. Once the taxi's on its way, I call Frank's house again. The phone rings out.

Try his mobile. Voice mail.

'Fuckin' pick up, you spaz.'

I kill the call.

When the cab arrives, I hop into the back, tell the driver to take me to Crumpsall and I'll give him directions from there.

TWENTY-FIVE

It's a bit of a drive, and despite the fact that I'm used to dropping him off around here at night, I'm still not sure where exactly Frank lives. So when I finally see a recognisable block of flats at the end of the street, it's a fucking relief. Not least to the driver, who looks like he's about to knock me out if I take him up one more cul-de-sac.

When I see Plummer's silver Merc in the car park, I nod to myself.

Frank's in. He's just not answering his phone. Which means that something went wrong and he's bottled telling me about it. I had a feeling something like that would happen, but I didn't want to say it out loud. I wanted to think I could trust the guy to stand in one place with a tape recorder running, but obviously that's beyond him.

The thing that really boils my piss, though, is that he didn't even have the balls to tell me he'd fucked up. What the hell did he think was going to happen if I didn't get him on the phone? He think I was just going to, what, *leave it?*

But he obviously doesn't think like that. He thinks like a kid, because that's his mental age. And what do kids do when it all goes pear-shaped? They run. Except Frank can't run anywhere, so he just hides in his flat and hopes that I won't come knocking.

I lean hard on his buzzer.

Wait.

Nothing.

So I lean hard on all the buzzers. There must be someone in this block who's either expecting someone or shit about security.

Right enough, through the chorus of irritation, there's the sound of someone saying, 'Just come right up.'

I push into the block, take the stairs because the lift looks like a death-trap and smells like a septic tank. Three flights later, I'm at his landing and out of breath, taking in the twisted mixed smell of chip fat and antiseptic in the air. My hip aches, spreads to the base of my spine. I can't remember the last time I took some pills, but reckon now's as good a time as any. Swallow them dry and straighten up slowly, take my time walking down the corridor to Frank's flat.

It's not bad up here. A bit cheap, maybe, but I've seen worse. Better than him living with his mum, which is what Frank was doing up until he got the job with Plummer. I never met the woman, but from what little Frank's told me, she sounds like a lovely woman with her claws so deep into her son, it's almost a sitcom. But then what do I know? It's not like my family's that close. Frank and his mum might be the norm.

As I get closer, I notice the front door to Frank's flat is open.

I wouldn't see the gap between the door and the frame if I was just passing. The door's barely ajar, but that gap's all it takes to put the fear in me.

Something bad happened here.

Not just kind of bad, either. *Really* bad.

I push the door with one hand. God help me, but it fucking *creaks*. I know I shouldn't go any further, feeling like a blonde in a slasher flick.

Telling myself that Frank's just been burgled, because I don't want to think about the alternatives.

The hallway's dark. And a strange smell in here, cloying.

Sweat. Whisky.

And cigarette smoke.

As my eyes adjust, I see strips of light under the door at the far end of the hall, and the door to my right. I turn, nudge the door open and the smoke smell is stronger in here. I squint against the light, my entire body tense, ready for a fight-or-flight moment.

Frank's living room. A portable telly in the corner, cheap three-piece. Coffee table with a bowl sitting in the middle of it, over-flowing with cigarette butts. I stare at the bowl. Don't get it. As I get closer, I see most of the dog-ends are roll-ups, roaches made out of the cardboard from a pack of Rizlas.

The fuck's gone on here?

I step back out into the hall, turn towards the other lit door. Must be his kitchen – the layout of the flat would point to that – but it's been a while since I was last here. Then I think, have I *ever* been here?

The answer: probably not.

And my survival instinct kicks in – go no further. Get out. Bad stuff happens in kitchens. Anywhere with wipe-clean surfaces and a handy array of knives.

A blast from the past: Rob Stokes with his pants around his ankles, blood already congealed down his chest.

Get out.

Get out now.

I clear my throat instead.

'Frank?'

There's a sound from the kitchen. A voice, maybe, but shot through with a thick dose of phlegm and cracked with pain.

'*Ghagum.*'

I freeze.

There's a thump from the kitchen. A sharp exhalation of breath, comes out like a hiss, then another thump, closer.

The door moves.

'Frank,' I say. 'That you, mate?'

A groan, then another hard thump against the door. It bounces against the frame, then swings open.

I can't see, the light blinding me for a moment.

There it is again, that sound: '*Ghagum.*'

Can't make out who just spoke, can't see anyone in the doorway until I look down.

Frank.

And he's had a proper hiding.

His face looks like it's been chopped down the centre, a rusty blood trail running down a mashed nose. Cracked lips and teeth. His mouth drops open and he's staring at me with his one good eye, the other already puffed shut. One arm wedged up against the door, holding it open.

'Fuckin' . . . *hell,* mate. Jesus Christ.'

I can't move for a couple of seconds, can't believe what I'm seeing. This big bastard of a bloke on the floor, looking like he's been run over.

He says, '*Ghagum.*'

And I get it now.

I move forward, ease Frank onto his back. His shirt's been ripped open, the buttons scattered across the kitchen floor. I grab him under the arms, shuffle round and grab one of the kitchen chairs for him. Takes a while, but I finally manage to get him sitting upright. He pulls at his shirt with one hand, trying to close it, keep some modesty. I cover him up, noticing as I do so the patchwork of yellow and purple that make up his ribs and gut.

Once he's settled, I take a step back, and get a better look at the kitchen.

There was a hell of a struggle in here. A block of knives lies broken and scattered, blades reflecting in the strip light. Smashed glasses in bloody shards on the floor, more blood pooling in the corner, against the sink, around the door. Red handprints on the kitchen table and chairs.

There's the smell of cigarette smoke again, mingled with sweat and blood. Something else. A brief look at Frank, and he's trying to cover up the fact that he pissed himself. And the smell of whisky, too. Something I caught in the living room, but it's like someone smashed a litre bottle of the cheap shit in here, it's that overpowering.

Right enough, there it is, a broken bottle of Glen Rotgut by the door. It was a big bottle, too.

I look at Frank. He's pawing at himself. Uncomfortable, in too much pain to think straight.

'What the fuck happened here, mate?'

Frank opens his mouth, his bottom lip splitting in the middle. Cracks his jaw, the sound loud as the bones scrape together. Frank's jaw locks. He raises one grazed hand, massages just under his ear, his eyes screwed shut. The lock breaks with another loud crack. A ragged breath of relief spills from Frank's mouth.

I grab the only glass in the place that hasn't been smashed, fill it with water and set it on the table. Dig around in my pocket and shake two codeine into the palm of my hand.

Jerk my head at him and say, 'Get these down you.'

Frank reaches for the pills, but he can barely see them. I help him with the water. He grimaces and looks at me, probably wondering why I've got prescription pills to hand, his head all over the place.

Like maybe I set him up for this.

'Who was it?' I say.

Frank opens his mouth to speak, blood on his teeth.

Nothing comes out.

'C'mon, mate . . .'

He shakes his head slowly. Looks like he's about to tap out, all the energy drained from him.

'Frank, tell me who did this to you.'

He raises an eyebrow. Waves one hand at the kitchen cupboards.

'What, you want a drink?'

A couple of fast waves, his shirt falling open again, then his hand drops to his side.

'What is it?' I go to the cupboards, open them up. Big lad's got more cereal than Seinfeld. 'There's nothing in here but Shreddies, man.'

He breathes out through his nose. It whistles. Looks at the floor, then brings his head up and grunts, like he's angry at me. He waves his hand at the kitchen cupboards again.

I pull out the cereal boxes, put them on the kitchen counter.
Then, right at the back of the cupboard, I find it.
The tape recorder.
And it's still in one piece.

TWENTY SIX

Frank was at the meeting, just like he promised. From the tape, I can make out that they had coffee – 'Kwiksave No Frills instant,' says Frank – and a tea that he couldn't place. From the sounds of it, caffeine's the last thing these people need. Sounds more like a zoo than a community meeting.

Frank motions me to fast-forward.

'Nothing happened?' I say.

He shakes his head, keeps motioning.

'I read the paper, man. Says there was a brawl.'

Another shake, another fast-forward gesture.

I do as he says, the hiss of the tape hitting the sound of voices suddenly. Frank waves at me to stop and rewind.

Whatever happened at the meeting, the tape recorder didn't pick it up. Too far away, maybe – there's just white noise and the occasional raised voice. That fucker at Dixons scammed me. But the way Frank's acting, the meeting's something I can strain my ears listening to later. He's more interested in afterwards, what I'm guessing he did to get himself kicked to shit.

'. . . was saying in there . . .'

Frank's voice.

'Yeah?'

A male voice. I don't recognise it.

'Just saying, y'know, I thought you was right, like. We're in trouble. Tell you, I'm worried.'

'You're worried. Right.'

Some laughter. Loud and kind of obnoxious.

'Big bloke like you, you're fuckin' worried . . . Jesus, I don't hold out much hope for the rest of us . . .'

'Yeah, I'm worried,' says Frank on the tape. 'I mean, Phil Collins, right, he's acting like he knows what's happening round here. But that's not what I've seen, is it?'

'He's a politician, mate. He'll say black's white. Besides, he's old-school, he's not one of us. Fuckin' Phil Collins is more concerned about keeping the fuckin' peace than he is owt else, the cunt.'

'Got to be something I can do about it, mind.'

Laughter, but not from anywhere near the microphone. Frank's speaking to more than one bloke, it sounds like. And the background noise – not a church hall, more like a pub. The voices raised not in anger, but to be heard over the general noise. So the meeting's over. And Daft Frank went to the pub.

'Tell you what you can do, Frank. You can vote ENS next council election. Get Jeffrey Briggs on the fuckin' case, you'll be fine.'

More laughter, and I wonder what's so fucking funny.

'Briggs is a politician, too.' That's Frank.

They don't hear it. 'Yeah, get Briggsy out from Bolton. Here, I knew that cunt when he was a fuckin' boot boy. Fucker were down the terraces at Maine Road, he'd be the first to kick off given half an excuse. Taking them cunts from the ICF right the fuck down.'

Someone else chimes in. And I think I know the voice: 'To the fuckin' pavement, Frank. Think on.'

'And look at him now, eh? Billy Big Bollocks. Right fuckin' top dog, eh? Mister fuckin' Suit.'

'Ease up, Russ. Briggsy's legit now. He's establishment. He has to be else they won't give him the fuckin' airtime.'

Jesus, it's Eddie. Frank's been hanging out with Eddie.

Before I can ask Frank about it, this Russ bloke interrupts: 'He's legit. Like fuck he's legit. He looks legit, he sounds it, too, but he's fuckin' not. Not really. And that's what makes him the fuckin' man, know what I mean? You was inside, Frank?'

'Yeah.'

'Then you know about it, don't you? There's a mate of mine, Jimmy Figgis . . . You know Jimmy Figgis?'

'No.'

'He knows Jimmy.'

'Yeah, you know Jimmy. You don't know the name, you'll recognise the cunt when I describe him. Got a face like all burnt up an' that. Pink gnarly skin, he's a proper fuckin' horror show on account of some fuckin' Paki scalded him on the inside, right? Fuckin' screws did fuck all about it an' all.'

'I heard it was acid, Russ.'

'Where'd you hear that, man?'

'I don't know.'

'Jimmy?'

'Maybe, yeah.'

'Right, well, that's why it's wrong. Jimmy's a fuckin' liar – he got scalded. And the screws did fuck all 'cause if they put force on a Paki, they're up on the old race hatred, am I right?'

'You're right.'

'Am I right, Frank?'

'Yeah,' says Frank, but he doesn't sound sure.

'Now what I'm saying is, Jimmy's a fuckin' lying knobhead an' that – proper fuckin' New World Order cunt reckons acid's a harder thing to get burned by – but he were bang on about some stuff. And Jimmy Figgis, you took notice of him.'

'Had to with that face.'

'Fuck up, Eddie-mate. Trying to tell Frank summat. Anyway, he was saying, like, it's not that big of a stretch to think that maybe the Pakis are tooling up for summat.'

'Don't get you.'

'C'mon, Frank. You heard what I was going on about in there. We're gonna have to circle the fuckin' wagons soon enough, mate. That burn in Longsight, there's rumours flying about: Pakis reckon us lot had summat to do with it.'

Eddie laughs.

'I know. It's a fuckin' job, innit? We're not like that, Frank. I mean, I don't want you thinking we're thugs just 'cause of what happened in that meeting. Just 'cause we're a bit rough and fuckin' tumble, that don't make our opinions any less fuckin' valid, does it? Thing is, the vocal minority have to be heard, don't they? The majority of people in Moss Side, they couldn't give a fuck, am I right? They're too busy working, keeping their heads down and being all fuckin' ignorant.'

'Apathetic.'

'They couldn't give a fuck. More people voting in *Britain's Got Talent* than any election. So someone's got to stir the shit a little. And if we don't do it, there'll be nowt done, you get me? They need to see the big picture.'

'Ah. No.'

'Fuckin' hell, he's a slow lad. And don't take that wrong, Frank. Here, I'm fuckin' dry. You get a round in, slow lad, we'll talk some more.'

Frank makes another fast-forward motion.

And stop.

'I knew Jimmy Figgis, Frank,' I say.

He motions for me to press play.

'Just so you know.'

Another 'play' gesture.

'. . . to the march, right?'

Stop. Rewind. Frank tells me when to play again, his head cocked to one side, listening hard.

Now.

There's the rustle of cloth against the microphone.

'. . . you going?'

'Got to go to the bog. Lager, mate. Goes right through us.'

The sound of Frank moving into the gents, the squeal and thump of the toilet door closing. Another rustle of clothes and his voice is as clear as it was when he told me what kind of coffee they had at St Dominic's.

'Two of 'em, Cal. You got Russell, he's the one what's talking the most. And that skinny bloke called Eddie – think he's the one you were talking about, the one from the garage. Got ink all over his arms. I got a good look at it and them tattoos are like full-on White Brotherhood.'

A click. Then another one.

'Did you turn the tape off to take a piss?' I say.

Frank nods.

'Thank you.'

Another click.

The sound of him walking back to the pub.

'Fuckin' hell, you're a horse, ain't you?'

'Oh, yeah. Listen, lads, it's getting on for last orders. I'm starving. You want to get a kebab?'

'Wouldn't say no, like. Get these down and we'll go.'

Fast-forward. Then play.

'. . . Bell's alright for you?'

A muffled affirmative from somewhere. The sound of glasses clinking. No other pub noise, so I'm guessing they're at someone's home. Probably Frank's, judging by the smell in here and the hall. From the sound of Frank's guests, the drink has hit them both hard. And Russell's taken the floor.

'You think the Pakis are gonna stand for a burn on their turf? No, they're gonna blame the first white man they see . . .'

'That burn,' says Frank. 'Who did that?'

'Fuck knows.'

'I thought it was . . . concerned citizens, y'know.'

'You pointing fingers, Frank?'

'I'm saying I wouldn't blame them.'

'Fuck's . . . Eddie, this cunt been listening to a single word I just said?'

'I dunno, Russ.'

'What, I look like I'd burn a fuckin' house down? What –'

'I didn't say that.'

'Didn't say that, you fuckin' *meant* it. Nowt to do with me. I need a fuckin' ciggie. You got a ciggie, Frank?'

'I don't smoke.'

'Eddie?'

'Rollies.'

'Fuck's sake. Give us a top up then.'

The sound of Frank coughing. Russell must've cadged a roll-up from Eddie.

'Cheers. You're coming to the march, right?'

'March?'

'Yeah, the march. The fuckin' march. You know about the march.'

'It's Briggsy. You not listened to the fuckin' radio, Frank?'

'I missed it.'

'Briggsy's got this bright idea, he's gonna get a bunch of the ENS together and we're gonna march on down to Rusholme.'

'Fuckin' genius set-up, you ask me.'

'March about what?' says Frank on the tape.

'We're gonna march in protest.'

'Protest against what?'

'Against the fuckin' busies, man. A Paki lad gets his arse kicked, a fuckin' Paki house burns down it's like, shit, we better do summat about this because otherwise we'll have all them fuckin' liberal bastard council people on our arses, right? But you see all them Pakis beating the shit out of people in the city fuckin' centre, right in everyone's fuckin' faces, and the police do nowt.'

'Right.'

'So Briggsy's got this march, right, on Friday. They can't stop him marching. Can't stop us protesting. And I'll tell you right off the fuckin' bat, you are coming. Because you are now a mate. And we're gonna get beered up –'

'Too fuckin' right.'

'We're gonna do some fuckin' damage. Hit them before they hit us. Show them who the fuck they think they're fucking with. 'Cause I'm serious about this, Frank – it's only a matter of time, you mark my fuckin' words, son. Them lot're gearing up for summat, I can smell it.'

The sound of Frank clearing his throat close to the microphone. 'Yeah. I'll be there. No bother, Russ.'

'Fuckin' *sound*. I knew you was a good bloke.'

'I need the bog again.'

'You got the bladder of a child. I'm after you.'

The sound of Frank getting up. He goes into the bathroom, the acoustics switching. The rustle as he moves the tape recorder.

'Cal, I'm scared, man. Look, I'm going to put this in the kitchen cupboard, right, and I just hope you got what you wanted. But I can't keep doing this. They're smoking. I can't breathe in there.'

A thump. 'Who you talking to in there?'

The click of the tape recorder as it turns off.

Silence.

I press stop, look across at Frank. Looks like the painkillers are kicking in.

'They caught you, didn't they?' I say.

He feels his jaw. It clicks once more, then he can move it properly.

'You want to tell me what happened? You up to it?'

Frank nods.

'They caught me,' he says. 'And then some.'

TWENTY-SEVEN

Frank tells me what happened. In detail, apart from what Russell and Eddie said. Even when he's quoting people, Frank tends to replace swear words, but I know what he means.

The way it worked out was this:

After Frank switched off the tape recorder, he flushed the toilet. Stepped out of the bathroom to find Russell standing in the hall with a face on.

'You talking to your knob?' he said.

Frank tried to shrug it off. 'You've had too much to drink, mate. I was talking to nowt.'

'You called it Cal.'

'What's that?' shouted Eddie.

'Cal, man. Frank here's named his fuckin' cock.'

Eddie came into the hall, a big grin on his face. 'You named your cock, Frank?'

'He called it a Cal.'

Eddie stared at Frank, and that was when Frank knew he was fucked. 'Cal? What, like *Callum*?'

Frank had never been a good liar. He said, 'Nah.'

'Callum like Callum fuckin' Innes?' said Eddie.

'Who's Callum Innes?'

'Phil's been on about this cunt Innes, man,' said Eddie. 'Been around the garage with his shitty little Micra. He was at that Longsight burn, you must've read about him in the paper.'

'That bloke? He's police or summat, right?'

Eddie drew closer to Frank. The smell of tobacco and whisky on the man's breath made Frank's gut flip. 'He's a PI. Isn't he, Frank?'

'PI?' says Russ. 'Fuck off.'

'Serious. He's been asking questions round the garage. Phil's been chewed on it, man. Reckons he got grassed by someone 'cause Plummer's been saying it's him what organised the burn. Doesn't have the foggiest why anyone would think he wasn't an old-school socialist.'

'You trying to fit us, Frank?' said Russell.

'Course he's trying to fuckin' fit us, Russ. Give your head a shake.'

Frank pushed past them into the kitchen. 'You two lads, you're paranoid.'

He opened one of the cupboards in the kitchen, stuck the tape recorder in behind a box of Shreddies. He could hear the pair of them talking in the hall. Russ and Eddie still trying to work out if Frank was suss or not. Frank had just managed to shut the cupboard door when Russ came into the kitchen. He had the bottle of whisky in his hand. Gripped tight, his knuckles pale around the neck of the bottle.

'So who's Cal then, Frankie?' Russ's mouth hung open.

'How'm I supposed to know? You're the one heard something. Wasn't me. Must've been your brain playing tricks on you. That's what you get for drinking the blended stuff, mate.'

'Mate?' said Eddie, coming up behind Russ. 'The fuck you know about mates, Frank?'

Russ shook his head and looked at the lino. He held the bottle up to his head for a second. 'What'd we say to him?'

'Eh?'

'What'd we tell him? I said we didn't do that fuckin' burn, didn't I?'

'Don't matter, man. Cunt's still gonna try to fit you up for it.'

Russ squinted at Frank. 'You seriously trying to do that, Frank?'

'I don't know what you're talking about. I thought we was having a chat, having a drink.'

'You drink,' said Russ. 'You had a drink?'

'Aw, *fuck's* sake,' said Eddie, doing a pained dance. 'He's had a drink. He's had *one* fuckin' drink all night, carried the bastard thing around. Y'know what, we should've known better, man. That cunt's acting all pally an' that, he's just trying to make us talk.'

'You got a wire on you or summat?' said Russ.

'Nah.' Frank held up his hands. 'And you ask me, Eddie, you're a nasty drunk.'

Russell looked at Eddie. Weighing up his options. Like even then, the way Frank tells it, Russell wasn't sure he believed his drunk mate. But Frank must've either thought too much of his act, or Russ decided he wasn't going to take any chances, because he went straight for the big man. The smell of smoke on Russ's breath made Frank cough. Spit flew into Russell's eye.

'Fuck you doing, gobbing at us, mate?' said Russ.

Frank started, 'I didn't mean to –'

Russell put two hands at Frank's collar, tugged his shirt open. The face on Russ, he was expecting the full body wire.

He was disappointed.

Frank made a move, planted both hands in Russell's chest, put his weight behind it, shoved the bloke across the kitchen. Russ slammed into and then over the kitchen table, bringing it onto its side as he grabbed onto a chair for support. The bottle of whisky dropped, smashed. Russell brought the kitchen chair to the lino as he fell.

'Get out of my house,' said Frank.

He'd figured his bulk would be enough to put them off, a show of force confirming it. But there were two of these blokes, and they were both drunk enough to figure they had a shot.

Eddie ran at Frank, caught him in the side. The skinny bloke stuck his elbow in Frank's gut, backed him up against the sink. Russell pulled himself up to his knees, his right hand glistening with blood, glass and whisky. He planted a hard right in Frank's face, snapping the big guy's head back. Eddie threw his weight against Frank, kept him pinned as Russell threw another right, the glass digging into his hand, into Frank's face.

Frank yelled, hunkered down and tried to barrel past. He made a grab for the knives on the kitchen counter – reckoned a weapon, a couple of choice slashes, and these fuckers would leave him alone. He caught, fumbled, the knife block dropping to one side and spinning across the counter, the knives falling to the floor. Eddie brought his knee into Frank's gut. Russell kicked him hard in the ribs.

And Frank – big Daft Frank, never took a fall in his life – hit the floor. Tried to crawl away, but he was caught on both sides.

Heel-kicks. Their coordination killed by the booze, but the blows hard enough to crack ribs, smash features. Frank's lungs screamed for air. Each heel took the breath out of him.

Frank knew well enough from his time inside that when you're down, you stay down. No room for Cool Hand Lukes. You play possum, you wait it out, you get to breathe again.

And Frank did breathe again. But only for a second. Then a kick to the jaw blacked him out.

He's still rubbing his jaw right now. He says he doesn't think it's broken, but he'll never eat toffee again. I take that as a sign he's feeling better.

'You been here since last night?'

Frank nods. The story's pulled him lucid, the codeine numbing most of the pain. 'Glad you made it.'

'Shit, Frank, I'm sorry, man.' I need a cigarette, but even I'm not that much of an arsehole that I'd smoke around Frank right now. 'You need to get yourself to a hospital.'

'I'll be alright.'

There's a long silence. I stare at a blood splatter on the lino.

'Why'd you do it, Frank?'

He blinks. 'What?

'I told you to go to the meeting, right? Report back. That was it. I didn't tell you to go undercover, did I?'

'I didn't get anything from the meeting.'

'Then you should've left it.'

He lets out a ticking sigh. 'I thought I did a good job.'

'I didn't say you did a bad job, mate. What's this bloke Russell look like?'

'Moustache. Stocky.'

'Just a 'tache? No beard to go with it?'

'They didn't burn that house down, Cal.'

'I know.' I dig around in my jacket, pull out the envelope that Plummer gave me. A stack of notes. Three hundred quid. 'Here.'

I drop the cash on the table. Frank glances at it, then looks at me. 'That's more than you said.'

'Call it a bonus.' I pull out my prescription bottle, shake some pills into my hand. Pick up the tape recorder. 'You sure you don't want to go to the hospital?'

He moves a hand. 'I'm fine.'

I slap six codeine on top of the money. 'In case you need 'em.'

'I don't need drugs.'

'Don't be fuckin' Amish about it. Take them if you need them. Your front door still on the latch?'

'Yeah, just pull it closed.'

I move to the door. 'Cheers, Frank.'

'No bother.'

And his lips part into something that passes for a smile.

TWENTY-EIGHT

The cab driver has the radio on as we head to Moss Side, and the DJ who's telling us that we're looking at Manchester's hottest summer on record is fond of old news. We've been told this time and again the past couple of days. The hotter it gets, the more we're told. And in weather like this – where there's a perpetual sweat on your skin even when you're not moving – the last thing you need to know is that it's getting hotter. Might as well tell a drowning man he's wet.

Or a beaten man he's bleeding.

The cab drops me off outside Collins Motors. I watch it go before I head into the garage. Looks empty, but I can hear people pottering around. That same DJ I heard before is on a radio somewhere in the building.

A mechanic, all grey stubble and sick eyes, comes out from the side office and frowns at me. He's wiping his hands on a Lake District tea towel. Chewing something, too. From the smell that follows him out, I'm guessing it's a fried egg buttie.

He jerks his chin at me, grease shining. 'Y'alright?'

'Eddie about?'

'Why?'

'Out the back, is he?' I walk past him, head through to the back yard.

And speak of the fucking devil.

Eddie's tinkering with a Nova, working on something under the bonnet. The mechanic I just saw says his name as I step out into the yard. Eddie straightens up. Sees me. Roll-up in his mouth as always. He squints against the smoke.

'Just come round to see how the car's doing,' I say.

'Your car?'

'Yeah.'

He chews his lip. Looks behind him. My Micra's parked by the entrance to the alleyway. Looks like the window and mirror have been replaced.

'Yours is the Micra,' he says.

'That's right.'

'Looks finished.'

'How much is it going to set me back?' I say.

'I'll get the bill for you.' He heads off to the garage office. There's some noise from within. I look around the place for a potential weapon. There are a couple of spanners in the garage, but I don't want to be seen going for them just yet, so I light an Embassy while I'm waiting for Eddie to get back.

He doesn't take long. He holds the bill out to me. 'Here y'are.'

I take one look and say, 'Got to be some mistake here, Eddie.'

'Nah.'

I stare at him. 'Then you've padded the fucker.'

'Not me.'

'Phil, then.'

'It's all itemised,' says Eddie. He points at the bill, but looks over my shoulder at something behind me. When he points, he shows the knuckles on his right hand. They're scraped and a little swollen. 'You got your wing mirror, your window, your tune-up and your labour.'

'I didn't ask for the tune-up. Scratch that off.'

'I can't scratch nowt,' he says. 'That's a usual. Standard, the tune-up, like.'

'Not for me.'

'For everyone, mate.'

'I'm not your fuckin' mate, you cunt.'

Eddie keeps quiet. His lips go thin and he stares at me.

I stare right back. 'Tell me something, Eddie. Were you at that meeting the other night?'

'What meeting?'

'St Dominic's church hall. The community meeting. You know the one.'

'No,' he says. 'Not really my thing, is it?'

'You're not into local politics?'

'No.'

'Who added this tune-up?'

'It's standard.'

'So Phil did, right?'

'Yeah.'

'And where's he?'

'Out.'

'Where's out?'

'Not here.' Eddie shifts his weight back. I can almost see him wind up for a sucker punch. 'Here, you want to pay the bill, sweet. You don't want to, we can hang on to your car.'

'Oh, you can do that, can you?'

'That's our right, like.'

'How'd you fuck your hand up?' I ask.

'You what?'

'Your hand. Noticed that it's skinned. Wondered who you'd been fighting with. Or if you got it dragging your knuckles on the fuckin' floor.'

'How's that your fuckin' business?'

'Just wondering.' I open my wallet, pull out some notes to cover the bill, saying, 'You charge everyone the same round here, I'm not surprised you don't do much business.'

Eddie's still not sure how to take me. Which is precisely how I want him. He might think he's on his guard, but he's not clever enough to maintain his calm. I hand him the cash. He counts it himself.

'You want a receipt?' he says.

'Yeah, why not? Be a nice souvenir of the time I got fucked by a stranger.'

'Not a stranger, mate.'

'And I told you, you're not my fuckin' mate.'

He nods, sucks his teeth. Then he heads back to the office. I check the work on the car. Can't complain, apart from the price, the gouging bastards. Look around, and I'm sure there are blokes out there in the garage watching me, waiting for me to leave. Let them watch. If they were going to do something, they would've done it by now.

When Eddie comes back, I snatch the receipt out of his hand, nod at the car. 'You fill her up?'

'Oh, you took the platinum service, did you?'

I grab my car keys off him, thinking even if he hadn't done what I know he did, I'd still want to smack him. 'Forget it.'

I get into the Micra, start the engine, and there's a rattle somewhere that wasn't there before. One of those repeat customer plants, probably, a final fuck-you from Eddie to me. He's about to head back to the Nova when I call his name.

'Just one thing,' I say. 'When you see Phil, you tell him I'm sorry that I couldn't make it to the meeting the other night.'

'Right,' he says.

'But I sent a mate of mine along to cover it for me. So I've got the edited highlights to look forward to.'

Eddie nods. He looks almost relieved.

'Just so he knows.'

'I'll tell him,' he says, smiling.

Bet you fucking will.

I throw the Micra into gear, then struggle to get the car back down through the alley. I drive a little way up the street, then kill the engine. Sit watching the garage in the rearview mirror. Eddie emerges from the garage, sees my car and folds his arms.

We both stare at each other for a few seconds. He's waiting for me to leave. I'm not going anywhere.

I light an Embassy and wind down my new window. He stays there for a while, staring at me, then he shakes his head and turns back towards the garage.

So what now?

There's a lad I know, he wasn't big on the whole revenge thing. A lot younger than me, acts a lot older. More mature, like he's made enough mistakes and learned from every single one of them. He wouldn't do what I'm about to do. He'd think it was a waste of time and energy, that there were other ways around it.

But the fact remains that when someone beats the shit out of your partner, you're supposed to do something about it.

Or something like that.

TWENTY-NINE

I smoke the cigarette down to the filter and chuck it out of the car. I get out, slam the door and head back towards the garage again.

If Eddie had done a runner when I came round, I wouldn't be back. If he'd showed some fucking guilt at what he'd done, I wouldn't be grabbing a large spanner from the garage and heading through into the back yard right now.

But he thought he could ride it. See him ride a fucking spanner in the head.

Eddie's back at the Nova. I could rush him now, but I want him to know about it.

'Eddie.'

Eddie freezes. Then thaws almost immediately. He slams the bonnet of the Nova harder than he needs to. Sounds to me like he's making a point. 'Fuckin' hell, mate. I do not get you at all.'

'How's that?'

Turns back to me, takes the cigarette from his mouth and blows smoke at the ground. He looks amused with me now. 'Come out with a fuckin' spanner, is it? So what d'you think you're gonna do with it? It's not even your spanner. You just picked it up from in there.'

'Did I?'

'Yeah, you did. That's Tony's spanner, that.'

'How d'you know that, then?'

Eddie grins. 'Because it's got his fuckin' name on it, *mate*.'

I don't check. Positive someone's going to jump me the moment I lower my head. I can hear crunching gravel behind me. Tony's come out of the garage and, from the sounds of it, he's brought reinforcements.

Which means I'm flanked. And fucked if this turns nasty.

'So what you doing with Tony's spanner?' says Eddie.

I smile. Even though my arse is eating my boxers with fear. 'Tell you the truth, it kind of depends on you, Eddie.'

'Is that right?'

'Yeah. Depends on what you want to tell me about last night. See, I couldn't make it to the meeting. But you know that, right?'

'What meeting's that again?'

'You know the one.' I change my grip on the spanner. 'St Dominic's. You met a mate of mine there afterwards.'

He looks at my hand. He raises the cigarette back to his lips. When he opens his mouth, I catch a glimpse of yellow-streaked teeth.

'Went to the pub,' I say. 'Got talking to him properly, went back to his flat and then you and your pal beat the shit out of him.'

There's movement on the gravel behind me. Someone shifting their weight. I pause, brace myself to move quickly if that weight shift is accompanied by something aimed for my head. Eddie doesn't look behind me, so I suppose I'm safe for now.

'Can't say I remember,' he says.

'You need a reminder, I've got it all on tape.'

He doesn't say anything. But there's tension at the corners of his mouth. A tiny movement, but seeing as I'm watching his face like a fucking hawk in case he nods at someone behind me, I catch it.

'You knew he was wired for sound,' I tell him. 'Just didn't know where, did you? Fuckin' stripped him down. Like a couple of grab-arse poofs. You strike me as the kind of bloke that did time, got fucked and liked it a little too much. What d'you say, Eddie?'

Eddie blinks. Slowly.

'Talking fuckin' hard, eh?' he says, breathing out through his teeth. 'But you got nowt.'

'I just wanted to tell you.'

'You got nowt.' Shaking his head slowly now, pushing his mouth up to his nose. 'You got fuck all, you just come round here to try and put the shits up us. Reckon you see these fuckin' tats, I'm scared of going back to stir, you'll fuck with me head a little bit, right?'

'Hit them before they hit us?' I say.

Eddie drops his cigarette to the gravel, steps on it. 'You fuckin' heard nowt, mate. Making it up.'

'Frank wasn't wearing a wire, Eddie,' I say. 'But he *was* recording. You just didn't bother checking the rest of the house, did you?'

'Fuck off.'

'What was it?' Another change of grip, my palm slick with sweat. 'You take one look at him, think he was dead and fuckin' bottle it?'

'You don't know what you're talking about, mate.'

Eddie looks behind me. I don't say anything. Listen for sudden movement.

If they come at me now I reckon I've got one clear throw at Eddie's head, watch the spanner connect and put him down. Then maybe a few decent kicks to the fucker's balls and face before I'm pulled off. All dependent on how many of Eddie's mates are now standing behind me, and how committed they are to the cause.

'You know I'm telling the truth here, Eddie,' I say.

'So, what d'you want, mate?' Eddie sticks his tongue under his bottom lip as if he's fishing for food. Then he sucks his teeth and takes a few steps forward. 'You want to fuckin' come at us, or what?'

'Take a swing at you?' I say.

'Yeah. Fuckin' that's why you got Tony's spanner, innit?'

'One of the reasons.'

'So, you gonna ask Tony if you can use his fuckin' tool?'

'Tony, can I use your spanner to brain this cunt?'

'Cunt, is it?' says Eddie.

'Nah,' says Tony. 'Think I'll have it back.'

'Fuckin' *cunt,* is it?' Eddie gets closer. He's breathing through his mouth now. Working himself up for something bloody. 'Here, you want to be the fuckin' hard lad, you come ahead. Do not fuckin' bottle this, alright? Your mate took a few kicks, reckon he took 'em because you were too much of a fuckin' bottler to get the job done yourself, eh?'

I keep it calm. Don't even twitch with the spanner. Difficult now Eddie's close. One quick swing is all it'll take, and him pushing the bottle button doesn't help his fucking case.

'So what's stopping you now?' says Eddie.

'I didn't come here to deck you, Eddie,' I say.

'Fuckin' looks like it.'

'That's because you haven't been listening. I've got you on tape.'

'I heard that.'

'But you didn't *listen.* I've got you on tape. Russ, too. And I've got you both saying that this march tomorrow night is going to be a fuckin' bloodbath.'

'We never said that.'

'You said enough. You said Briggs has organised this to be a fuckin' riot. Can't stop you from marching, right? And if you march down where you're not wanted, and people happen to be out there chucking things at you, *provoking* you, you reckon it's perfectly alright to fight back, don't you? Because that's all you've been doing all this time anyway. Fighting back.'

Eddie doesn't say anything.

'I'm not on anyone's side here, Eddie. Way I see it, you're all as fuckin' bad as each other. But I *am* warning you to get the word out. Call off the march. Else I'll make that tape available to the press.'

'What tape's this?' says Collins.

I see him moving in my peripheral vision, reckon it's safe enough to chance a look. Collins is sweating hard under his suit jacket. The stains have already started to spread from his armpits to his tie, which hangs around his neck like a tugged noose. The gravel crunches louder under his feet as he walks round to face me. Eddie backs off a few steps at Collins's approach.

'Eddie didn't tell you,' I say. 'Course not.'

'Tell me what?' says Collins.

'About this march tomorrow night.'

'I know there *is* one, yeah,' he says, looking at Eddie, then around behind me. 'But I don't see what it's got to do with Eddie.'

When I look back at Eddie, I can see the fucker boiling, wishing Collins wasn't here. I take the opportunity to turn round, see who's behind me.

Three mechanics. The stubbly guy who I reckon is Tony, two others I've seen in the shadows of the garage, only noticeable because of the oil shining in the dark.

I turn back to Collins. 'Right. Because you're the politician, right? You're the one worried about his community. You're not part of this shite.'

'I don't know what you're talking about, Mr Innes.'

I stare at Eddie as I say, 'Well, to warn you up front, Mr Collins, Eddie and some of the other lads are going out down the curry mile tomorrow night. Reckon they'll call in sick the day after, and you'll have the press on your doorstep.'

'And why's that?' says Collins.

'Because –'

'Fuck yourself,' says Eddie. 'You want to talk about grab-arse poofs, you watch out for your gay mate up in Salford.'

'You what?'

'Fuckin' sort that poof out good and fuckin' proper –'

I bolt for Eddie, swing the spanner as hard as I can. The tip connects sharply with Eddie's face and he drops like a bag of rocks. Hits the dirt with blood splattering out of his nose onto the ground, one hand up, the other breaking his fall.

I take another swing at him, but there's arms around my waist, forcing me forward into the Nova. A jolt of agony up my spine as Tony barrels me into the car. I drop the spanner and cry out. Then there are more hands on me, dragging me away from the Nova. I can see Eddie still on the ground, up to his knees now, one of the mechanics demanding that he move his hand away from his face so he can check the damage.

I brace myself for a volley of kicks, a little solidarity violence for their fallen comrade, but all I get is held tight.

Collins turns to me, his face tight. He gestures for the mechanics to let me go.

'What the hell was all that about?'

I look round at Tony and the other mechanic. They've backed off. They don't want to sort me out in front of their boss, but they *do* want to sort me out.

Back to Collins, and I realise he's the only thing stopping me from ending up like Frank right now. 'We should walk and talk.'

Eddie switches round in the dirt. He's being helped to his feet, one hand clamped to his face, his eyes wild in their sockets. He points at me, doesn't have to say anything.

You're fuckin' dead.

I walk with Collins towards the alley. 'You know there's going to be a protest march tomorrow night. Jeffrey Briggs is organising it.'

'I told you, I don't have anything to do with –'

'I believe you. I think. But your boys here do have something to do with Briggs, and your fuckin' ignorance isn't going to save you. I'm asking you to talk to those lads for me. They'll listen to you more than they'll listen to me, obviously. Tell them to pass the word on, I have it on tape that this march is going to be a forced riot.'

Collins's face pales. 'That's got nowt to do with me.'

'It will do.' I stop by the entrance to the alley. Look across at my car. 'Because if you don't manage to persuade these lads from attending, if you don't use whatever pull you have with Briggs to stop this march, then I'll get the *Evening News* to do to you what they did to Plummer.'

'You can't do that.'

'With a fuckin' tape of your employees, I can. Now think about that.'

I head off towards my car. Stop as I'm about to get in.

'And tell Eddie, I see him anywhere near the Lads' Club, I'll put him in the fuckin' ground.'

THIRTY

Sitting in my darkened living room, waiting for boot boys to kick the front door in. I've tried to tell myself I'm not doing that. Went so far as to actually cook something to take my mind off it, fried the blood out of a steak, got surprised at how long it took to do a potato in the oven. Then I settled down in front of the telly with a beer.

Now the beer's drained, and I've moved on to the vodka, straight from the freezer, the greasy dinner plate on the coffee table in front of me. Watching the news with the volume turned down, got a pleasant codeine-vodka haze going on and a chair wedged under the handle of the front door. Not that it'll make much of a difference, but it should be an early warning if Eddie and his pals decide to pay me a visit in the middle of the night.

PROTEST MARCH PLANNED FOR FRIDAY EVENING.

That's the caption underneath footage of Jeffrey Briggs leaving what looks like the Manchester law courts. He meets a huddle of reporters, tries to fend them off as he walks right through the middle of them. His face has the burst blood-vessel complexion of a serious whisky man. A small knot in his tie, which hangs from a thick neck. His suit jacket barely covers his gut. The man's trying his best to keep a smile on his face, but it's not a natural expression and makes him look like he's been sipping vinegar.

I take a drink, talk into my glass: 'Cunt.'

See a brief standing next to Briggs now, a shabby guy, looks like a welder in a cheap suit. Briggs comes up to a clutch of microphones, clears his throat and brings up a piece of paper. Some kind of prepared statement, but I'm not going to hear it. I double-check that the volume's turned right down. I don't need to hear what he's saying to know it's most likely bullshit.

Besides, the papers have been full of it recently. When they're not talking about how hot it's getting, how the temperature's breaking all known records, they're talking about how crazy people are getting about the race situation. We're so scared of the influx of immigrants that we're not dealing with it, we're withdrawing, terrified of car bombs, ricin and crazy brown guys with explosive vests on public transport. We're barricading ourselves into our homes and watching telly, letting all this shit fester.

And that can't be good.

I finish my drink. Feel the bubble where my brain should be.

Look across at the front door, squint to see if the chair's moved.

No. We're good. Safe for now. But I'm still slipping out here, feeling the edges blur a little too much. I lean forward, put my glass on the coffee table, take a deep breath. I can't just wait around here. I'll keep drinking, keep swearing at the telly, get more and more fucked until I wake up screaming again.

So I get to my feet and stand there for a bit, looking at the television. Swaying in the half-light. I look down at the ashtray, see it clogged with filters and wonder when I smoked all those cigarettes. I check my pack, find I'm running low and decide I'll go out, get some more.

I shouldn't drive, but I try anyway. What I end up doing is leaning over the steering wheel and looking at the road through narrowed eyes. Turn the radio on to keep me from losing my mind at the wheel, and I'm grateful it's a music station. I don't think I could take more news at the moment.

I find myself heading to Cheetham Hill. When I see a garage up ahead, I don't trust myself to manoeuvre the Micra onto the forecourt without doing some serious damage, so I park up the street and stagger down to the shop. Buy a load of cigarettes, some chocolate and a couple of cans of Red Bull to shake some of the booze out of my system. All it does is wake me up a little. I still feel pissed.

I can see Strangeways assaulting the skyline from here. You can't walk around Cheetham Hill without seeing at least part of that shithole. When I first got out, I swore I'd never go near the place again, but since that close call in Newcastle, I've found myself driving back up here every now and then. It's a kind of therapy for me; I can look at the place now and not think I'm going to be dragged back.

Not without a fucking good reason, anyway.

I light a cigarette, head for my car. As I'm walking, I notice someone at the end of the road, hear the scrape of heels as she walks towards me. As the light catches her, she's one of those women who look a lot older than they actually are. Dark hair frames her face, which is pale, but made up. She's holding onto a handbag that doesn't match what passes for her outfit, a denim skirt and trackie jacket, halfway zipped, revealing a pinkish cheap top.

'Got a light, love?'

I look at her. Nod. She shakes a cigarette to her lips. I light it for her. When she breathes smoke, she looks up at me as if she expects me to say something.

When I don't, just swaying and staring aimlessly, she says, 'What you after?'

'I don't know,' I say, smiling. 'Have not got the foggiest.'

She pulls the cigarette from her mouth. 'You want prices first or summat?'

I shake my head. 'It's okay.'

She tries to keep talking, listing it out. Hand jobs, blow jobs, fuck jobs, no anal, no bareback . . . and I can afford it all.

'No, it's okay. I'm not interested. Really.'

It takes her a while to process that. She looks at the cigarette in her hand, then smiles at me, but there's a touch of pity on her face that I'm not keen on. 'Did you think I was just asking for a light?'

'No.'

'Then what?' She's already looking around, wondering if she should keep talking to me. Getting ready to flinch if I make a move for her.

'You know something, I don't know.' I follow her gaze, then up to the prison. 'I just thought I'd help you out, I suppose. Be that one bloke who actually gives you a light, so you remember.'

'Why would I want to remember that?'

I nod. 'You're right. Sorry I bothered you. You take care of yourself, alright?'

She cocks her head at me, then sticks the cigarette in her mouth and continues up the road, glancing every now and then over her shoulder to make sure I'm not following her. I take a drag on my Embassy, blow smoke, and look at the 'Ways again.

Stupid. *Stupid.* Can't play the same game with her that I can with other women. What fucking game? What other women?

Fuck off.

It doesn't take, so I have to say it out loud: 'Fuck off.'

And now I feel like a headcase.

Which is why I'm no good with women, right? Fucking head-cases don't tend to pull that often. If I want to justify it to myself, I could say that I got locked up before I got the chance to live the life of the single bloke. Didn't get a chance to get beered up with my mates – fuck it, didn't *have* any mates except my smackhead brother, and he wasn't much fun to be around. So I didn't get a chance to hit the pubs, cracks on with the drunk lasses for a quick fumble up an alley or in a bus shelter.

The time I should've been doing that, I was shacked up with a bunch of fucking lags. Blokes talking about sex as fantasy – 'I'd fuck that' about a picture on the cell wall. They treated their women like wishes, afraid that talking about them would make them disappear.

Scared, angry and desperate. Prone to things that'd make them sick on the outside.

But fuck that. Don't get on it; keep it locked. Now's not the time.

I dump the cigarette and get back into the Micra. Sit listening to the radio for a moment, trying to recognise the songs by the first few bars and failing miserably, then pop the second can of Red Bull and guzzle it till my eyes water.

When the news comes on, I kill the radio and start the engine.

Feeling slightly better now. Clear enough to drive home without killing anyone, anyway.

THIRTY-ONE

First thing the next morning, I call Frank's mobile. This time, it doesn't go to voice mail. Which is immediately gratifying, because it means he's doing better than the last time I saw him.

'How you doing?'

He keeps his voice low, but he seems better. More alert. 'I'm good, Callum. Bit stiff, bit achey. Nothing too bad.'

'Why're you whispering, mate?'

'I'm . . .' The rustle of the phone against material. Then: 'I'm round my mum's. She's not happy.'

'Right. Course not. She said something. She noticed you were –'

'Well, it's not like it wasn't obvious,' he says. 'I look like that bloke from *The Goonies*.'

I laugh. Grab my jacket and head out of my flat. 'Well, you get her to look after you, mate. Bed rest. You need any money or anything, you let me know, okay? Least I can do.'

'Appreciate it.'

I hit the car park, head for the Micra. It's a cool enough morning to wear a jacket, so I shrug into mine, pop my mobile in the pocket and get into the car. The idea this morning is head over to Paulo's, apologise for not going round yesterday to help with the new rings, and see if there's anything he wants me to do. If I'm going to be moving into the back office, it's best I get on his good side.

Start the engine, and the radio kicks in. It's a talk show, one of those topical phone-ins where the insane and the ignorant call up thinking they're experts because they read a book once.

Or they've heard the latest news – some guy in Bolton, asylum seeker, just been found guilty of four counts of possessing material of use to terrorists, plus two further charges of similar offences and two counts of money laundering. The charges are all very vague, but the evidence isn't.

Talk about fucking red-handed. Apparently the guy had the equivalent of the *Terrorist Almanac*, how to maintain multiple identities, advice on how to carry out suicide bombings on bus and train networks, pointing to other targets such as stadium exits, colleges and cinemas. Home-made bombs and internet chemistry lessons – how to poison the country in three simple steps.

What made me stop is that he supposedly downloaded all this from a secret Al-Qaeda website. Wonder if they're on Facebook, too.

Some bigwig in Manchester's counterterrorism unit – which I didn't even know we had – says: 'He appears to have been a *sleeper* remaining in the shadows, waiting and preparing for action. It's clear to us he had support and links with terrorists across the world.'

That's the main topic of conversation at the moment. Various callers ranging from the narked to the homicidal, both sides of 'Manchester's race divide' as the DJ puts it. Way to pull communities together, you daft prick.

Thirty seconds into it, and I'm already annoyed. And I'm not the only one. Some of the callers with limited vocabularies are throttled in the middle of their sentences, a profanity caught in the five-second delay. As for the rest of them – especially the ones bandying rhetoric around like it's their own show – I'd gladly choke the lot. I check my watch, wonder why these people aren't at work like the rest of us.

'Not just the recent terror arrests to talk about,' says the DJ. 'We also heard a lot earlier on about the attack in Rusholme. Bit of a hot topic for a warm morning, this one. Keeping the lines open, so have your say. You know the number to call.'

I turn it down, keep it as background noise so that it almost matches the engine.

Catch the words 'student' and 'beaten' . . .

My back hurts. I take a couple of pills, have to dry-swallow them because I've run out of water. Or someone from the garage nicked the bottle I had in the glove compartment. When I rattle the remainder of the codeine around in the bottle, I realise I'm running low. Wonder how the fuck I managed to take so many.

'On the line, we have Del Shickley –'

'Shikely,' says the caller. Then slower, for the benefit of the DJ and anyone else who needs it: 'Shick-ay-lee.'

'My apologies, Del.'

'Absolutely fine, Robin. Happens all the time.'

'Now, you found David, is that correct?'

'I did, yes, but that's not why I'm ringing in. I've been advised not to talk about what happened. For legal reasons.'

'You have something else you'd rather talk about?'

'Yes, mostly to counter what one of your callers was talking about, uh, this being a *racist* attack . . .'

'Jeffrey Briggs.'

'Yeah, well, he wasn't at the hospital,' says Del. Quickly, as if he's positive he's about to be cut off. 'He said he spoke to David last night. Well, he didn't. I found him, I spent most of the night at the hospital and Mr Briggs wasn't there. So he didn't talk to David, much less get his side of the story.'

'David was beaten, wasn't he?'

Del pauses. 'I'm not sure if I'm able to talk about that.'

'There's no need to be coy, Del. It's in all the papers.' There's a rustling sound as the DJ picks up a newspaper. 'Says here that David was found beaten in Rusholme.'

'If a white man is beaten up in Rusholme, that doesn't necessarily mean it's a racist attack.'

'But there have been incidents where students have faced discrimination and sometimes even *violence* in South Manchester, haven't there?'

'I wouldn't know.'

'Well, what Mr Briggs was saying was that he's had students

approach him. They've told him that they've felt under siege for quite a while. And perhaps we shouldn't look at David Nunn's attack as an isolated case . . .'

I reach for the radio, turn up the volume.

Jesus.

David this, David that. Didn't realise it was David fucking Nunn they were talking about.

But it's true.

I swing by the newsagents on Oldfield Road, pick up another bottle of water and the early edition. It's only a small story, the bare facts, really. I dread to think how badly it'll have snowballed by the evening papers.

David Nunn, second-year politics student, found beaten to shit in Rusholme last night. Assailants unknown at the present time, and from the tone of the story, I doubt they'll be caught. An otherwise unmotivated attack, the police haven't got the first fucking clue, as per usual. The ENS mouthpiece who's been given far too many column inches agrees with me. Except he's convinced that it's a racist attack, that there were racial slurs shouted before the kicking took place.

Which means he knows more than the police, or he's just leaning on hearsay to make a point.

'If it's white on Asian, there's an outcry. Culprits are found and tried. Cast the situation in photo negative, and those politically correct and castrated institutions turn their heads.'

Segue into how South Manchester isn't safe for students any-more, the same shit the DJ was flinging. They can't find affordable housing anywhere, a situation made worse by the recent allegations surrounding Donald Plummer.

They always shoehorn Plummer into the proceedings. Makes me think he's actually got a point – maybe the press are persecuting him. At the very least, they seem to have found a bad guy who's in no real position to fight back. I'd feel sorry for the bastard if what they were saying wasn't true. To cap it all off, the Manchester University student representative have announced that they're boycotting any letting agency handling a Donald Plummer prop-erty.

Flick back to the David Nunn story: the student's in a coma, which kind of puts the kibosh on the ENS ever talking to him. Just like Del said.

Something there, though. A connection, definitely. I just don't know how tenuous it is. And my brain tends to weave conspiracy at the drop of a fucking hat these days.

Swig from the water. Tap the newspaper as I think about it. I don't like it that David Nunn was in Rusholme, unless he lives there. It bothers me, and I don't know why.

I start the engine, chuck the water bottle onto the passenger seat, and set off for the University of Manchester.

When I get there, I pay through the nose to park and head for the union bar. Reckon, if I was a student, that's where I'd be right now. A couple of years of exams, I could've come somewhere like this. Don't know what I would've done outside of drinking, mind, but I'm sure some subject would've cropped up.

I get into the union bar, see students dotting the place, but none of them looks familiar. Ideally, I want to talk to one of David's mates, reckon if I see anyone from the picket, that'll be a good start. But this lot don't look like they leave the house much. If they had, they wouldn't be looking at me like I just crashed my spaceship outside.

Yeah, I don't belong. That's getting more and more obvious. Christ, whatever it is that's playing on the union jukebox hammers that point home – an acoustic guitar and what sounds like a trapped cat on vocals.

Feeling about as comfortable as I would've felt at that Moss Side meeting. And knowing that even if I'd stayed on at school, all that, I wouldn't have been one of this lot. Because even when I was kid, I knew that being clever didn't stop you from getting your arse kicked – in fact, in a lot of ways, it fucking caused it.

So they can give me the eyes over their lattés as much as they want. I don't care.

I keep walking, head into a long corridor off the main bar, one wall glass, the other crammed with noticeboards.

Start checking the boards out one by one.

There's one for a lesbian-gay society, another for the am-dram – auditions for *The Gut Girls* by Sarah Daniels, along with character types. I'm guessing that there aren't many actors in the university because most of the characters are female. Band societies, DJ societies, job vacancies for events and booze night coordinators.

And then the political boards. You name the party, they're represented here, plus a few more that must've been made up after a night on the drink.

'Mr Innes, isn't it?'

I turn at the voice, recognise the skinny girl from the letting agency. She's watching me with wide brown eyes, head cocked to one side. If it wasn't for all that shit in her face, she'd be pretty in a waif-like way. A messenger bag hung over one shoulder. It looks heavy. She's holding a bright yellow piece of paper with the word MEETING on it, but that's about all I can see.

'Yeah, you were at the picket, weren't you?'

She nods, tucking a strand of hair behind her ear.

'You a friend of David's?' I say.

She looks uncomfortable at the mention of his name. 'I'm his girlfriend.'

'Right. Shouldn't you be at the hospital or something? I mean, no offence, but –'

'I've just come back.' She holds up the notice: MEETING CANCELLED. 'Supposed to be a meeting tonight, but we can't have it without David.'

'How's he doing?'

'He's in a coma, Mr Innes.'

'I read that.' I show her the newspaper. 'But it says some bloke from the ENS talked to him. I just wanted to get my facts straight.'

'The ENS?' She frowns. 'I don't think so.'

'That's what it says here.'

'You think he's in any state to have visitors? If they're not even letting *me* in . . .' She shakes her head, then holds out her hand for the newspaper. 'Sorry, can I have a look at that?'

I hand her the paper. 'Page two.'

She reads the story, a crinkle appearing between her eyebrows. When she's finished, she folds the newspaper and hands it back to me. 'You're a private detective, right?'

'Investigator, yeah.'

She looks like she's thinking hard. Then she tacks up the notice to the board, makes a move to leave. Stops.

Looks at me again, cocking her head. Almost squinting at me. 'You want to get a coffee?' she says.

I nod, and let her lead the way.

PART THREE

×××××××××××××××× ××

ALL YOU FASCISTS (ARE BOUND TO LOSE)

THIRTY-TWO

The girl's name is Karyn. She was adamant about the 'y', dropped
the cash to change it legally from Karen. Brought up in one of
Chester's leafier suburbs, a two-car family, mother a stay-at-home,
father with his own consulting business that meant they didn't have
to worry about money. What he consulted, I didn't ask. I wasn't
that interested. But Karyn likes to talk, mostly about her sister.
Emma's studying at Oxford and, by God, are the family proud of
her. But Karyn, well, nothing she ever does feels good enough. Not
that she cares what her parents think.

All this as Karyn sips a decaf soya-milk tall latte, picking at an
apple-cinnamon muffin without any of it actually reaching her
mouth. Baked goods as fretwork, building up to something she
doesn't want to discuss.

'You look like you want to be somewhere else,' she says, a small
smile on her face.

'Now that you mention it, I thought you wanted to talk to me
about something.'

'And your time's money, is that it?'

'Something like that.'

'What is the going rate these days?'

'For what?'

Karyn stops picking at the muffin, the top of it lying in crumbs
on the plate. 'I don't know how to go about this, Mr Innes. It's not
something I've had that much experience with . . .'

'You want me to find out what happened to David.'

She shakes her head and laughs. 'Sounds daft now. Forget it.'

'Okay.'

'I know what it sounds like.'

'Sounds like you don't believe what you read.'

'The paper?' Karyn stabs the newspaper with one finger. 'No, I don't believe *that* version of events. Bugs me that they can get away with making stuff up like that.'

'Well, he got beaten up. That's true enough. And if he lives in Rusholme –'

'David didn't – *doesn't* – like Rusholme.' Karyn sighs, resumes picking at her muffin. 'He lived there last year, but he told me there was no way he'd go back.'

'Any particular reason?'

'I don't know. I didn't know him then. He doesn't like to talk about his first year. Family problems, course problems, discipline problems.'

'He likes a drink.'

'There were a couple of nights in the cells, yeah,' she says. Smiling as if it's a walk on the beach. The smile disappears when she sees the expression on my face. 'But that's pretty normal, Mr Innes. We all have it to a certain extent. No matter how much you might want to leave home, the reality of it is still difficult. And the sudden freedom, nobody telling you you can't do things . . .'

'I can imagine. So David went to Rusholme last night and didn't tell you about it?'

'No. I mean, yes, he didn't tell me about it, but I'm not his guardian, am I?'

'You don't live together?'

'No. We've only been seeing each other for a year.'

'Right, you didn't know him before that.' I nod. 'You told me that already, didn't you?'

'Yes.' She looks at me. 'Do you think I'm wrong?'

'Wrong how? Like do I think you should believe what the paper says? No. Not if you don't want to.'

'You must be getting a lot of work from that newspaper story, right? Everyone wants their own PI?'

'I got some work, yeah.'

'A lot of work?'

'Why are we sitting here, Karyn?'

'I wanted to hire you.'

'Then you could've said that right at the start and saved yourself the trouble of flattering me. I'm too busy.'

'So what are you doing here?'

'Another case entirely. Can't really talk about it. Thought your boyfriend might be involved.'

'So it's the ENS,' she says.

'Not necessarily.'

'Got some wanker from the English National Socialists saying he's talked to David, so you jump to the conclusion that he's connected.'

'It's not such a fuckin' leap, is it? After what you just told me about his temper —'

'What temper?'

'You said he'd had a couple of overnighters.'

'God, just *drunk* stuff.'

'No, it's never just *drunk* stuff, Karyn. If you're locked up, you're a fighter.'

She leans forward. 'Let's get this straight, and you can write this down if you feel you have to take notes for your *other case*. The English National Socialists will latch on to anyone if it means votes.' The trace of irritation in her voice becomes something more militant. 'David's not a person to them, he's a demographic. In fact, David's been speaking *against* the ENS for a long time. If they knew anything about him, they'd know that. He's been very clear that he's in no way connected with that kind of political thinking. And he's not the type to engage in . . . *random* violence.'

'Okay,' I say. 'That's all I needed to know.'

'But nobody's going to hear that because of that stupid fucking story.' She narrows her eyes at me. 'You know the Conservatives are telling people to vote Labour or Lib-Dem rather than BNP or the ENS? You ask me, that's one of the few laudable things they've done in the last twenty years, asking people to vote for the opposition.'

'I wouldn't know. I'm not really up-to-date. It doesn't concern me.'

'It should. If you don't vote, you're leaving it up to the gullible to make your decision for you.'

'Very socialist, Karyn.'

She shrugs. 'I don't care what it sounds like. A majority of any general public will do exactly as it's told. And I'm telling you, David would have *nothing* to do with Jeffrey Briggs. It'd be like Guevara hooking up with Hitler. But I'm worried that people might see it like that, think the ENS is a party to be trusted, you know what I mean?'

'You think David Nunn has that much sway over people?' I say, trying to keep the amusement out of my voice and failing.

'Why not? He's the one who organised the city-wide picket of the letting agencies. And he did it without the student rep's permission, because getting them to do anything like that takes forever. And the reason he managed to do that is because David *does* things. He's a natural leader.'

'I'm sure he's very charismatic.'

'But it's not as if David's in any position to tell anyone what really happened, is it? And in the meantime, those fuckers are going to use him as some sort of *mascot.*'

I finish my coffee. 'Blame a politician for bending the fuckin' truth. What a novel idea.'

'But you can prove them wrong. Discredit them, make it public.'

'I'm not about to get caught up in any fuckin' agenda here, Karyn.'

'You want to be a hero, be heroic,' she says, her voice raised. Trying to get attention from other people, trying to tarnish the image she thinks I care about. 'I mean, if you're working on something to do with the ENS, it shouldn't be too much extra work. Might even help you.'

'You talked to David's mates about why he was in Rusholme?'

Karyn smiles, as if I've just accepted the job. 'I haven't had a chance. As you can imagine, it's all been so hectic. You could talk to Ben. He might be able to help. Whatever he won't tell me, he'd certainly tell you. He's like David in that respect.'

'I met him, didn't I?'

'Ben? Probably.'

'You know where he lives?'

'Didsbury.'

'He share a house with David?'

'Yeah. I'll give you the address.' She hefts her messenger bag onto her knee, pulls out an A4 pad and writes down the address for me. 'Phone number's on there too, if you need it.'

I fold the note, put it in my inside pocket. 'You know, if this does turn out to be what the paper said –'

'Then I'll have to accept it, won't I?' She tucks the pad back into her bag. 'I love David, Mr Innes. He has ideals, and he's working hard to achieve those ideals. Most of the blokes I meet here, they're interested in booze and tits – David's interested in *people*. He's all about putting things into place that will help them despite themselves. Like this place. You know he was the first to campaign for a campus-wide smoking ban? Not just indoors, either.'

'Really,' I say. 'Fascinating.'

'I mean, he got me to quit smoking, which is more than a dozen teachers and my parents ever managed to do. Because he has this way of telling you the truth and making you understand, d'you get me?'

Not at all, but I pull a face that I hope conveys some understanding.

'And it would be a shame if all that work ends up flushed down the toilet because of some bogus affiliation with the ENS.'

'You sold me, Karyn. I'll see what I can do.'

She smiles, showing both her teeth and her youth. 'My number's on the paper too.'

I promise to give her a ring if anything turns up. As I'm walking out of the coffee shop, I pull out an Embassy and light it as soon as I'm outside. Puff hard on the filter. Fuck the smoking ban.

My back tweaks at me. I take a pill to shut it up. Catch a dirty look from someone as I'm heading off-campus. I don't know whether it's the cigarette or the pills that have annoyed this young man, but I'm not going to bother my arse to find out.

I get into the car, dump the filter on campus. Head for Wilmslow Road. And start trying to find out why David Nunn was beaten into a coma.

THIRTY-THREE

I pull into Rusholme, park outside a restaurant called The Balti King. I'm a white guy with short hair, not quite the skinhead but close enough to draw some glances from a couple of Asian lads across the street. I don't meet their eyes, look at the ground. Keep walking, try not to look too threatening.

Canvass the shops on Wilmslow Road. The same introduction, a flash of the one business card I have left, and the questions.

'You working the other night?'

'You hear about that student getting beaten up?'

'You see anything?'

A big fat fuck all from everyone I talk to. Either they know something and they're keeping quiet because they don't trust me, or they're as clueless as they make out. Tell the truth, I'm probably asking the right questions to the wrong people. It's unlikely those who worked in the mornings would be on the night shift too. But it's worth a try. I've got to do something. Keep my hand in. Hope for a fucking miracle.

One bloke in a place called Plaza Kebabs doesn't understand English. That's what he tells me – 'No English'. When nobody's forthcoming in translating for me, I wave my hand at him, tell him it doesn't matter.

'You want something to eat?' he says as I'm heading out the door.

Yeah, doesn't speak English. Fucking hell.

I shake my head, step out onto the street. They're already suspicious of me. And there's my problem.

I don't blame them. The last time someone asked these

questions, it was the police and the press. Probably pretended they couldn't speak English then, too. But they don't want to deal with the same questions again, especially when it makes the entire community look bad.

Can't say their silence is doing them any favours, mind.

I hit the end of Wilmslow Road, so I start the long walk back up to my car. Meanwhile, the glances have turned to full-on stares. The word's spread.

I pass a car, a blue VW Beetle. One of the new ones, the old model melted into a more Japanese shape. In the back seat, something bright yellow catches my eye.

A pamphlet reading: GOT PLUMMER PROBLEMS?

David's car.

There's something shining on the dashboard. I have to turn back, glance in through the window again.

A brass Zippo, catching the sun. I reach into my pocket, pull out my cigarettes and light one. A campus-wide smoking ban, David managing to persuade Karyn to give up the tabs. I blow smoke, wondering what a militant non-smoker's doing with a Zippo in his car. I look into the car again, just to make sure I'm not seeing things.

I'm not. It's a Zippo, the smoker's lighter. And it's battered. Now, maybe it's a family heirloom, but then heirlooms are kept in locked drawers.

I try the driver's door. Locked.

Figures.

'Help you with something, mate?'

I look up. An Asian guy, about my height, staring at me. Concerned frown on his face, his eyes half-closed. Black T-shirt, biceps pushing against the fabric. Clean blue jeans.

'Nah,' I say, 'I'm good.'

'That your car, is it?'

'What car?'

He gestures towards the Beetle.

'Nah.'

'You're looking at it like it's yours.'

'I'm just having a smoke, mate.'

'You sure?' He comes closer, his shoulders rolled back. 'Because it looks to me like you were planning on nicking it or something.'

I laugh. 'Not me.'

'You tried the door.'

'No, I didn't.' I start walking away, keep the Embassy wedged between my lips. I don't want to take it from my mouth, my hand's shaking too much. I can see the bloke in my peripheral vision, moving closer.

'Here,' he says, 'do I know you?'

'Nah, you don't know me.' I walk faster. My car just up ahead. 'That's my car just up there.'

He drops back. I can't see him anymore, but he says, 'Right.'

A Zippo in a locked car. Plummer leaflet in the back. That's too much not to connect. I unlock the Micra, get in. Watch the bloke cross the road, glancing back at the Beetle, probably wondering what's so fucking special about it. Then he glances my way. My first instinct's to duck down in the seat, but I wave and smile at him instead. Roll down my new window and put my arm out. Tap ash.

I dig out my *Manchester A-to-Z*, look up Wilmslow Road, then pull the list of Plummer addresses from my jacket pocket. I smooth the paper down, suck on the filter. Sure enough, just below the cigarette burn, there's an address in Rusholme.

Could well be a coincidence. Like I said, a night without decent sleep, the kind of week I've had so far, my thought processes are all over the shop. I might be looking for links where there aren't any. There's no proof that David knew about these addresses, never mind that he was visiting one of these houses. Could be, he was down here to get a curry. By himself. And he got beaten up before he got a chance to make it to his car.

His car with the Zippo in it.

The lad made no secret about the fact that he was pissed off at Plummer.

Yeah, but there's a difference between being pissed off and

burning property. Collins might be completely out of the loop when it comes to what his staff get up to when they're off-duty, but he had a point there.

I flick my smoking filter out the window and reach for my mobile. A bastard of a headache starting behind the eyes, which I put down to all this thinking. I massage the bridge of my nose as I call Dobson & Main. A receptionist answers. I ask for Meg.

'Tell her it's Mr Innes,' I say.

There's a pause. Voices in the background, just for a couple of seconds, then the receptionist sticks me on hold. Classical music playing. I don't recognise the tune. Didn't really expect to. I stare at the VW Beetle up the street, part of me hoping that I don't get the confirmation I'm expecting.

'Mr Innes,' says Meg.

'You got a second?'

'If it *is* a second.'

'Your student pals still picketing outside?'

'No,' she says. 'Look, we're very busy.'

'Why's that then?'

'Excuse me?'

'Why aren't they still picketing? They all rallied round David's bed, are they?'

'You heard the news.'

'Absolutely. Kind of escalating, isn't it?'

'They're not here,' says Meg. 'Is that why you called?'

'No.' I shift position in the car, straighten my back out a little more than usual. 'I wanted to know if you'd managed to get anywhere with that list I asked you about.'

'I told you, Mr Innes, I'm not allowed to give out that kind of information.'

I sniff. 'Right. I forgot. Just, I read in the paper that the Manchester University student representative are boycotting all of Plummer's properties.'

'That's correct.'

'So how do they know which ones to boycott?'

Silence at the other end. It goes on so long, I think she's hung up on me.

'Hello?' I say.

'Bear with me just one second.'

'Take your time.'

Meg doesn't hear me. She's stuck me on hold again. That same music, and I realise they've only bought a section as hold music. After a minute, the music loops back to the beginning. And after six minutes by the clock in the dash, I can feel sweat prickle the sides of my face. I'm about to hang up and call again when Meg comes back to the phone.

'Mr Innes,' she says.

'Still here.'

'Looks like I owe you an apology, but we really didn't –'

'You gave a list of Plummer's properties to the student representative, didn't you?'

'Not me, no. My boss. And direct to them, yes.'

'That's all I needed to know. Thanks, Meg.'

She starts to ask me something, but I hang up on her. If the student rep have a list of properties, it's not entirely implausible that David Nunn could get his hands on it. But it's still not enough. If I want to push this further, I'll need more than a handful of coincidences.

I call Plummer at his office. He picks up on the fourth ring. The gravel in his voice makes me think he's either just woken up, or he's hammered already. Could be both.

'What?'

'Don, it's Cal. Look, do me a favour –'

'Where the fuck is Frank?'

'He's off sick.'

'You heard from him, then?'

'Yeah, I saw him.'

'Where is he?'

'He's not well, Don.'

'I'm sick of this taxi shit. I don't have the money or the fucking patience. You see him again, you tell him I want my car back. He doesn't want to come to work, that's fine. You two go off, go play whatever the hell you want to play at, but I want my car back. It's my car. I deserve –'

'Don, shut up for a second. I need you –'

'Who the fuck d'you think you're talking to, telling me to shut up? I'm telling *you*, Callum, you're still in my employ. And so's Frank. I know he's your mate and everything, but he needs to understand that he has certain duties. I'm skint, alright? I can't afford to keep taking cabs. Christ, I might even have to sell the Merc. You know what kind of blow that's going to be?'

'You want to find out who torched your property or not?'

There's a pause. Plummer seems to sober up a little. He clears his throat. 'You know who did it?'

'I have an idea, but I still need proof.'

'Who did it, Callum?' He coughs, then shouts down the phone at me. 'Who started all this? I'll have their fucking legs broken.'

'You'll have a job. The bloke I think did it, he's in the hospital already. But I need you to check something for me. You ever rent to a David Nunn?'

'David Nunn? Why's that ring a bell?'

'Did you or didn't you?'

'Whoa, wait a second – David Nunn's that fucking student, isn't he?'

'Yes.'

'He burned the Longsight house?'

'I'm not getting into it, Don. Just do me a favour and see if you've rented to him. You said you've got records of your tenants. Nunn would have rented last year, probably. Guessing at a place in Rusholme. He's a second-year student, and he doesn't live there anymore.'

'I can't go through those files, Cal. You saw them. They're all over the place.'

'Well, you need to get your arse in gear and do it anyway. If you find anything, let me know.'

'Christ,' he says.

I start the engine. 'What is it?'

'That break-in –'

'You said it was vandals.'

'But I'm thinking now, I'm thinking –'

'That it was a bunch of students. Fuck's sake, Don. Look through the files anyway, I'll see what I can dig up at my end. There's light at the end of the tunnel, that's the important thing.'

I hang up on him, stuff my mobile into my jacket pocket. Head down Wilmslow Road to the property on the list.

I try to tell myself that this lead, it's probably nothing. My fucked-up perception, coupled with Don's, everything's thrown out of whack. But then another voice rages that I'm onto something here. And I don't know what I'm going to do if I manage to prove this, but I'll deal with that when the time comes.

First, I need to get someone to tell me what I think is already the case. That David Nunn, for all his left-leaning politics, was down here in Rusholme to set fire to a house.

THIRTY-FOUR

Parked outside 16 Viscount Road, another nondescript terrace in what seems to be a city of them. A short drive from Wilmslow Road, but I've taken it slowly. Watching for any miraculous clues to make themselves apparent. You never know, I might be on a roll.

There's a gang of kids, up and about early to make the best possible use of the last of their summer holidays. They're banging a football against a garage door, making a hell of a racket. The kid in the makeshift goal tries to grab at the ball, but the other kids delight in kicking too hard for him to risk a catch.

I get out of the Micra, lean against the car and stare at number 16. The house doesn't look like one of Plummer's properties. It's well maintained for a start. Whether that's down to Plummer, the letting agency or the tenant is another matter. Then again, as Meg said, Dobson & Main aren't in the business of letting slums.

I push off the side of the Micra, open the small front gate and head up the short garden path to the front door. Press the bell. I can hear it sound inside the house, so I step back and wait.

The door opens on a chain. I can see a guy in the gap.

'Yes?' he says.

'My name's Callum Innes. Wonder if I could have a wee word with you.'

'What's it about?'

'It's a little delicate actually, kind of private. I need to ask you a few questions. Probably best we do it inside.'

He looks at me. Up and down, trying to gauge how important I am. Then he says, 'Are you police?'

'No, I'm a private investigator.'

He laughs, then narrows his eyes at me. 'You're serious.'

'I am.' I show him my business card.

He laughs again. 'I know you. You were in the newspaper.'

Might as well use it to my advantage. 'Yeah.'

'You work for Donald Plummer.'

'That's right.'

He nods, then slams the door in my face.

I stand there for a moment looking stupid, then I press the doorbell again. From inside the house, I can hear him shouting, 'I paid my rent.'

I use the letterbox as a makeshift intercom. 'I know you did.'

'I told Mr Plummer, I told the letting agency, I paid my rent.'

'I'm not going to evict you,' I say.

'Direct debit.'

'I know.'

'To the letting agency.'

'I'm not here to chuck you out of your house, alright?' A twinge in my back. 'Look, can you open the door so I don't have to shout?'

'No.'

'It's not about Plummer, it's about the student that was assaulted the other night. I need to ask you some questions about it.' Really shouting now, half out of trying to make myself heard, half just because I'm pissed off. The kids have stopped playing football, decided that I'm far more entertaining. 'Look, it won't take up much of your time. And I don't have to come in if you don't want me to.'

The door opens. The chain's on.

I straighten up. 'Thank you.'

'I didn't see anything.'

'Were you at home?'

'The boy was found on Wilmslow Road,' he says. 'This isn't Wilmslow Road.'

'I know that, but I have reason to believe he was here.'

'Why?'

'Did you hear anything?'

'I heard nothing. I saw nothing. I don't know why you're asking me these questions.'

He makes a move to close the door; I stick my foot in the gap.

'You're sure you didn't see or hear anything out of the ordinary?'

'That's what I said. I have to be at work soon. I would like you to leave. Take your foot out of the door.'

'If you didn't hear anything that night, you heard anything since?'

'Please, remove your foot. I don't know anything.'

'People talk.'

He shakes his head. Stares at my shoe. Doesn't say anything else.

'Fine.' I take my foot from the gap in the door, hold up my hands. I'm not a threat to him, want him to know that.

'Thanks for your help.'

He frowns, and slams the door.

Wanker.

It's one thing to be wary of strangers, but this is ridiculous. I should've told him that Nunn was planning to burn his fucking house down, see if that jogged his memory. Nothing like fear to get the old grey cells motivated. I walk back down the path, don't bother to close the gate behind me. I look across at the kids, and they seem to start moving all at once.

'You got something to say, lads?'

The kid holding the football, taller than the rest, could be twelve or thirteen, he jerks his chin at me.

Says, 'What's it worth?'

I stop walking. 'Depends on what you've got.'

He bounces the ball to one of his mates, walks towards me. As he gets closer, I can make out a strip of hair across his top lip, pulled back in a sneer.

Thinks he's a hard lad, this one.

'Fifty quid, and I got a fuckin' witness statement for you,' he says.

'Witness statement, right?' Lad thinks he's got the jargon down, too. It'd be sweet if he wasn't so fucking annoying. I nod. 'What's your name?'

'Tariq.'

'How old are you, mate?'

'What, you trying to pick us up or something, eh?' He grins, looking around at his mates, wagging one hand. 'Ain't into that, man.'

There are a few giggles, nothing too much. Nerves in this gang. Anxious about being out in the open talking to me. Which means they might have something.

'I'm not trying to pick you up, Tariq. I'm just wondering what the fuck a twelve-year-old's going to do with fifty quid.'

'Whoa, fuckin' fourteen, innit?' he says. 'And back up, mate, 'cause I ain't in the mood for a lecture.'

'Not about to.' I reach into my jacket, pull out two twenties and a ten from Plummer's envelope. Christ, but it's feeling light these days. 'But how come you were out the other night?'

'What, 'cause I've been grounded, yeah? My father says, I don't go out unless I got a good reason.'

'So you weren't out?'

'What you smoking?'

'Nothing.'

'You smoke.'

I give him an Embassy. He lights it up, sucks on the filter. Turns the lit end of the cigarette to his palm like a soldier. Or, and this is probably the effect he's going for, a con. Playing it up for his mates.

'I don't listen to him, man,' he says. 'He's not the boss of me.'

'So you were out.'

'Wants me to stay in and do homework. He's like, I'm gonna be a lawyer, but I'm like, no way, man.' He grins at his mates, and then his voice drops. 'He's a fuckin' *machood*.'

'What'd you see, Tariq?'

Another jerk of the chin. 'Show us the money again.' He grins, catching a riff. '*Show me the money.*'

'I'll show you the money, yeah,' I say, holding up the fifty. 'But you look with your eyes, right? Get to look with your hands when you tell me something I can use.'

'You're a *businessman*.'

'Whatever, mate. What'd you see?'

'Don't tell him,' says one of Tariq's mates. Dressed head to toe in Adidas, kid thinks he's a gangster, but looks like he's about to piss himself with fear. Shifting his weight from one leg to the other. 'Y'ain't a grass, man.'

'Nah, you're a fuckin' rudeboy, aren't you?' I say.

'What d'you know about it?'

'Tariq, you want to tell me something, you tell it. You want to also tell your mates to back the fuck off, then we can talk.'

'Naz. Chill.'

'Yeah, Naz. *Chill.* This has fuck all to do with you, mate.'

'You calling me, man?' says Naz. None of the fear now, fronting with his trackies in a fucking twist, face following suit. '*Bhanchood.*'

'You want to call me a fuckin' name, son, try putting it in a language I understand.'

'Fuckin' *racist*, man. Fuckin' calling me 'cause I don't speak your English.'

'*My* English?' I shake my head, tuck the fifty in my jeans. 'You know what, fuck this. Wasting my time, bunch of fuckin' mobile thieves, am I right?'

'Hang on,' says Tariq.

'Nah, think I come down here to play gangster with you lot . . .' I keep walking. 'Forget it, son. Had your chance, but you had to keep bucking your gums.'

I'm almost at the car when I hear someone coming up behind me. Turn, and it's Tariq. Look over his shoulder, and the rest of his mates are still by the garage. Naz watches the ground, knocks the ball between his feet. One of the other lads takes it off him and the game starts up again.

'This don't go no further, right?' says Tariq.

'Whatever, mate. You think I'm going to tell your dad, I don't know him.' I lean against the Micra. 'And if there's someone else you don't want me to tell, chances are I don't know them either. So anything you say, it's more than likely private and confidential.'

Tariq opens his arms, then lets them flop to his sides as he takes a breath.

'In your own time,' I tell him.

'There's this bloke, he's called Saeed, right? Real gangster, get me?' He chews his lip. 'Me and Naz, we do some work for him every now and again. Just deliveries, nothing heavy. He gave us a couple bikes to do the running on –'

I gesture: *skip to the end.*

'Right, so I'm out there, I'm waiting on him.'

'Where?'

'Up by the garage. Always meets us there. And Saeed pulls up in his car, and he's got this bloke with him, I never seen him before. Says this is his mate, he just got out the 'Ways, he's sound, gonna be doing some business, yeah? So I do the handshakes an' that, y'know, *introducing* myself. And then there's this noise –'

'What noise?'

'Like shouting an' that, 'cept it's not really shouting. Like, arguing. But they're trying to keep it quiet.'

'Right.'

'Then there's these two white lads come round the corner and they're proper at each other.'

'Uh-huh. You remember what they were arguing about?' I pull out my cigarettes, hold the pack to Tariq, who takes one and slips another behind his ear. I light an Embassy.

'Summat about that house, weren't it? I didn't catch it.'

'What house?'

'That house you was at.'

'If you didn't catch it, how d'you know it was about that house?'

'Just thought it was, didn't I? It was summat important, and they were like coming from around the back, like.'

I look at the house. Right enough, there's that alley that leads round the back. I blow smoke.

'You said two of them?'

'Yeah.'

'So what happened then?'

What happened was that Saeed and his big mate just out of prison, they took offence at the two white lads. Nothing more than that, really. Same as if a couple of Asian lads were looking suspicious in Ordsall and a couple of tap-headed scallies saw them. Saeed and mate looked at David Nunn and *his* mate, saw a couple of strangers with something to hide.

'Describe them,' I say.

'One of them, he was the bloke you were talking about. The student.'

'What'd he look like?'

Tariq frowns with the top half of his face, grins with the rest. 'What, you don't believe me?'

'No. Convince me. What'd he look like?'

Tariq sucks his teeth, moves his hand over his chin, stroking a beard that isn't there. 'Had one of them beards, fuckin' *tramp* beard. Dressed like a student. What else d'you need? He looked like a student.'

'You know what a student looks like.' But right enough, Nunn had a beard. Not in any of the photos I've seen in the papers, though.

'I seen plenty of them, man. They all live round here.'

'What about his mate?'

'No beard. Biggish.' He laughs. 'Fuckin' hell, I knew you'd be asking me all these questions, I'd have took a photo, know what I mean?'

'Biggish like what? Like a bouncer?'

'Like Jonny Wilkinson big. Like thick neck an' that. Looked a bit like him.'

'Like Jonny Wilkinson, right. And Saeed and his mate, they just laid into these blokes for no reason?'

Tariq shakes his head. 'Weren't no reason, man. Them bastards, they was up to something, you could tell. *We* could tell. So Saeed's all like, "What you doing, lads?" Trying to shit 'em up a bit, y'know? And it was working, they was getting proper scared. 'Cause Saeed's a psycho bastard once he gets going, and him having that mate with him, tell you they were putting the shits up *me*. Pfffft.'

'So they kicked off,' I say.

'Shouldn't have been there in the first place. They should know, we all got bredren in Longsight, man.'

'Saeed and this bloke kicked the shit out of them,' I say.

'You judging us? You hear what I said?'

'I heard some macho fuckin' bullshit, Tariq.' I look at him. 'I'm after what happened, there's you spinning me a cunt's yarn. They did the beardy student, so what happened to Jonny fuckin' Wilkinson?'

'He took off.'

'Didn't just look like him, ran like him too, eh?'

'Once that student started giving it back with the mouth and Saeed kicked off, he was out of there. Yeah, he fuckin' took off running.'

'What's Saeed's number?'

'No, fuck off. I ain't doing that. I ain't a grass.'

'I need to corroborate this, mate.'

'You don't believe me, you can get fucked.' He backs up a few steps. 'You just give us my money and that's it.'

'You gave me nowt, Tariq. Two white students, they start some shite, one of them takes off running, the other one gets a kicking. Then they dump him on Wilmslow Road? Meantime, there's people looking at this like it's a racist thing –'

'Nah, man, don't be feeding me that bullshit –'

'I'm feeding you nothing. I'm telling you the truth. The fuckin' news is all about it, son. You're about to have a march in your own back yard because of this. And let me tell you something, those marchers see a brown face, they're going to stomp on it until the white meat shows, you get me?'

'Nowt to do with me, man.'

'You going to be out on the streets tonight?'

'Me and the boys, if what you say is true, we'll be doing *something*. And what d'you mean I gave you nowt, man? I told you what *transpired*. Just 'cause it's not what you want to hear, doesn't mean you don't pay us.'

I pull out the fifty, frown at Tariq. We both know I don't need to corroborate any of what he told me. 'Do yourself a favour, mate. Get a DVD or something, get drunk, sniff some aerosols, have a night in. Because there's nothing you told me that I can use to stop them coming down here with fuckin' sticks.'

Tariq plucks the money out of my hand. Closes his fist around it and pokes his bottom set of teeth with his tongue.

'I mean it, man. You care about your fuckin' *boys*, don't make this into a war. You're too young to be fighting that hard for fuck all.'

I get into the Micra, start the engine.

'See you tonight,' says Tariq, giving me the wink.

I shake my head, pull the car away from the kerb. Fucking kids.

THIRTY-FIVE

Heading towards Didsbury when my mobile rings. I turn the radio down, check the display. Not a number I recognise.

'Hello?'

'Mr Innes? This is Karyn.'

'Right. How are you?'

'I'm okay. I just wondered if you'd managed to find anything out yet.'

'About David?' I shift in my seat, think about what I've just seen. 'No, I haven't had a chance to look into it yet, Karyn.'

'No, I know, that's fine,' she says. I swear I can hear a voice in the background. 'I'm glad, actually, because I was going to tell you that it didn't matter. *Doesn't* matter.'

'What doesn't matter?'

'The job.'

I straighten up a little. 'And why's that?'

'Please, Mr Innes, I'd rather you didn't bother yourself. You're right. You know, you're busy, you don't have time to investigate properly, I fully understand.'

'It's not even been a day yet, Karyn.'

'I appreciate that, but I'll still no longer be needing your services. It's okay, really. Look, I just wanted to thank you for the work you've put in so far.'

'Who's that with you?' I ask.

She doesn't say anything. The line falls totally silent, no background noise either. Then: 'There's nobody here apart from me.'

'Then what happened to change your mind?'

'Nothing. I was just . . . upset. I wasn't thinking right.'

I chance something. 'If it's the money, that's fine. I'll do it for free.'

Again, there's a pause. 'It's really not the money.'

'You just want me to drop the case.'

'That's right.'

A pause. She's floundering. Then she takes a deep breath.

'Because I don't think you're up to the job,' she says. 'I wanted someone trustworthy. And your prison time is an issue.'

I let that particular lie hang between us for a while, just so she realises how fucking ridiculous she sounds.

'Okay,' I say, sounding suitably hurt. 'If that's the way you want it. Who told you I was in prison, by the way?'

'It doesn't matter.'

'I'd like to know.'

'I'm sorry to have wasted your time.'

She hangs up. I'm left with a dead phone and a very live lead.

Shouldn't take me too long to get to Didsbury, but I still have to pull in and pop the glove compartment. Rifle around for the piece of paper that Karyn gave me. I find it wedged against a bag of glacier mints that've gone sticky.

I also find the flyer for tonight's opening. I tuck it in my jacket pocket.

Dial the number, wait for Ben to pick up his mobile. Watch the birds at a feeder in someone's garden. See them splashing around in the bird bath and remind myself that I need to take a shower before I head over to the Lads' Club. When I turn my attention back to the inside of my car, I realise that the place is starting to look like Plummer's office. Everywhere I turn, there seems to be a pile of loose paper and no filing system to speak of.

And for one second, I actually look forward to moving back into an office at Paulo's place.

Fuckin' dream on, son.

'Hello?'

Jesus, about time.

'Ben?'

'Who's this?' he says. Wary.

'Callum Innes.'

'Who?'

'Don't know if you remember me. We met outside the letting agency the other day.'

A pause, then it sounds as if Ben remembers. 'Oh, right, Mr Innes. Sorry, yeah. How'd you get this number, by the way?'

'Karyn gave it to me. She said to give you a call.'

'Did she now?' Ben's voice drops a little in volume. Sounds like he's moved his mouth away from the phone.

Which makes me think Karyn's in the room and he's looking at her right now.

Which also makes me think that if Karyn's hanging around now, it's not that much of a stretch to think Ben was in the room when she called me.

'You still there, Ben?'

'Sorry,' he says, back at the phone now. 'What was it concerning?'

'She was after hiring me to find out who put David in a coma.'

'Really?' Ben sniffs, clears his throat. 'That's interesting.'

'Yeah. Thing is, though, she phoned me this morning to tell me I was doing a shit job. That I should probably let it lie.'

'Oh, I see.'

'Yeah, that I hadn't done enough since she hired me this morning. Something like that, anyway. I mean, she didn't go into any detail. Which seemed a little suspicious to me. She was so adamant about me working on it before . . . I don't get the change of heart.'

'Well, she's like that sometimes,' says Ben. 'A bit flaky.'

'I didn't know that. She doesn't come across that way.'

'Comes and goes.' Ben clears his throat. 'Look, if she wants you to drop the case, then you should probably drop the case, right? I mean, it's not your fault you didn't do anything. You're probably really busy right now.'

'Actually, that's kind of why I was ringing. I just cleared a case, so

I thought, y'know, Karyn might not be able to afford me, but I'm not above doing some *pro bono* work.'

'That's very kind of you.'

He doesn't sound very grateful.

'Yeah, well, she bugged me with that whole ENS thing. I didn't want poor old David to be tagged like that. He's a politics student, isn't he?'

'Yes.'

'Well, that kind of thing sticks with a lad.'

Ben doesn't say anything.

'But I need some help,' I tell him. 'I tried a few leads this morning, but they're pretty much dead ends as far as I can see. I thought if I popped round, we could have a wee chat.'

'I'm kind of busy right now, Mr Innes.'

'No, I appreciate that. You've probably got a lecture or something, right?'

'Yeah.'

'Tell you what, Ben, it won't take up much of your time. I just wanted to ask you a couple of questions, put our heads together, see if there's anything I've missed. Nothing to get worried about.'

'I'm not worried.' Ben makes some thinking noises. He's not keen. I don't blame him. 'And I don't know . . .'

'Look, the way it's going at the moment, the ENS have David Nunn as a poster boy for their cause. And that cause is going to go marching through South Manchester tonight on some kind of rabid crusade. People are going to get hurt, Ben. And I'm guessing that, when all's said and done and the dust has settled, you and Karyn don't want David to be associated with all that.'

'Of course,' says Ben. 'David's not about that.'

'And neither are you. So help me out.'

'Really, I haven't –'

'Look, I've already got your address. I'll come round, we'll talk and I'll be out of your hair in half an hour, okay?'

Ben sighs. He doesn't want to sound like he's trying to put me off. He also knows I'm not going to give up.

'Okay,' he says. 'But it'll have to be quick.'

I ring off. Pull the Micra in at the top of his street and wait for a few minutes. I don't want to force it, but I also want a view of his house, just in case he tries to do a runner.

I take a pill, light a cigarette. Fill the car with smoke as I pull the tape recorder out of my jacket. Test it once more.

'Testing, testing, one-two-three.'

Play it back, and it seems okay. Even if my voice doesn't sound the way I always thought it should.

It certainly wasn't Karyn with David that night. Tariq reckoned the other guy was a Jonny Wilkinson lookalike, and the only guy I know who looks that much like a rugby player is the guy who just tried to put me off coming round.

And thinking back, wasn't that the same guy who looked worried as fuck about that kid I saved?

Yeah, me and Ben, we need to talk.

One last chance, and I'll play it like Frank. Get the fucker on tape. Then I'll be able to do something with it. The only difference is I'm not going to be dealing with a couple of hardcases, like Frank did.

No, this guy's just a student who ran out on a mate when things looked hairy. Should be a doddle if I play it right.

I just hope he speaks loud enough to record properly.

THIRTY-SIX

Ben's house has rugs in the window instead of curtains. I wonder how that became a staple of student living, then wonder how I'm supposed to know that's a staple of anything. I just suppose it's the kind of thing students do. Ben does it. Just like it's still light outside, but I can make out the glow of a lamp between the wall and the rug. I do another quick level check on the tape recorder, play it back and rewind.

Should be okay as long as I'm close enough and speaking clearly.

I drive up to a parking space outside Ben's house. Get to the front door and give the wood a sharp knock. Ben opens up.

'You alright?' he says. 'That was quick.'

I don't answer as I step inside. Immediately get the whiff of something that must be incense, as well as the distinct impression we're not alone.

'Karyn about?'

'No.' Ben opens the door to the living room, his hand on a poster of the Simpsons as Tony Soprano and family. There's a battered sofa, probably came with the property, a throw covering it. An overstuffed chair, the same deal. Heavy rugs on the window, a bare light bulb hanging from the ceiling and a brand new CD player on a table in the corner. I look at the posters on the far wall: *The Motorcycle Diaries*; that one of Bob Marley with lips around a spliff and the prerequisite Che Guevara icon, black on red. Books litter a large dining table. 'Revolution' and 'isms in the titles. I pick one up: *Writings on Guerilla Warfare, Politics and History*.

I read aloud: 'It is not necessary to wait until all conditions for making revolution exist –'

'The insurrection can create them,' finishes Ben.

'Very good. You know it off by heart?'

'One of the key points.' Ben takes the book from me, flicks through it as if he's read it more times than he cares to admit. 'Have to study it, some of it's got to sink in, eh? All the stuff about the time and situation where there's no room for civil debate. When you have to fight for your social goals in another way.'

'You can't start a revolution from your bed,' I say.

Ben smiles. 'Noel.'

'Don't know if that's the right quote. I can't fuckin' stand Oasis. If I want to listen to The Beatles, I'll listen to The Beatles.'

'Right.'

I pick up another book. 'Not that I ever want to listen to The Beatles.'

'Mr Innes, I'm sorry.' Ben looks at his watch. 'You said you wanted to ask me some questions?'

'Yeah,' I say, putting the book back down. I reach into my jacket, press record. Bring out the list of Plummer's houses and look at it. I make a point of not showing it to Ben. 'There's really just one thing I wanted to clear up.'

'What's that?'

'What's the deal between you and Donald Plummer? I mean, you hate the bloke, fair enough. He's not the easiest fella to get along with, I should know. But what did he do to you?'

'Plummer? He's a blight –'

I wave at him. 'Yeah, I know all that. David told me that line when I talked to him. But people don't just get pissed off at other people's business practices.'

Ben squints at me. 'You can't seriously be calling them *business practices*.'

'Well, it's something to call them, and I'm not about to start debating words with you, Ben. So you don't like the phrase, you think Plummer's unethical, whatever.' I smile at him. 'But the thing is, these pamphlets, they don't get printed without something personal behind it, you know what I mean?'

'We had a good reason,' says Ben. 'The man's –'

'I'm not making myself clear. How's about this: did you ever rent from Plummer?'

Ben folds his arms. 'I don't see what this has to do with David.'

'I'm interested.'

He thinks about it.

Then: 'David and I rented from Donald Plummer, yes.'

'Last year?'

'Yes.'

'And he fucked you over?'

'You could put it like that.'

'How should I put it?'

Ben pulls a face. 'He fucked us over.'

'That's what I thought.'

'Why're you asking me this if you already know?' says Ben.

'Did I evict you?'

'No,' he says. 'Someone else. A big bloke. Scared the shit out of David. Said that we hadn't paid our rent. I mean, we paid it every month, direct debit. What are we supposed to do when someone comes round the house and says that?'

'Show them a bank statement.'

'You have bank statements handy?'

'No, but then I don't rent from a dodgy landlord.' I move a little closer to him. 'So all this leaflet bollocks, it was personal.'

'Donald Plummer is in the wrong, and he shouldn't be allowed to get away with that kind of practice.'

'That wasn't the question.'

'But that's the answer you're getting.'

'David come up with that?'

'Yes.'

'And you agreed with him?'

Ben nods.

'You agree with him on most things?'

'Politically?'

'Yeah.'

'Yes, I agree with him on most political issues. We're in the same seminar groups. David can be very persuasive when he puts his mind to it.'

I smile. 'Yeah, I know. Karyn told me about the smoking thing. Wish I'd known when I talked to him.'

'She makes it sound like he hypnotised her. And there's people on campus who think David has that spark about him, like he's some kind of cult leader. Fact is, I just think Karyn was sick of the early morning hacks. She used to cough so hard, she'd get these headaches.'

'So you can't make someone quit if they don't already want to, right?'

Ben purses his lips, says, 'I don't know what you're getting at.'

'Nothing,' I say with a shrug. 'Just thinking about myself again. Been meaning to give up. What with the no smoking in enclosed spaces thing. David didn't smoke at all?'

'No,' says Ben. 'Never did. Why?'

'I wondered, because I saw his Zippo, thought he might've smoked at some point.'

Ben looks at me. 'What Zippo?'

'In his car. His is the blue Beetle, right?'

'I don't know —'

'I mean, it had one of your leaflets in the back, and I remember seeing it by the picket line. New car like that, I've got to wonder how he could afford it.'

Ben shakes his head. 'His parents bought it for him.'

'Man, you think they'd buy me a new car? Mine's been through the wars, let me tell you.' I wipe my nose. 'But the thing is, if David doesn't smoke, what's he doing with a Zippo in his car?'

'It's mine,' says Ben.

I point at him. '*You* smoke?'

'Yes,' he says.

I regard him, then look around the room. 'Oh, okay. That makes sense.'

'Was that all?'

'Yeah, I think so.' I back up a few steps, look at the poster of Che Guevara. 'So you knew his car was still on Wilmslow Road?'

Ben's face is calm. Otherwise, he's hugging himself so hard it looks like he might crack a rib any minute. He nods at me.

'You know he was there, then,' I say.

'I assume so. You said his car's there.'

'He didn't tell you anything about going to Rusholme.'

'I'm not his carer.'

'You're not? I thought you two hung out together.'

'What're you getting at?'

'You're seriously telling me that if David decided to go down to Rusholme, you wouldn't tag along?'

'Yes, I'm seriously telling you that,' says Ben. 'We're not joined at the hip.'

'Lucky for you, else it could be the pair of you in the hospital.'

'I suppose.'

'But the problem is, I did some digging and turns out David wasn't in Rusholme alone. Turns out, he wasn't just messing around on the curry mile, either.' I wait for a reaction from Ben. He's doing his best not to give me one. But there's something, a ripple in that calm exterior. 'He was at a house. With a mate. Got caught doing something he shouldn't have been doing, two guys cornered him, and his mate took off.'

He works his mouth now, weighing up what he thinks I might know. 'Why are you telling me this?'

'You tell me, mate. Your lighter in the fuckin' car, isn't it?'

'Yes.'

'You're the one who did a runner.'

He shakes his head.

'You're the one who told Karyn to call off the job, right?'

Ben's eye twitches. He rubs it with his thumb. 'I didn't tell Karyn anything of the sort. And I know what you're doing here.'

'What am I doing, Ben?'

A half-smile pushes up the left corner of his mouth. He wags his finger at me like he's just caught the punchline to a joke before I said it. 'You're still working for Plummer, aren't you?'

'Doesn't make any difference who I'm working for.'

'Trying to . . . *discredit* those few people who actually stood up to him.'

'No, Ben, I'm trying to find out why you and David burnt that house.'

He folds his arms again. 'I didn't say anything like that.'

'But you did it, though. You were there in Longsight, you helped him then. No reason to think you weren't in Rusholme too.'

'Mr Innes –'

'I'm not saying you knew anybody was in the house,' I say. 'In fact, you probably thought the place was empty. Lots of Plummer houses that are supposed to be empty – those are the ones that he keeps rolling tenants through. No paperwork to snag him, either. And the first thing out of your mouth when you knew who I was: "How's the kid?" So I know you're not the kind to jeopardise people like that.'

Ben shakes his head. 'No, you're putting words in my mouth.'

'Then tell me, why'd you burn the house, Ben?'

Make sure to get it on tape. Make sure my voice is loud enough, make him raise his to match it.

'I didn't –'

'Don't fuckin' lie to me. You burned the Longsight house. I have proof. You were in Rusholme with David the other night. I have proof there, too.' I hold up the piece of paper. 'Got a list here only you two really had access to through the student rep. I *know* you did it, I just want to know why. I'm giving you a chance here, Ben.'

'This isn't anything to do with finding who beat up David, is it?'

'You know who beat him up. You were there.'

'I didn't . . .' He catches himself, bares his teeth, like the thought on the tip of his tongue is too bitter. 'You don't have any proof.'

'There were people in the Rusholme house, too.'

Ben stares at me.

'Was that why you were arguing? Saw a light go on or something, knew there was people in there, but David wanted to pull the burn anyway?'

'I don't have to talk to you.'

'I wouldn't worry. Plummer's already ruined – he's getting evicted from his own office building. He's up on criminal negligence. You probably read about it in the papers already. So there's nothing I can do to keep him out of prison or get his business back. You already won, Ben. Only reason I'm asking you now is for my own peace of mind.'

'Bullshit.' Ben gives me a tight smile. 'I mean, you don't agree with my politics, that's fine –'

'Your *politics* have fuck all to do with it, mate. Doesn't matter if I agree with them or not. I'll tell you, past couple of days, all I've heard is fuckin' politics. You can't move in this city right now without someone telling you what's right and how you're wrong, who's to fuckin' blame for whatever invisible evil's in our blood. The media, the Muslims, the police, the fuckin' *landlords*. I couldn't give a shit if you're strapping Semtex to kittens or giving blood to the fuckin' orphans, that's got nothing to do with my job.'

'You can't be apolitical,' says Ben. 'Even George Orwell said –'

'Fuck George Orwell. Why'd you burn the house?'

'Look in the books,' he says. 'The only way to hurt a capitalist is to take away his capital.'

'And you thought you were bringing down Enron when you were just fucking about with Arthur Daley.'

'Donald Plummer was hurting people.'

'And you weren't? You killed an old woman, that's not hurting people?'

'There wasn't supposed to be anyone in the house.'

'Yeah, well, these things happen. That kid wasn't supposed to be in the house, the granny wasn't supposed to be in the house, *I* wasn't supposed to be in the fuckin' house. But sometimes it just rains shit, doesn't it? You got the Longsight community up in arms, you gave the ENS something to fight against, and now you've got David in with them –'

'I didn't do that!' he shouts. 'David isn't like that, I'm not like that. We're about as socialist as it gets, alright?'

'Like I give a fuck –'

'Look, when I finish university, I have a job. I'm going to work for the Labour Party. Christ knows they need all the left-wingers they can get these days. Just administration, but do you honestly think that they'd have anything to do with me if I had ties to the ENS?'

'I'm not saying you're a Nazi, Ben.'

'Good.'

'I'm saying you're an arsonist.'

Ben twists his face and breathes through his nose. 'I can't be held responsible.'

'You put a match to a house.'

'David did it. He was the one that started the fire.'

'You were there.'

'I didn't want to be.'

'But you were there and you didn't stop him. And when he got caught, you fucked off. Why didn't you take the car?'

'It's David's car. He had the keys. Still does.'

I stare at Ben. Let him work through it, give him a break from the questions. I think I've got all I need. And he knows I've got him, except he thinks I don't have any evidence. He *hopes* I don't have any evidence. Something like this, I can tell it's been weighing on the fucker. He's looking around the room, anywhere but at me, but he can't avoid me for long. Every time he comes back, I'm staring right at him.

'We were supposed to be having a look,' he says finally.

'At the house?'

Ben nods. 'I asked David, I wanted to make sure there was no one in there. So we went to have a look at the house.'

'And there was someone in.'

'David didn't give a shit about that. He called it collateral damage. But when I told him I wasn't going to do it, he kicked off. And then we got caught. I didn't know what else to do, so I ran.'

'Right.' I nod at him, keep my voice low. Let him know it's alright. For the moment. 'What'd you use to pull the burns, Ben? Petrol?'

He grunts an affirmative. I'm losing him here – he's too busy replaying the other night.

'Where is it now?'

'In the car.'

I make a move to go. Ben grabs my arm.

'You don't have any evidence,' he says. Sounds like a threat.

'Get your fuckin' hands off me, Ben. You're a runner, not a fighter.'

'You don't get it. Plummer was single-handedly turning this city into a place where students couldn't afford to live –'

'Yeah, you and everyone else, Ben. Do I look like a fuckin' freshman?' I prise his hand off my arm. 'Like I'm going to swallow that shite.'

Ben rears up to his full height now. 'Who the fuck d'you think you are? Think you're a fucking hero because you saved some Paki kid? I know you, did some homework on you. You were in *prison*.'

'Yeah, and you told Karyn, too.'

He grabs me again. I batter him off. He grabs. 'Don't think I'm going to take shit from an ex-con who thinks he's something special. And don't think for a second about going to the police because they'll laugh you out of the fucking station. You think us *talking* is proof enough? I'm doing politics and *law*, Mr Innes. It's *hearsay*. Your word against mine.'

I stand there, brush him off. 'You're right, Ben. I don't have any evidence.'

That's when the tape clicks.

'What was that?'

'Nothing.' I head for the door. 'Thanks, Ben. You really put my mind at ease.'

He moves quick for a big bloke, grabs the back of my jacket. I spin around, knock him with my elbow, but he lets go, wraps his arms around my waist and tackles me to the floor. I wriggle backwards, kick out at him, catch him a square foot in the face. A sick crunch and blood from his nose, but he's dogged, this fucker. Keeps throwing himself at me, and that's a lot of weight. Trying to pin me down, scrabbling at the inside of my jacket. He grabs the tape recorder. I throw my head back, snap it forward into his broken nose. Feel the blood on my forehead and him lurch away from me. The tape recorder drops to the carpet, bounces away from us.

I lunge, throw my hand over the tape. Hang on for dear life.

Roll over onto my hands and knees, push against the floor like a sprinter, try to get upright.

Then a flash of pain, exploding white just behind my eyes. Can't see, so I put my free hand to the side of my head. My fingers come away wet. I twist, my vision clearing up, see Ben's eyes wide with fear. There's a large pub ashtray in his hand.

I try to move out of the way, but the world's moving too slow for me to catch my balance.

Ben swings with the ashtray again; the room shatters out.

And I'm left with one thought: Should've got the MP3 one.

THIRTY-SEVEN

Bad dreams, but nothing concrete. The world catching on fire like the *whoosh* of a match to gas. Burning bright and fast, an orange flame turning yellow turning white in a split-second.

And then a lifting sensation, like I'm weightless.

'Mr Innes.'

I open one eye. Can't open the other one – something's gummed it up. I try to raise a hand to the sticky part of my face, but I miss my entire head somehow, end up touching the fabric on the sofa. It seems to be loose. Now that the vision in one eye's coming back, I can make out a big lad, his ruddy face moving in and out of focus. I smile at him. Fuck it, he looks friendly enough. Nasty bruise on his face, mind.

'Y'alright?' I say.

He looks worried, this lad. Behind him, there's a girl, pretty in a skinny way. Like she should be on a magazine cover about ten years ago. They're both familiar, but they might just look like people I saw in a film once. Got that kind of shifting recognition thing going on.

Right, yeah, the bloke looks a bit like that rugby player, what's his name.

Jonny Wilkinson.

And the girl looks like what's-her-face from that telly thing. Maybe it's not a telly thing. Maybe it's a film. Probably a film. Or she could be a singer. She looks like a singer. One of those folky types. Something shiny in her nose. I stare at it.

'We should call an ambulance,' says the girl.

'He's okay. You're okay, aren't you, Mr Innes?'

More of a plea than a question. I look around me. I'm laid out on the sofa, and the reason the fabric felt loose was because the sofa's covered with a throw. One of my legs hangs off the side. I turn back to the lad and say, 'What happened?'

'You fell,' he says.

'Right.' My brain feels like it's floating in my skull. It's not entirely unpleasant. 'Right, course I did.'

'Ben, he's not okay,' says the girl.

'I'm fine, love.' That name ringing a bell, but I can't place it. I try to sit up, my gut lurching. 'Shit, hang on.'

'Get the bowl,' says Ben. 'He's going to be sick again.'

'No, I'm fine,' I say.

Then I throw up on myself. Not a lot, but enough to make me feel like I've had enough to drink already, thanks very much, and it's probably time for me to call it a night.

I check my watch – it's just gone four.

Christ, I must be starting earlier and earlier these days. I need to cut down on my drinking, especially if I'm getting hammered in front of total strangers.

Except they're not total strangers, are they?

I dig around in my jacket. Ben looks worried.

'I just need my cigarettes. You seen 'em anywhere? Hang on.' I find my Embassys in the inside pocket, struggle like a bastard to get them out – my limbs won't do what I want them to do right now – and then stop. 'Shit, I forgot. It's alright to smoke in here, isn't it?'

Ben doesn't say anything, but I see a pub ashtray on the table next to me. It's cracked but serviceable, got a weird brownish pattern on the side of it. I light the Embassy, take the smoke deep.

'Fuck me, that's the ticket.'

I rub at my gummed-up eye, look at my hand. There's blood on my fingers.

'I'm sorry,' I say, looking at the bloke. 'It's Ben, isn't it?'

Ben looks at the girl, who's sitting there with a bowl in her hands just in case I throw up again. She hands me some kitchen roll. I dab the blood from my fingers and the vomit from my shirt.

'I'm sorry, mate. I didn't think I'd throw up. Just –'

'It's the fall,' says the girl. 'You're just a bit nauseous from the fall.'

'Right. Anywhere I can wash up, d'you think?' I pull at my shirt. 'I'm minging.'

And then I remember.

'No. Wait. Shit.' I look at the pair of them, stick the cigarette in my mouth and say, 'Look, I'm sorry about this, but I've got to be off.'

The girl says, 'Mr Innes, I don't think you should go anywhere.'

I throw my other leg off the sofa, fight back a rising tide of nausea, try to breathe deeply.

'I have to.'

I've got an appointment. Got to get back to the flat, get changed and go to this opening at Paulo's. Can't go there stinking of vomit, can I? I've got to get my head clear, too. Don't know how long that's likely to take.

'Probably best to stay where you are for a bit longer,' says the bloke.

'That's kind of you – was it Ben?'

'Yes.'

'That's kind of you, Ben. But I think I made enough of an arse of myself already this afternoon.' I push on the arm of the sofa, rise unsteadily to my feet and smile at him. Try to keep my distance – my breath probably reeks, but I need to continue the deep inhale-exhale to keep the sickness at bay. 'I'll be good. Going to sound like a daft question, but did I bring my car?'

The girl narrows her eyes as she glances from Ben to me, and back again. Then she seems to relax, but she still doesn't believe that I'm actually walking out of here. 'It's outside, but you shouldn't be –'

'He'll be fine,' says Ben.

I catch a warning look.

Shit, I really must've acted up. This bloke – nice bloke too – wants me to leave. The state I'm in, I must've been a right twat. I hope I wasn't the one who gave him that bruise. I know I get a bit lairy when I've had a few, reckon I can punch out of my class. I put a hand on his shoulder to keep myself steady. Lower my head to stifle a belch that could turn liquid.

'Ben, I'm sorry, mate. I don't know what I did, but I'm sorry for being a twat.' I breathe out. 'It's these pills I'm on. Fuckin' doctor must've doubled my dose and not told me, eh?'

'Sure you don't need anything?' says the girl.

'Nah, I'm good. Thanks for looking after me and that, but I think I've got somewhere to be and I reckon I've outstayed my welcome.'

I head towards the hall, feel my way to the front door. My legs don't work, my head spinning, but I'm not going to look weak in front of these two. Got that terrible clenching sensation in my stomach that means I did something daft and I can't remember it, the same throbbing behind the eyes means I got drunk, got doped up, something, and I fell. Don't know what I fell on, but my head hit something sharp. Each step threatens to throw me on my arse, but I keep going, the smoke from my Embassy rising up into my eyes.

Fumble with the front door, and I'm out. I hang onto the doorway, turn to see Ben and the girl in the hall. Ben is breathing through his mouth; the girl's standing next to him with her arms across her stomach. Looks like she's going to start throwing up too.

Students. Must be. I know what they're like when it comes to drinking. Probably some fruit punch with more punch than fruit, even though I didn't see any evidence of a party.

The pain increases as I stumble back to my car. I shake four codeine into my hand and swallow them back with the taste of puke. Look in the bottle, and there's only a few left. I wonder what the fuck I've been up to that would make my back spike that much.

It doesn't matter. I know a man who can hook me up. I just have to drive there without killing myself.

THIRTY-EIGHT

Greg's my friend. He's my pal. He's the one with the key, the pills, the fucking *answers*. Driving back to my flat is an assault course, like one of those on *The Krypton Factor* or like one of the other things they had on that show, like the blocks you had to put together to make a giant K or those observation tests where you had to . . .

I've lost it. Whatever it is.

Like the old joke. Why did the supermodel stare at the carton of orange juice?

Because it said: Concentrate.

Hunched over the wheel, my back scraped. Squinting at the road through my one good eye. Couple of close calls with parked cars, my door-width distance creeping into an inch. Almost took off more than my fair share of wing mirrors.

I leave the Micra parked at an angle and fumble with my keys to swipe into the block. Take the stairs slowly and seriously. No fucking about when my coordination's this sketchy.

When I reach the landing, I look across at Greg's flat. There's the glow of his lava lamp. The little beauty, he's in. I ease myself round to his front door, leaning on the railing every step of the way. Ideally, I should've gone home, got cleaned up first, but this is more important. I knock sharply on his door, then retreat to the railing. Turn around, look over the side. I feel like throwing up again. In fact, I do, but the puke doesn't make it past my teeth before I gulp it back.

'Jesus Christ,' says Greg.

I turn around and smile. 'Greg, mate.'

'Jesus *Christ*,' he says.

'How are you?'

'What the fuck happened to you?'

'I had an accident, mate. Nothing that could've been helped. Look, I need to buy.'

Greg shakes his head, his arms folded. I can smell weed smoke wafting out from his flat. The sweet stink turns my stomach.

'No?' I'm still smiling. Still got the taste of vomit in my mouth. Can't quite register the word 'no'. Playing around with it in my head.

Get the old 2 Unlimited song in there: 'No, no, no?'

'You're fucked, Cal.'

'I haven't been drinking,' I say. But I have. Must've been. A bloke doesn't just fall over if he hasn't been at the booze. And I'm slurring, dizzy. That doesn't help my case right now, so I try to watch it. 'I swear to God, Greg, I have not been drinking.'

Over-enunciating now. Get a grip on yourself.

'Are you *bleeding*?'

'That's the least of it,' I say, touching my head. 'C'mon, I just need to buy. You want to bump up the prices, that's fine by me. It's kind of an emergency.'

Greg watches me for a second, then looks up and down the landing. He pulls a face, then pushes open the front door. 'Get inside.'

'Cheers, mate. You won't regret this.'

'Broad fuckin' daylight, you're coming round.'

I walk into his living room. Greg's sacked Cat Stevens, got himself some James Taylor, singing about fire and rain. It's mellow. I like it, sing along a bit in my head before I run out of words.

I lean against the wall. I don't want to chance the sofa. If I sit, I'll have to get up again. I don't plan on being here that long, and I'm having enough of a job standing upright.

Greg looks like he's about to say something, so I interrupt: 'I know, it's getting harder to get the codeine. You said that the last time.'

'You want the same as last time?' he says, crossing to the ashtray and picking up a spliff. Annoyance in his tone. He tries to melt it out with a hefty drag. 'Or d'you want what I've got left?'

'There a problem?'

He exhales a thick stream of smoke. 'I don't know. You come in here, broad fuckin' daylight –'

'You said that already, mate –'

'And you're all fucked up. I didn't think you'd do that.'

'Do what?'

'Act like a fuckin' junkie.'

I step forward, but keep my hand on the wall. 'Don't call me a junkie, Greg. You know I don't like that, mate. It's fuckin' rude.'

'You act like one, I'll call you whatever the fuck I want.'

'It's just that *word* –'

'Callum, don't think you can come round here and demand shit, alright? What'd I tell you when you first came to me, eh?'

I shake my head. 'This isn't the time –'

'I said I was glad you come round, mate. You were one of the few. Most of the bastards I deal with, they got their pupils in their back pocket. I got a reputation and a front to keep up, you think I got that rep because I let fuckin' junkies come round all hours of the day –'

'It's half four.'

'I'm *discreet*, I'm professional. I keep a low profile.'

'I know that, man.'

'And I maintain that low profile because I don't have people who look like they need a fuckin' fix hanging around plain as you like. Plus, I liked you coming round because you live just up the way and it was kind of like having a mate pop by who just like bought as a sideline thing, right? Got a medical condition, couldn't get it legit on account of how the government are fucking up our National Health, so you came to me. It felt like I was doing you a favour rather than taking your money.'

'Nothing's changed, Greg,' I say.

'Bollocks.' He points at me with the spliff. 'Maybe the other night when you were screaming up the fuckin' walls, you could still play off that medical thing. But a bona fide *condition*, it doesn't make fucked up and stupid, does it?'

'Who's fucked up and stupid?'

'Prove my fuckin' point, why don't you? Look at yourself, man. You're covered in puke, you're bleeding. You stink like you've been sleeping in your clothes.'

I wave a hand at him. 'You selling or not? 'Cause if you're not, I'm leaving. I can't be doing with this shite. I've got places to be. And yeah, I'm stinking. But you *lecturing* me's not going to get me clean, is it? You want to talk about fuckin' ethics, we can do it some other time when I've had a shower and I'm not in such a hurry. Until then, could you please do what you do best and get me my fuckin' pills?'

Greg looks at me, takes another draw off the spliff. He shakes his head, looking at me like I just asked him for crack. Hands me the spliff as he walks out the room. I take a puff on it, then a deeper drag, hold it in my lungs as long as I can. Calm me down, whatever it takes. My gut revolts against the taste and I cough out the smoke, grab onto the back of the couch. I notice gob on the upholstery, wipe it off with my free hand.

I ease myself round, put the spliff back in the ashtray and stick an Embassy in my mouth. Light it with a shaking hand. I can feel the back of my neck start to prick now, a knot above my eyebrow.

Greg better hurry back soon. I don't know how long I can smell myself and the smoke in here before my head goes too light to stand. I look around at the wall.

There's a bloody mark on his paintwork.

Greg appears, bag in hand. He holds it out to me. 'That's the last of it.'

'You doing me that lot?'

'Same price, take it off my hands. You're the only bloke I get it for. No call for codeine, but you know that.'

I reach for my wallet. 'You're doing me a favour then.'

'Nah, you're doing me a favour.' He presses the bag into my hand.

I give him money, try to smile. 'Always glad to help out.'

'That's not the favour.' He tucks the cash into his back pocket, crosses to his chair and slumps into it. 'The favour is, you don't come round anymore.'

'Come on, man.'

'Alright, so it's not really a favour, I'm telling you. You don't come around anymore. You want to score, you find someone else willing to put up with your shit.'

'What, because I'm a bit worse for wear? The fuck do you get off, Greg?'

He looks at the end of his spliff, blows the rocks aglow. James Taylor's still trying to mellow everyone out, but there's a place for his brand of homespun porch-folk, and this isn't it.

'Greg,' I say. 'C'mon, mate. You wouldn't believe the day I had. Trying to work this fuckin' case, I got all sorts of bizarre shit happening to me –'

'I don't care,' he says.

And that's it. Final word on the matter.

'We'll talk about this later,' I say.

Greg doesn't say anything. I push off the couch and guide myself to his front door. I'm already trying to calculate how long these pills are going to last me, but mental arithmetic was never my strong point, especially when my head's in the shed.

Lucky for me I don't have a long walk back to my flat. Any longer, and I'd be in serious trouble. I pull myself along the railing, bent double. When I can make out my front door, I tuck the pill bag in my pocket and grab the prescription bottle. I'll need to take the rest before I get in the flat. I've still got a shitload to do before I'm needed at the Lads' Club. I fumble with the child-proof cap, can't get the fucker open.

'Fuckin' *open*.'

I flick the cap, feel the bottle flip out of my hand. Swipe at it, trying to catch, but the prescription bottle spins into the air. I touch with the side of my hand but can't get my fingers to close. The bottle drops over the railing.

I watch it fall, spinning. Then it connects with the concrete, bounces out of sight.

Doesn't matter. I've got a bag of pills here. I take two, one at a time, slow and sure, then head for home.

THIRTY-NINE

My phone's ringing when I push into the flat. I dump the pills on the coffee table.

'Hello?'

'A courtesy call, Mr Innes.' There's the sound of heavy machinery in the background. 'Just to make sure you're still coming to the grand opening tonight.'

My fucking brain's gone foggy. I have to take a second to think about what I'm going to say.

'Course I am. Wouldn't miss it for the world.'

'I heard a pause, Callum.'

'Then you're going fuckin' mental, mate.'

'You remembered, didn't you?'

'Absolutely.'

Paulo yells at someone in the club. 'Lift and place the fuckin' table against the wall, don't try to fuckin' hump it there.' Back to me: 'You promised me you'd be here, Cal. Means a lot to me, this does. And from the RSVPs, it looks like we're going to be thin on the ground.'

'What happened?'

'This march,' he says. 'Got people too scared to leave their houses. Hang on a second.'

He puts his hand over the mouthpiece of the phone and yells at some more people. When he comes back, he sounds distracted.

'You know what, you pay peanuts, you get monkeys.'

'Who you got helping you out?'

'The usual lads. Would've thought by now, all this time I taught 'em how to smack people, they'd be able to take simple fuckin' instruction on where to put tables. But no, these lads are fighters, not movers. And you, you're positive you're going to be here.'

'How many times you going to ask me the same question, Paulo? When d'you need me there, mate?'

'We're not starting till seven.'

'So six thirty, right?'

'If you could. And I expect you to be presentable when you turn up.'

'When am I not presentable?'

'I mean wear your good duds. There's going to be a press presence.'

'Oh, fuckin' marvellous. I get to have my photo taken again.'

'You love it,' says Paulo. 'It'll keep you in the papers, and it can only be good for business.'

There's a terrible crash on the line. I have to move the phone from my ear. When I move it back, Paulo's turning the air blue at his end, telling someone to get the fuck out of the way, he'll sort it out, just *leave it*.

'What happened?'

'Nothing,' says Paulo, half to me, half to whoever's just fucked up. 'They're just setting up the trestles and they *need a fucking manual to do it*.'

'Trestles, eh? Going all out for the *Evening News*.'

'Yeah.'

'Great stuff. I should start getting ready.'

'Remember, *six thirty*. Don't make us come looking for you.'

'See you later.'

I put the phone down, lean on the table. This is not going to be fun.

Hot water beating against my back and neck, stinging against cuts and scrapes, my head down. I've already checked my face in the mirror. A wee gash above my eyebrow, but it doesn't look too serious. I'm not worried about the damage, just the appearance. I don't need to be noticeably beaten, don't want people to talk about it.

My clothes lie in a smelly heap on the floor of the bathroom. Means I'll have to streak to the bedroom, but I'm okay with that. Now I've soaped up and rinsed off, I've got a glass of cold water just within reach. I'm taking more pills to balance out the aches, the thumping behind my bad eye.

I need to maintain, even if it's just for a couple of hours. And I can feel the clouds parting, less like my brain's made of cotton wool. I can start to think again.

Greg's a wanker. That's all there is to say about that. He's a judgmental wanker. Who the fuck is he to get on my back about fucking ethics? He deals drugs. I don't see that as a humanitarian vocation. Don't see too many crack dealers popping down the hospice to give blood to the orphans . . .

Wait.

I run a hand over my head, open my mouth as water streams down my face. A memory jogged somewhere, but only a flash before it flies off somewhere else. It can't be important if I can't hold onto it. Another pill, another swig of water, then I step out of the shower and towel off, the skin on my face tight.

Look at myself in the mirror and reckon it'll do. I promise myself that I won't drink too much. My body's already taken enough of a beating from booze today.

Christ knows what I was doing drinking with students in the middle of the day. I should know better. But then after that weird longing I had when I was walking around the student union, the old what-if-life-had-turned-out-different bit, I probably just lost the plot a little.

It happens.

I check my watch – should be going. Shake my jacket and it feels light. I've got my wallet, my pills, my cigarettes, my lighter and my mobile. So, what am I missing?

I shake my head. Nothing. Got everything I need.

Check my watch again because I forgot the time. I'm doing okay.

On schedule. And everything's fine.

When I pull up outside the Lads' Club, I'm immediately disappointed. For some reason, I expected more excitement, people milling around outside the club, an Oscars party vibe, but the place is deserted.

I park the car, get out and head to the double doors. I push through into the main club. There's a couple of lads in the corner. Some more at a long trestle with glasses of red and white wine laid out, orange juice in wine glasses for the teetotallers.

There isn't any sign of a hedgehog. And while I knew there really wouldn't be, it doesn't stop that twinge of disappointment. It looks like I'm not the only one, either. Apart from the two lads I recognise from the club, there are a few more groups of them, mostly wearing school shirts and shoes. Milling around, look like they'd rather be at church than here right now. They're talking amongst themselves, but their voices are kept low, almost like they're plotting to tunnel their way out.

I see Liam standing by the sound system. He sees me, too. The kid keeps growing, it looks like. Last time I saw him he was tall enough, but reedy with it. Paulo's been working the lad into another weight class or something, because Liam's turning into a brick shithouse. I don't really want to talk to the kid, don't know what I'd talk to him *about*, given our previous shared circumstances, but before I can pretend I haven't seen him, he nods my way. I nod back.

Paulo's at the end of the room, talking to Andy Beeston. I head over, grab a glass of juice on the way.

When Paulo sees me, he smiles. 'You're on time.'

'Just about.'

'No, you are.' He's trying for jocular, but he can't quite manage it. 'Glad you could make it.'

'Not a problem.' I smile at Beeston.

We all stand there for a few moments, not talking. Beeston in particular looks uncomfortable with the situation, looking around the room. If he's searching for something to talk about it, he doesn't find it. So we keep standing there, Paulo and I sipping juice, Beeston with his white wine.

It's all very sophisticated and unbearable.

When Paulo clears his throat for the third time, I have to say something.

'Alright,' I say. 'What's going on?'

Paulo attempts another smile. 'I don't get you.'

'You sent out invitations, didn't you?'

'Yeah.'

'So why isn't this place packed?'

Paulo moves his shoulders. 'People, Callum. Never underestimate the power of apathy.'

Beeston shuffles his feet, looks into his glass of white wine.

'I thought you had a thing in the paper,' I say.

'He did,' says Beeston, not looking at me. 'More than one article. It's a good thing, this place, but you can't blame people for not wanting to come out tonight.'

'Why's that then?'

Paulo puts a hand on my shoulder. 'It's alright, Cal. Tell you, I don't think I'd be here if I could help it.'

I stare at him. Then Beeston.

Smile and say, 'Okay, someone going to tell me what's going on?'

'You didn't hear?' says Beeston.

'No. I didn't.'

'The march,' he says. 'You must've heard about it. Everybody's that scared they're going to come through Salford. No big deal, really. Just bad luck had to hold his opening the same night.'

I frown. 'What march?'

Beeston looks at me like I'm drooling. 'The ENS.'

Time for a shrug. 'ENS?'

'English National Socialists.'

'Right.'

The name rings a bell, but both Paulo and Beeston are looking at me like I should know all this. I put it down to my bad drunk, and then start to wonder how long I was actually out. When I catch Paulo about to ask me what's wrong, I say, 'They're the ones that're marching.'

'Yeah,' says Beeston.

'Oh, right, yeah, I remember now,' I say.

Beeston sips his wine. 'It's been in the papers all week, Callum. Of course now, it's a solidarity march for that student.'

'I know better than to read the papers,' I say, grinning.

Throwing it around the inside of my head. Trying to remember why that organisation rings a bell. And why it's tied to a student. Thinking now, I met a couple of students this afternoon, maybe they've got something to do with it.

Ben and what's-her-name.

Did she tell me what her name was? I think she did. I just can't remember.

When I look at Beeston, he's talking. And I realise I haven't heard a word he just said.

'Sorry? I didn't catch that.'

Beeston squints. 'I said, if you ask me, anyone who's locked themselves into their homes, they've got the right idea. I said I was already booked to cover this thing, otherwise they would've had me down in Rusholme tonight.'

'You're welcome,' says Paulo.

'Too right.'

I don't get it. What's Rusholme got to do with anything?

I'm about to ask when I remember.

'Rusholme,' I say. 'That's where they found . . . *David*, right? He's the student?'

It's starting to come back to me now, a headache coming along for the ride. Bits and pieces, but I can't quite grab onto the connections anymore. There's a march, and there's Rusholme, and there's this student David, but none of it fits together.

'It'll be carnage tonight, you mark my words. It's not often the ENS feel they've got a real reason to go marching. Things're going to *burn*.'

Something clicks.

'What'd you say?'

Beeston moves his head, brings Paulo and I into a huddle. He smells of aftershave. 'Keep this under your hat, but it's going to kick off bad tonight. Coppers've got the riot gear out. They're not taking any chances.'

'Been there,' says Paulo. 'You bring out the shields, they're brick magnets.'

'When were you there?' says Beeston.

I shake my head, try to focus. My fucking head is pounding now.

'Where's this again?' I say.

'Rusholme. Longsight.'

Rusholme. Longsight. Both places jarring memories loose.

'I was down in Rusholme today,' I say, and as I'm talking, more comes back to me. 'I think it was today. I talked to a lad down there, he said it was a couple of blokes who beat up David.'

There's a moment where Beeston seems to transform into a teacher I once had. She was a patronising bitch with a smile that I wanted to punch out, even when I was nine.

'Oh, you know who did it, do you?' he says.

I stare at him until he switches back to normal. Then I say, 'I'm not sure.'

'I've been asking the police about it. They've given me nothing as usual. Still pending –'

'An investigation?' I say.

'Something like that.'

I shake my head. The headache starts creeping out behind my eyes. 'Some bloke called Saeed and his big mate. They did it.'

Beeston looks interested. 'You got a surname for this Saeed?'

'Seems to me like you've heard of him already.'

'It's a common enough name, Callum.'

'Local gangster, or wannabe. I know his big mate's supposed to be just out of jail.' I look at Beeston. He sips his wine, waits for me to continue. 'You know David Nunn wasn't given a kicking just because he was a white boy, don't you? I mean –'

Ben. That girl with him.

Karyn.

Yeah, Karyn with a 'y', because she wants to make herself seem different. And it works because the 'y''s what makes me remember her now.

Trying to call me off the case because she only fucking knew that her boyfriend tried to burn down a house in Rusholme. *Did* burn down a house in Longsight. Her looking all worried because she thought Ben had done me some serious damage. And he *had* done serious damage, except I was too fucked up to notice it.

Me acting like I was drunk. Thought I *was* drunk. Covered in puke, not sure where I was, it was a good enough guess. More likely that than concussion.

I rub my good eye. When I look at Beeston, he has one of those wee tape recorders in his other hand.

'You don't mind if I get this on the record, do you?' he says.

The tape recorder.

Fucking *bastard*.

'I need to go,' I say.

'You feeling alright?'

'You look like you're about to throw up,' says Paulo. 'You want to have a sit down, mate.'

'I'm fine. I just need to go. Right now. I'll be back, okay? And none of this is on the fuckin' record yet, Andy.'

I don't turn around. Don't want to see the look on Paulo's face as I'm leaving. I push out through the double doors, light a cigarette and squint against the sunlight. Christ, it's not even seven yet and it feels like mid-afternoon. There's already sweat building in my collar.

I can't go back to Ben's, not unless I want another hiding. Besides, he's probably listened to the tape and erased it by now.

No, that's not the priority anymore.

David left his car in Rusholme. There has to be some evidence there, something I can use.

Problem is, the march has already started.

FORTY

The more I see, the more I think I'm not going to get out of this alive.

Police vans already congregating around the city centre. Policemen in full riot gear, just as Beeston said. Batons, shields, helmets scuffed from a thousand close encounters with bricks, bats and bastards. I ease off on the speed once I hit the southern part of the city, slow as a police van draws up behind me. In the rear view, I can see the driver, his hands gripping the steering wheel at the official ten-to-two. He's staring at the road with hooded eyes and probably seeing none of it. Thinking about the night ahead.

Already slipped past the main barricades now, and I start to wonder what the fuck I think I'm doing. What happens if I find the car? David's the one with the keys, so since when did I know how to flick an ignition? Can't even work the DVD player half the fucking time, and now I'm going to play at car thief?

No, all I need to do, I need to get some proof, that's all. Ben's got the tape, so that's out of the window, unless I drive back there and take it by force, which is highly unlikely considering he already fucked me over once today.

Maybe I won't get to the car at all. Rusholme could be a war zone by the time I get there. But if that's the case, then me lobbing a brick through a car window wouldn't look suspicious. Christ, everyone'll be doing it. And then I can grab something from the car. There's got to be something they left in the Beetle.

But self-preservation is a priority. No point in me doing this if it's going to be unsung. I need the papers on my side. I need them to make me into a fallen hero if this all goes pear-shaped.

Just in case. Always thinking, just in case.

I pull out my mobile and call Andy Beeston. Instead of hello, he says his name. Very professional. I can hear the background noise of the Lads' Club, what little there is. Doesn't sound like a lot's going on.

'You want a scoop, Andy?'

'You feeling alright, Callum?'

'Uh-huh, but that's not the story. You said yourself, there's more exciting stuff happening elsewhere.'

'Where are you?'

'On my way to elsewhere. Wilmslow Road.'

'Jesus, why would you be doing that?'

'Because there's a car down there that's more than likely got a bunch of petrol bombs in the boot.'

The sound of Beeston switching ears. The click of his tape recorder.

'Turn it off, Andy. I mean it. You keep taping me, I'll hang up.'

'I thought this was a scoop.'

'You turn off the tape recorder, I'll tell you more.'

Another click.

'Thank you. Now you're wondering why all this can't be on the record: I'm not sure of anything right now and I don't want to be quoted. Besides, it concerns Plummer. Donald Plummer came to me, he said there was someone threatening to burn his properties down. They'd already done one –'

'Longsight.'

'Correct. And they'd sent him a list of addresses with a cigarette burn in it, right? A ransom note without the ransom.'

'I didn't know this,' says Beeston.

'Yeah, you thought it was an insurance job. Well, that's not the case. Turns out the guy who did the Longsight house was going to do a house in Rusholme when he was interrupted. Now he's in a fuckin' coma. Name's David Nunn.'

'You what?'

'Got his arse handed to him in Rusholme because he was acting all suspicious and he got the attention of the wrong lads.'

'Hold on a second,' says Beeston.

'Haven't got time, mate. Write quicker or remember quicker, whatever the fuck you're doing. David Nunn used to rent one of Plummer's houses. You want to double-check, I'm sure the university will have a record somewhere. Now, Nunn was evicted. Not by me, but by the bloke you saw with me at the hospital. Name's Frank Collier.'

'Was the eviction legal?'

'Probably not, but who really gives a shit? Doesn't matter. Bottom line, the one file we had to tie Nunn to Plummer, it's been nicked. Anyway, the lad had a grudge, he was a fuckin' militant with it, decided that there wasn't enough being done about Plummer so him and his mate burned one of his houses. Trouble was, there was someone home.'

'You have any proof?'

'I had a confession. The other lad confessed, and I got it on tape.'

'Where's the tape?'

'I don't know. The lad lamped me with an ashtray. I think. I don't know where the tape is. He's got it. I think he's got the ashtray, too. Probably has.'

'Callum, you're not making any sense here.'

'I will if you fuckin' *listen* to me.' Shake my head. Can't seem to keep my thoughts straight. There's a growing pain at the back of my head, feels like it's spreading around under my ears. 'Rusholme, they tried to burn the house. They didn't. They argued. Some bloke stepped in. Saeed. The other lad did a runner. But his *car's* still there. It's a blue Beetle. That's the one that has the petrol bombs in the boot, I fuckin' know it. There's a Zippo in the front, but David doesn't smoke. Ben *does* smoke, because he's got an ashtray.'

A warning bleep from my mobile. I glance at the display. The battery's dying on me. Fucking typical.

'There's a Zippo,' I say again. 'He doesn't smoke, you get me?'

'Cal –'

'Just do some digging, alright? Do some *investigating*. I'm right.'

I pull the phone from my ear, beep him off. No point in trying to explain it any further. Too much for my brain to process, and it's difficult enough keeping my mind on the job, without having to do it for someone else. I chuck the phone onto the passenger seat as I reach for the painkillers in my pocket. I've got to shake this headache. Need to be lucid when I get to the car.

Into Rusholme now, and the streets are starting to fill with people. Supposed to be behind closed doors, all safe and tucked up at home, but nobody let these guys know. A quick scan of some of the people as I pass them in the Micra. They're wearing hankies or bandanas around their necks, some of them pulled up over their nose and mouth. Look like bandits, the lot of them.

I turn on the radio. White noise of barely controlled hysteria, translated into reportage. The march has already started, coming through the city centre. Coming south. Police are blocking off roads. There's already been some violence, the odd skirmish. It's the hottest night of the year so far.

And I'm stuck behind the barricades.

Another codeine. Can't shift the headache. Thinking that I've had one too many knocks to the old noggin recently. Wondering if these pills Greg gave me are any good. I wouldn't put it past the fucker to dose me with placebos, wouldn't put it past *God* to fuck with my medicine when I'm feeling like this.

I'm about to turn onto Wilmslow Road when a police van trundles in front of the Micra, blocking my way. I put my foot to the brake, stop the car before I hit anything. A copper looks my way. He must be roasting in all that gear he's got on. I unclick my seat belt and sit there for a second, trying to breathe. Then I wind down the window and gesture to the copper in the van.

'What's up? I can't go into Wilmslow, officer?'

'Cordoned off.'

'The march coming down here, is it?'

'It's coming close enough.'

'What am I supposed to do then?'

The copper shrugs under his stab vest. His shoulders barely move.

'Thanks,' I say, duck my head back inside and throw the car into reverse. A five-point turn later, and I'm pointed back towards the rest of Manchester. I take a jaunt around the block, find an alley that doesn't look like it would interest many people, and leave my car parked in the shadows. Grab my mobile and stuff it into my jacket pocket, get out of the car. Might be a daft thing to do, but I lock the car.

Start walking, see if I can circle round to a bit of the cordon that isn't quite so heavy. Further on down the road, maybe, where they're not as prepared.

Fuck it, you never know who's out this time of night, especially when there's going to be trouble on the streets. Reckon maybe I can smash a few heads before I get pounded into the concrete. And I *will* get pounded into the concrete. I'm painfully aware of that now. Whether I meet up with Eddie or Russ or any of the other marchers coming down here to burn the fucking place to the ground, someone's going to put me down tonight, I can feel it.

Call it a sixth sense, whatever. But I've been knocked around enough times that I can smell it coming now.

I keep walking, though. Because it's my job to keep walking, find a way in and get that car.

And why? When I already told Beeston everything I needed to. Why am I walking into the fucking riot to get this car? I don't need evidence that badly, do I?

Yeah, I do. Because as much as Beeston sounded interested, he'll do fuck all to prove it. Guy might paint himself as a crusading journalist – and fuck it, he might've actually thought of himself as one at some point – but he's just like every other jobsworth in the world. He gets told to write what's popular and easily digestible. He's not in the business of shocking anyone unless it helps whoever's in charge.

So they need something else. They need solid proof that a couple of fucking students were behind these fires, that it was a couple of naïve, angry wannabe revolutionaries that caused the riot that's about to happen. That it wasn't anything to do with racism or grand political statements, that the fear this city's feeling has nothing to do with the fires, and everything to do with how they're being sold to their 'enemy'.

And there's the chance that I might not make it out of here. In fact, if I'm going to be straight with myself, that chance is turning into a certainty the more I walk. Passing through into Viscount Road now, and I can already see the curtains twitch at the white face. There are people out here who've been waiting to put the boot into someone like me for a long time, because that kind of racism, it's not just the fucking province of the white blokes out there. Your man Saeed's living proof of that. See him and his ex-con mate round here, I'll have some trouble. And I don't think I can run that fast with this head and my back scraping at the same time.

I pass number sixteen and keep on. Take another pill for my head.

Feels like it's getting warmer the closer I get to Wilmslow Road.

And I can see the police lines already forming. The vans pulling up, blocking alleys and side roads. I can see riot shields and batons, helmets and boots. Like the entire constabulary are out in their gladrags tonight.

I keep as low as I can, duck into the end of Wilmslow Road as a police van approaches behind me. Keep expecting someone to shout at me, but I don't hear anything except my heart thumping in my ears.

Duck behind an Escort as a police van rolls past. Keep my head down, my face out of sight and grit the pain in my back away.

Yeah, there's a chance I'm not going to make it out of here. I knew that when I left the Lads' Club. And I couldn't give a fuck. Here's the thing – I've been trying all this time to live up to that fucking label they gave me, so I reckon maybe it's time I either live up to it, or die trying.

Sounds dramatic, but what the fuck.

Better to cark it and prove a fucking point, and in case I do, that should push Beeston to do something more than a two-line footer.

When the van moves away, I get to my feet and head into Wilmslow Road.

FORTY-ONE

I can hear the sound of the march coming like an approaching storm. The sky has the last glow of the evening replaced with false light.

They're coming closer. Christ, I can almost feel the tarmac rumble under my feet. The English National Socialists chanting. Something to do with justice. Their right, not their privilege. I keep to the walls, see the police arriving at the top of the road. They look like soldiers, except they're not armed that I can see. Lined up in the street, shields at the ready. Once they're in position, there's the odd shuffle of feet, but they're otherwise motionless. Just this implacable wall, something to guide people. Not riled yet.

In the opposite direction, right at the other end of the road, I can see the Beetle. Nobody's touched it and everything's working out so far. Nice and quiet, but it won't stay that way for long.

I make a move, take my steps with my back to the shop fronts. Behind me, I can see placards arriving as the marchers round the corner. The police already bristling as a unit, getting nervy. At the other end of the road, there's those blokes again, the bandanas up over their noses. Coming out of nowhere, disparate elements congealing into one mob, a glut at the end of the street.

But not moving forward, not yet. Just growing larger and staring beyond me as I hear the ENS marchers spill into Wilmslow Road.

A glance behind me: the police move now, forming a corridor, funnelling the march straight down the middle of the street. One of the uniforms at the end of the line is gesturing towards something out of sight. There's an engine sound forming a throbbing bassline to the chants, so I guess it's one of the police vans I saw earlier.

I can't walk now. Have to pick up the pace. Sprinting towards the Beetle.

If I can get in that car, fucking *break* into it, maybe get it off this road, somewhere safe, I can go through it. If not, I've got to grab whatever the fuck I can and get out of there. Something to prove the students were behind this. The Zippo, the leaflet, something else. I already told Beeston about the car. If he's got any sense, he'll call the police.

But then a lack of police really isn't the problem right now.

There's got to be a way of saving this. And that hope is enough to keep me moving.

A stone skitters off the tarmac next to me. I react to it, swerve but keep running. My lungs already tight against the inside of my chest, I have to stop, duck behind a Volvo.

Another stone, bigger, bounces off the bonnet of the car. Whoever it is, they're fucking aiming at me. I hazard a glance at the stone's origin – see that the gang of Asian lads at the end of the street have started a march of their own. Moving towards me, looking to meet the ENS head on.

And me in the middle.

I hunker down, skip to the pavement side of the Volvo and duck-walk my way to the Beetle. Hoping that the mob of National Socialists will keep the gang busy.

Another object thrown, this time a brick.

Nowhere near me now, this time connecting with one of the riot shields.

The chants from the ENS grow louder. I can't make out the words anymore, only the attitude. They've seen the Asian lads, the locals, and they're spoiling for it. Like Russ and Eddie said, beered-up and looking for a little blood in their mouths. So they might as well be chanting that there ain't no black in the Union Jack, the kind of front they're putting on, as well as the kind of reaction they get.

Shouts from the Asian lads, running feet.

Something slams against the road. There's a shout from the protestors. I can hear the clatter of riot shields now. Turning around, the police are trying to divert the march. It's not happening.

These guys didn't come here to protest anything; they came here to do some fucking damage. And these fucking busies are compounding the issue they came to shout about. So the marchers push against the police cordon. I look around and see the cop line stretch almost to breaking point. One of the coppers turns, and signals to the alley.

The roar of an engine, and one of the vans lurches out into Wilmslow Road.

I keep my head down, crouching by a car. The Beetle's within arm's reach, but I can't get there without giving away my position. And as much as I'd be fine with those Asian lads in any other situation, right now I get the feeling that they'll stomp the first white face they see.

Something's thrown at the police line.

That something multiplies quickly.

There's a tremendous groan from the police line. At least it sounds like that. Then a couple of the riot cops flip onto their backs. I turn to catch three coppers on the ground, trying to scrabble as the marchers stampede over their bodies. The other coppers stand as fast as they can, loose and warped links trying to bind back into a chain.

Enough is enough. This march is over. One of the brass has decided that the protest ends here. There's the sound of a loud-hailer squelching, *blaring*, someone with stripes on his uniform telling the English National Socialists and the Asian lads to disperse. That they should head home.

This is a disturbance of the peace.

Any further disturbance will be met with —

Too late. The floodgates are already wide open.

A fizz of a fuse, then the machine-gun staccato burst of

explosions. Bangers, fireworks, something like that. The rest of the police line back off, a flurry of red, white and blue sparking in a sea of busies. The assault's come from the ENS side, the police not expecting the white lads to kick off this early.

Another fizz. More fireworks. One of the marchers, a white guy wearing a hoodie, backs off, jumps and throws them at the Asian lads. The bangers hit the deck in front of the bandana gang, explode just as they retaliate with a volley of stones, bricks, whatever they can lay their hands on.

The protesters push halfway down the road. On either side, I can see the police ready their batons, clicked and swinging.

I switch, keep low, head to the Beetle and search the ground for one of the thrown bricks. Can't hang around here. If it's not fucking nasty already, it'll get here soon.

A cry from the crowd. One of the Asian lads with two coppers on him. One with the lad's right arm, the other taking his baton to the back of the lad's knees. Trying to buckle him, force him down.

The ENS have fragmented now, taking on the police line as well as the approaching Asian lads. I see the hoodie hit the ground under a dozen police-issue boots. One of the coppers kicks him face-up, the hoodie curling and screaming at the same time.

I grab a half-brick, pitch it through the Beetle's side window. Glass rains down onto the passenger seat and the alarm goes off. The noise bores right through my skull, jars the pain into agony. I hold onto the side of the car, the crunch of pebbled glass under my hand, try to focus, stop my knees from giving out.

Can't do it. The ground whips away from me in an instant, but I hang on, wait for it to whip back.

I need to get this car started. It's the only way. Drive the fucking thing out of this riot. Have a go at hotwiring it. It's about the only thing I can do now. Because if I don't have a vehicle soon, I'm going to get stomped to death out here.

If this headache doesn't kill me first.

I pull myself up, look through the smashed window. I can't see the Zippo anywhere. Last time I saw it, the lighter was sitting on the dash. No reason to think it'll have moved since then, not unless Ben's been back. But then how did he get into the car?

Focus.

A brick stots off the back of the Beetle. I turn at the noise, see the Asian lads fall back as the police push forward. I see the Met have regrouped a solid line, some of the marchers running in the opposite direction, some of them caught on the wrong side of the line. I see a couple of bandana-wearing lads putting the boot into a skinny lad. For a second his pained features flash into Eddie's.

'Go on, you take that fuckin' kicking, you cunt!'

Shouting cripples me. I scrabble at my suit pocket, my back hitting the Beetle as a gang of marchers barrel past me. I fumble out some more codeine, the world grown fucking small as soon as I see those pills.

Another brick bounces by my feet, hits me in the leg.

I twist, see the pills falling before I get a chance to react, my heart stopping for a split-second as they slip out of my hand.

I drop to the pavement. See a white guy in a Lonsdale shirt running towards me. Can't see his face, my vision's that wet.

I blink, and he's suddenly right in my face.

'The fuck, man?' he says.

I push him back. Hard. Watch him grab onto me as he goes. Kick him once in the kneecap and see him hit the bonnet of the Beetle at an angle. He creases his face.

'The fuck?' he's saying.

I turn, grab as many pills from the ground as I can and shove them into my mouth. They taste like talcum powder and grit. I swallow them with a parched throat, see the white guy dig into his pocket.

Thinking, fuck.

It's going to be a gun.

This is it. Happening again.

And this time, the guy isn't going to miss.

He's out of range for any Asian lads to come at him. I feel my bladder go. Just a little.

The guy brings a string of fireworks from his jeans pocket. A lighter in the other hand.

'The fuck, man?' he says. 'What you on?'

'I don't –'

He cranks the wheel on his lighter. And the fucking world's gone so slow, I can see the shower of sparks he makes as the flint catches. Then the flame, rising up to the fuse on the fireworks.

The fizz. Again so slow, the pitch rising as I realise where he's going to throw them.

He chucks the bangers into the car.

I see him break away from the Beetle, hurtle into the crowd, can't place the fizz of the fuse for a second before the bangers go off.

Then I pick up my feet and run. Back to the here and now, some more of the ENS have broken through to the Asians, who seem to be mostly wounded and back-pedalling.

But not beaten. Not yet.

A smash of glass and the sound of catching flames comes from behind me. I follow the noise to the Asians – they have their own fireworks, homemade, milk bottles filled with petrol. Fending off the ENS with everything they have. If their community's going to burn tonight, the Asian lads want to be the ones to do it.

One of the bottles smashes against the Beetle. The flames spread across the paintwork. I can already see the glow inside the car.

I'm slowing, pain in my chest. Pain in my head. Can't keep running, but I need to. I slam into one of the Asian lads, his face covered. He twists out of the way, reaching into his pocket. I see the flash of a blade and hold up my hands. All ready to fucking cry myself to safety if need be.

It's a sharp blade, but short. A fishing knife. But this guy's not going to use it. Too much water in his eyes – he's scared out of his mind. He pulls the bandana from his face. I can't see through the gloom, my head raging, my vision shifting in and out of focus.

I catch a crystal clear image for a moment.

Tariq.

'What the fuck did I tell you, man? I told you to stay at home.'

That's what I'm trying to say. Doesn't come out like that. I'm slurring, my speech lost, probably about the same time I lost the rest of my bladder.

'The fuck you doing here?' he says.

This headache, the pressure's fucking immense, feels like my skull's about to explode.

The car.

I remember the car.

I push him out of the way, start running again. My right leg buckles out from under me. I drop to the pavement, hit my right knee hard but I don't feel it. I fall further, try to break my fall, but my right arm refuses to take the weight. Hit the concrete with my shoulder and one of my front teeth. My vision blanks to a grey fuzz again, like I've had a gallon of vodka put straight behind the eyes.

Need to get out of the way.

My mouth filling up with blood.

My skull. It's going to crack wide open.

Can't hear much now. Can hear Tariq. He's shouting.

He needs to move. I need to fucking move. Try to get up.

Can't.

Try to twist onto my other side.

Can't.

Try to shout at Tariq, cry out for help.

Comes out spluttered, the right side of my face slack and numb.

And then the Beetle explodes. A flash of orange light tearing into the sky, it almost looks beautiful. I manage to roll onto my back, see the flames cut through the night. My vision flickers into clarity for a moment and I can see all the stars.

Tariq blocks them out, looks down at me.

'I can't move,' I say. I see the blood and spit spraying out of my mouth, but I can't feel it land. Just as I can barely hear myself speak. 'I can't –'

'Jesus,' mouths Tariq.

And, just before I die, I remember thinking that that's a weird thing for a Muslim to say.

FORTY-TWO

Dead for thirteen seconds. Unlucky for some.

Unconscious for a lot longer than that. Difficult to say how long, really. Once you throw in the trauma of resurrection, the whole shebang feels like a fucking decade. And when you finally crawl out of the darkness, when all your senses work to a degree, when you know where you are, what you're greeted with are the sterile walls of the local hospital and a mask over your face.

Makes you wonder why you bothered breathing again. Especially with that toxic smell of rubber in your nostrils and a raw throat.

Let the eyes focus in their own time: the coughers, bleeders, sniffers and moaners are everywhere. Might not be the same people, but they're familiar enough.

Surrounded by the dead and the dying, or at least playing the part with conviction. What's worse: I fit right in. I swallow painfully.

So what did me in?

It's not long before a doctor comes round to tell me in great bloody detail. I don't catch his surname, but he seems well versed in my medical history, so I leave it. And the answer to the question is, take your fucking pick.

Normally, the doctor tells me, it's easy enough to spot what actually kills a man. You can spot a knife wound, a bullet in the head (or what's left of it), the rictus of a massive coronary. It's also relatively easy to determine whether the dead man *stays* dead.

Hell, most of them do.

But my problem was my 'pluralistic' injuries.

He reels it off, a sad old song growing lyrics every day, it seems.

My bad back, that was a given. Jarring of the spine caused by a collision with a budget car. The ear – as well as the partial deafness caused by the close proximity of a gunshot – had the lobe blown off in a Californian desert. As the doctor points out, the ear looks worse than it is, but add it to my current complaints and I'm definitely out of the running to becoming Britain's Next Top Model.

Then there are the drugs. What the doctor calls my 'increasingly damaging attachment to Class B narcotics'. In my case, codeine and its derivatives.

According to the white coat, here's where I start being interesting.

Codeine in the bloodstream.

Doctor says that like I'm supposed to start blushing or something. Like I wasn't supposed to be taking it. If it's bad, I put it down to a dodgy batch from Greg. Otherwise, I don't see the problem.

Concussion. That's the next big word the doctor chucks at me. But I know what that one means. That's a serious problem, and the way the doctor tells it, I've had not one, but *many* potentially concussive blows to the skull.

Lucky me.

'Sounds . . . painful,' I say.

'It would be. Very painful. Which brings us back to the codeine.'

Right. Always back to that.

I get a lot of pain, I up my dosage. I up my dosage, I end up taking too many. An overdose, if you will.

Fine. I can handle that.

Except I can't. Obviously.

I try to ask him about the fucking stroke, but my sentences struggle out. Halfway through a word, I'll forget the sound, the meaning. Not all the time, but enough that I'm pissed off and scared in equal measure.

He sees it. Tells me it's dysphasia. Then waves his hand at me, tells me a little speech therapy'll do me the world of good. That all I need to do right now is think hard about what I'm going to say before I say it.

'What about . . . ?' I struggle.

What about me *dying*?

I draw a thumb across my throat, make a wet sound.

'Well,' says the doctor, smiling, 'that was an extreme reaction.'

I frown with both sides of my face. Only half of the frown is voluntary.

You ask me, he doesn't know why I died. Plus, he doesn't know how I managed to claw myself back into the land of the living.

The doctor leaves. I watch him go.

In the meantime, I have more pills. They keep me from moving, but smother that sensitivity to light and sound that he said was a direct hangover from the stroke.

Or the concussion. I lost track of what he was saying.

But I'm better. I *feel* better. Probably the new pills.

Plus the knowledge that I'd end up in hospital on a long-term pass at some point. Could have been physical or mental, but either way it was inevitable. I mean, I can't say I'm uncomfortable. I can't feel much of anything save the odd dizzy spell, a touch of creeping cold nausea and a flash-bomb migraine every other day. Otherwise, this ward's acted as a sedative.

It's just that realisation, I suppose – that we all end up fucked, one way or the other.

'Callum,' says Frank.

Still that problem with my attention span. I keep finding too many things that demand to be stared at.

Turn my head to see Frank shoving green grapes into his mouth. He's already got a bunch in there, he looks like the fucking Godfather. I don't remember him coming in, but he's sitting right by my bed, so I must've given him permission.

I nod at him. 'Y'alright?'

'I asked you a question,' he says.

'Uh-huh.' I look at the bottle of Lucozade on the bedside table and wonder where it came from. Then I get to thinking about how Lucozade bottles used to come with that yellow-orange plastic on them and how you don't see packaging like that anymore, like the little cardboard trays you used to get in Bountys.

'Callum.'

There's a newspaper sitting next to the pop. It looks unread.

I move my chin, like: *What'd you say again?*

'I asked you, did you see anything when you died?'

Right. Now I remember. Because Frank's impressed. He's never known anyone who died before. No one who made it back, anyway. Like that crazy old guy that bugged me for the first couple of days after I woke up, Frank's been wanting to know what it's like on The Other Side.

'Yeah.' I shake my head. 'Long tunnel. Floating. Violins. A choir.'

Look at Frank. He's rapt. Nodding.

'Bright light . . . at the end.' I point at myself, then pull a Superman pose. 'Floating towards it. And then . . . I saw my dad. All dressed . . . in gold. Like Liberace.'

'Cal, your dad's not dead.'

'My granddad, then.'

Frank pauses, a grape halfway to his open mouth, and his eyes narrow. 'You're feeling better, aren't you?'

'Makes you say that?'

'You're taking the mick out of us again.'

I smile with half my face. Must be pretty bad, because Frank looks at the bag of grapes in his lap.

Well, Christ, what was I going to tell him? That death was the ultimate nothing, as far as I can remember? No overwhelming sense of love or contentment, no feeling that I'd been a good person and could look forward to a pleasant afterlife.

Nothing.

Like there was no God, no heaven, just this eternity of darkness. And that didn't scare me one bit, because deep down, after all those years of hard pews, fire, brimstone and guilt, it was precisely what

I'd always wanted. No big man in the sky. No welcome party. No judgement day. No next life, just a lack of this one.

But I'm not about to tell Frank that. He's a Methodist. He wouldn't take it well.

'What about your face?' he says.

'Should be fine . . . a bit physio,' I tell him. 'S'what they told me.'

'My nan had a stroke, like.' Frank plucks another grape from the stalk, rolls it around between thumb and forefinger, then puts it in his mouth. 'She'd get words mixed up all the time, like instead of wanting chicken for dinner, she'd want pelican, stuff like that.'

'Right.'

'Her face didn't get better.'

'She didn't have . . . physio. Did she?'

'I don't know what she had.'

'I'll be fine.'

I raise my right hand to my right cheek. Feel the stubble growing there, rough against my fingertips. But everything else is slack there, my face dropped on one side. Now that I think of it, the doctor hadn't mentioned the physio working on my face. He just talked about the effects of the stroke as a whole.

And what a fucked-up word *that* is. You *stroke* a cat; it's a soft, gentle movement. Pleasant. What the word doesn't automatically bring to mind is the agony of the actual event. What it doesn't tell you is that you'll lose the feeling and motor skills in the right side of your body or that, when you eat, you'll have the after-dentist dribbles because of that paralysis. And it certainly doesn't tell you what you'll look like if you manage to survive. Frank's healing up, but he's still no beauty. And if he can bear to look at himself in the mirror every morning, there should be no reason why he can't look at me straight on now. I haven't seen a mirror yet. Don't want to. The sidelong glances are enough to tell me I'm not ready yet.

'I'm sorry about what happened,' says Frank.

'Not your fault.'

'Brought you a paper.' He nods at it.

'I saw. Thanks.'

'Should've been saving them for when you got better, but there wasn't that much about you.'

'Hey, maybe . . . if I'd *died*,' I say, trying to smile.

'Maybe.' Frank doesn't look at me, nodding. 'You want me to fetch it for you?'

'Yeah.'

He moves the bag of grapes from his lap, drops them on the bed next to me, then looks suddenly guilty as he sees the grapes are now mostly stalk. 'Uh, I ate some of your grapes.'

'Not a problem.'

'You sure?' Frank hands me the paper. 'Still some left if you want 'em. I just get a bit uncomfortable, have to do something.'

'Hospitals, right? It's okay, Frank. You did your bit. Appreciate it. You don't have to . . . keep me company.'

'It's my condition,' he says. 'The antiseptic smell and that.'

'It's fine.'

Frank nods to himself. 'It's just . . . There was something I wanted to ask you.'

'Shoot.'

He looks behind him. Wondering if he should take his seat again. He decides against it, looks at his shoes instead.

'You'll probably hear about it anyway, but Don's left Manchester.'

'For good?'

'I don't know. I mean, you didn't read it, but the papers were being pretty harsh on him.'

'He deserved it. He's a twat.'

'Well, he's gone. He took his car back and he went.'

'Right.'

Frank glances at me, clearing his throat at the same time. 'And, well, I was wondering, y'know, if that job offer was still going.'

'What job offer?'

'Remember, you said that maybe when you went back to the PI thing, you'd have an opening for me.'

'Did I say that?'

'Yeah. You did.' Frank moves his head, raises one hand. 'Look, sorry to bring it up. It doesn't matter, Cal. You're probably not in the best shape right now. I'll let you have your rest.'

He makes a move to go. I don't stop him.

'We'll talk. About the job. When I get out of here, eh?' I say.

'Right. I'll leave you alone, then.' He stops, points at the paper without looking at me. 'I don't know if you're interested, but there's a bit about you in the paper.'

Frank holds up his hand again, this time as a goodbye wave, then heads up the ward. I can see the slight limp in his walk. Yeah, he's healing, but there's some damage in him they'll never be able to put right. I don't remember promising him anything, but he was good on the doors, so I might have something for him.

Fuck it, who am I kidding?

I open the newspaper. Try to read through a squint; the light's too bright for me to focus for long.

David Nunn. Out of his coma. Much rejoicing. Family and friends look forward to welcoming him home.

And there's the picture: those same family and friends with David in the middle. He'd look more like a recently freed hostage if it wasn't for the fact that someone's taken the time to shave him. The skin's taut over his cheekbones. That's what a liquid diet does to a man.

The first thing he's going to do?

'Have a few pints with my mates.'

Nothing about the police. No mention of Ben. No mention of Karyn. I keep looking for their names, their photos. Anything with a gaudy headline. Talking of which, there's nothing about Donald Plummer either.

Getting to the point where I think I've just dreamt the whole fucking thing.

Then I turn the page, see the double-spread on the riots – THE AFTERMATH – and it's one week on. I check the date on the front of the newspaper.

Christ. Time has a way of melting away when you're under heavy sedation.

Back to the paper: police investigating . . .

I have to rub my eyes. Close them in a slow blink, then return to the newsprint.

Police investigating the car bomb on Wilmslow Road that took the lives of three Asian youths. Sources have indicated that the bomb – fucking hell – may have been a direct plant by the English National Socialists.

Sources. A wonderfully vague term, meaning they just made this shit up.

Witnesses say that a number of suspicious-looking Caucasian men had been seen loitering around the car – a blue Volkswagen Beetle – in the days prior to the explosion. Then there's a vague list of descriptions fitting these alleged bombers. One of them matches me, but I obviously haven't been taken in to help police with their enquiries, because it also matches half of Manchester. The other two I recognise as David and Ben. But again, that's only because I know who they are.

There's a picture of Jeffrey Briggs, his face twisted into full-on denial. Playing it Nixon, refusing to acknowledge the allegations. I stop, check who wrote it.

Sure enough, with words like *sources,* it's a Beeston byline.

And isn't that the problem with journalists? They spend so much time making shit up, when they're confronted with the truth, they don't believe a word of it. Probably thought I was off my head on medication. Playing it up, trying to hold on to my hero status. Or else he does believe me and the only way he can put it out there is through *sources.*

I don't know that I would've believed me, mind. Would've called myself deluded and left it at that, most likely.

Was I deluded, though?

According to what's sitting right in front of me, I was. There was me thinking it was David Nunn and his mate burning houses, but it can't have been. Had to be the English National Socialists, a militant strain of them, anyway. They were the ones who showed the foresight if not downright psychic fucking ability by planting a car bomb in the middle of a riot. It means they can be fingered for the attacks, too. After all, who's going to believe that a couple of students were responsible for one of the biggest race riots the city's ever seen?

Who would *want* to believe that? Especially when Briggs and his boot boys have been taking up too much airtime, making the place look bad.

No, Beeston knows his audience. They don't want a human angle unless it's either cute or tragic. Can't get their heads around anything that isn't black or white, spelled out for them in an eighteen-or-over headline font. Tell people students did the houses, the ENS did something else, that's too much information to process. Tell them it's all the English National Socialist party's fault, you're on safer ground. Now Plummer's out of the picture, and now it's obvious he didn't burn his own property down, Beeston and the *Evening News* lot need to give the public someone to boo. And Jeffrey Briggs is that someone.

As for me, Frank's right. There is a bit about me, but I almost miss it. The piece is buried on page sixteen, barely three lines. Saying I'm out of critical condition and should be back to work soon.

Above it, a huge article on the Eccles Youth Group and their new production of *A Funny Thing Happened On The Way To The Forum*.

Huh.

How quickly they forget.

FORTY-THREE

As Paulo opens the door, this weird smell hits me. Air freshener. Bleach. No smoke, no smell of spilled lager, vodka, vomit, pasties or Pot Noodles. A clean smell. Actually, it smells like the fucking hospital, if I'm going to be honest. But I don't say anything. The big lad's done a lot of work in here.

'Welcome home,' he says.

He ushers me into my flat, his hand on my arm. My other side's propped with a stick they gave me at the hospital. Just one item in a clutch of pensioner goody-bag souvenirs they foisted on me when I was fit enough to leave. It's the first time I've used the stick – the fuckers wheeled me to the door and Paulo took on pushing duties after that – and I'm still not comfortable with trusting my weight to a bit of wood. Supposedly the lifetime of physio appointments they gave me will make that better.

But as Frank said, physio doesn't help my face. Paulo hasn't mentioned it, but there was a definite reaction when he saw me in that fucking wheelchair. I looked like a basket case, most likely. Shaved, bathed and freshly dressed, but a basket case nonetheless. Maybe even worse for my clean and sober look – the terminal patient on one last day trip.

See, now. I should watch that. That's just the kind of negative thinking I've been warned about. The kind that Paulo's trying his best not to encourage. But also the kind that I can't help but drift into.

Especially when my flat looks like a show home.

He probably thought it was a good idea. And, on paper, it might well have been. Clean up the place for my return, I was bound to love it. Like starting afresh, the slate wiped clean. Like D:Ream once famously sang for Blair, things can only get better.

And we all know how that turned out. For D:Ream *and* Blair. No reason to think it'll work out any different for me. Still, it's a nice thought.

The trouble is, I come home to a spotless house, I'm reminded of the fact that I died. That it would probably be like this if I'd stayed dead, my possessions taken out or hidden away, some other tenant shown around within the month.

I don't say any of this. No sense in spoiling the moment, and what else could Paulo have done? Left it like the shithole it was?

'Thanks, man.'

He helps me to the couch. I rest the stick against the arm and it promptly drops to the floor.

'I got it,' he says.

I wave him off. 'Not a fuckin' . . . in-*valid*.' It doesn't sound right, so I try it again: '*Invalid*.'

'Okay.'

I don't look at him, but I can feel his stare. I need to think more about what I'm going to say. Otherwise I fuck up a word and it pisses me off.

Then we've got this long, uncomfortable pause. Him waiting for me to simmer down, me waiting for something to happen, sometimes drifting off.

Not now, though. Too busy feeling shitty for shouting at him. And knowing I have to swallow this back – have to stay positive.

'You want a drink?' he says.

I reach for the stick, say, 'Murder one.'

'Tea or coffee?'

'Stronger.'

'You shouldn't be drinking.'

I grab the stick, lean back into the couch and realise that I'm winded. I catch my breath and put my head against the back of the couch, look at Paulo. 'I think I'm entitled to a . . . beer. If there's one in the fridge. Besides . . . I've got a fuckin' throat on.'

'I thought you might say that,' he says, 'so I got some in. Didn't think you'd jump on them right away, mind.'

'Haven't had a drink. Fuck knows how long.' I reach into my jacket pocket, pull out my cigarettes, nod at them. 'Haven't had . . .'

Paulo disappears into the kitchen. I reach across to the stick – thought I saw it move in my peripheral vision – and make sure it's still leaning against the arm of the couch. Then I tug at the hospital bracelet. I hadn't realised I was still wearing it.

'Scissors?' I shout to Paulo.

'You want scissors?'

'Yeah.'

'Will do.'

He comes back in with a beer and some scissors, holds the scissors out to me handle-first. I take them, snip off the bracelet and hand them back. Then crack the can of Kronenburg, take a drink. Bubbles scrape up my throat, my back teeth twinge with the cold. I put the can down, light an Embassy. That first drag makes me grateful I'm sitting down. Been so long since I've lit up, my lungs must've cleared out. Time to put some tar down there.

'You settled in now?' says Paulo.

I take another swig and sit back on the couch. 'Just about.'

'Good. Your brother called.'

'Okay.'

'He left a message. Says can you call him as soon as you get it.'

I shake my head, look at the phone. 'Won't be important. Do me a favour. Delete it. Don't want the . . . big family update.'

Plus, I'm not in the mood to share my own bad news.

Paulo moves to the answering machine, deletes the message. He leans against the table, folds his arms. Watches me.

'So,' he says, 'what's happening, then?'

'With what?'

'With you,' he says. 'You going to go in for physio, all that?'

'I have appointments.'

'You going to keep them?'

I frown. 'Yeah. If I can. Why?'

'Just curious,' he says. 'Looking forward to having you back at the club.'

'How is it?'

'Fair to middling.' Paulo blinks. 'Some problems. Nothing that couldn't be sorted in your absence.'

'Kind of problems?'

'Nothing you need to worry about. Had a guy come round looking for you, name of Frank Collier?'

'Frank, yeah.' I'm about to call him Daft Frank, but it doesn't trip off the tongue the way it used to.

'Worked with you, am I right?'

I nod. 'Kind of.'

'Well, I set him to work in the back office.'

'Sorry, what?'

'Just keeping your chair warm for when you get back. Got your new office set up, put ads in the Yellow Pages, got the press involved for when you're up and about. When you walk through them doors again, you'll be as official as an ex-con's ever likely to be.'

'No,' I say.

The look on Paulo's face doesn't flicker. 'What's the matter?'

I have to concentrate, stare at the floor as I say, 'I can't do the . . . PI stuff anymore. Me and Frank.' Shake my head. 'Haven't got a . . . *functioning* . . . body between us. No way.'

'I don't get you. Frank's been doing great stuff while you've been away. And I don't know why you wouldn't go back to doing investigation work. From what Beeston told me, you solved the case –'

'Solved the case?' I flick ash, spiking my back. 'I got blown up. Two . . . *arsonists* got off . . . scot-free. How's that solving? Wrongs did not get righted. Wrongs just got more . . . fuckin' *wrong.*'

I'd stand up and walk out if I could. The way Paulo's looking at me, feels like I'm pinned to the fucking sofa. But then I was under the impression that given everything that's happened, I'd be coming back to a grunt job, something safe. I didn't expect this big poof to start making decisions for me. And I know it's a cunt's thing to think, just as I know he's probably put in a lot of work on my behalf, but the last fucking thing I want to hear is how anxious he is for me to go back to killing myself.

'Right,' he says. 'I get you.'

'Nothing against you. Paulo. I swear to God. I'm flattered. And grateful. For what you've done. And even Frank . . . Fuck it. The bloke wants to be a PI . . . I wish him the best of luck.'

'You're not in the best frame of mind right now,' says Paulo. 'You think about it.'

Shake my head again. 'No. Don't need to . . . think. About it.'

'Cal.'

'*Can't* fuckin' *think*. About it. You see me?'

Another pause. Him waiting. I suck my teeth, sit back.

'What did you think was going to happen?' he says. 'You think you were just going to go on the sick?'

I shrug.

'Man's got to work, Callum. You can't sit around here staring at the fuckin' walls.'

'No?'

'No.' He unfolds his arms, checks his watch. 'I should be going.'

'Right.'

'Don't drink too much. Give us a call on the mobile if you get into any bother, alright?'

'I won't.'

'Don't bother getting up.' He winks at me. 'I'll see myself out.'

I watch him leave the room, wait until he's out of my flat before I put the cigarette in the ashtray, feel around in my jacket pocket for my pills.

And come up short.

I take my jacket off, empty the pockets. Nothing.

The bastards must've taken the pills off me for some reason. And there's that twinge in my back already. I know it'll spread given half a chance. What the fuck am I supposed to do, subsist on beer and cigarettes?

Then I remember Paulo carrying my jacket for me as he wheeled me out of the hospital.

Jesus fucking Christ. I pull myself up on the arm of the sofa, grab my stick and struggle to stand. When I get onto both feet, I hobble over to the phone.

Pick it up and start dialling Paulo's number.

Full of hell, reckon I'm going to ask the cunt right out why he stole from me. Thinks it's a fucking joke, nicking a man's medication. And it's not like I'm up and about, walking around all healthy. I need those pills to get me through the day.

My back spikes. I suck in breath at the pain. Lean over the phone table and mutter about Paulo as I exhale. That fucking bastard, he's stranded me in the flat. He knows I can't go out. Even if I could, I couldn't go back to Greg again.

No, maybe I could. Maybe I could persuade him, tell him what happened. Fuck's sake, I was concussed. He'd understand.

I grab my stick, start for the door, but the pain doesn't let me get further than the couch. I ease down onto it, take a breath. This isn't good.

The pain's only just started. I grab my mobile from the coffee table and speed-dial Paulo.

'The pills,' I say.

He's calm. 'What about them?'

'Fuck you done?'

'It's for your own good, Callum.'

'Doesn't fuckin' . . . *feel* like it.'

'You in pain?'

'Yes.'

'You sure?'

I scream it: 'Fuck-in' *yes.*'

'I left you some cocodemol, Callum. Take those.'

There are pills on the table in front of me, alright. A box of them, prescription. A bottle of water next to them. There's a ball of pain in my throat. I try to swallow it back.

So much I want to say to him. Want to fucking beg him to bring my pills back, because I've tried cocodemol and they're nothing, they're useless. Sticking plaster on a fucking bullet wound. He doesn't have the right to take away my medication like this. He's not qualified to make those decisions. If the doctor didn't say anything about it . . .

'You can't do this.' Take a deep breath, concentrate. 'Got a . . . *medical . . . condition.*

'No,' says Paulo. 'No more excuses, son.'

Breathing hard through my nose now. Can't make my fucking mouth work. Can't tell him that these aren't excuses, these are reasons. Thinking he's a cunt for taking advantage. Trying to get a sentence out. Trying to get *anything* out.

'Take the cocodemol, son,' he says. 'Get some sleep.'

'Fuck –'

'I mean it. We'll talk later, okay?'

He disconnects.

I hold onto my mobile, stare at the pills on the coffee table. Might as well be fucking Anadin, the good they'll do. There's this tremendous pressure in my chest, like a scream trying to get out, and whatever burns in my throat can't be swallowed. Water in my vision now, I can't see properly. I press the heel of my hand to my eye and think.

There's got to be someone I can call. Someone who'll either sort me out or run an errand for me. Not Paulo, obviously. Can't trust Frank to do it, either. And there's no one else I can trust. Then I realise there's no one else in my life.

Stare at the carpet, rub away the tears. Then I look at my mobile, search through the contacts for Greg. It'll be okay. I'll just call him. We'll sort it out.

His name is missing from my phone. Someone's been in, erased it. And I'm guessing, but that someone's probably Paulo.

Fuck it. I don't need to speed-dial. I've got the number committed to memory.

I dial the 0161, then the first three digits of Greg's phone number. A brief moment where I think I've got it, then the rest of the number skips out of my head.

Shit.

I concentrate, try to remember, but it's no use. Meanwhile, the pain in my back gets worse. I leave it much longer, I won't be able to move.

No more excuses. Fuck him. Who the fuck does he think he is? Sounds like my bastard brother.

I lean forward, exhale slowly to kill some of the pain, then snatch the cocodemol from the coffee table. Tear into the box, uncap the water and take four pills.

Then I sit there, staring at the blank television. And hope the pain goes away.

Acknowledgements

As always, thanks to Team Polygon and Team Harcourt, for the filthy lucre and encouragement. Thanks especially to Alison and Graeme Rae for not letting this particular book wander out there with its ignorance showing. Team Publicity & The Printed Word, and the double-team of Sarah and Kenny for reminding me to breathe. Helen Stanton for babysitting at the launch party and introducing me to her mam, and everyone who attended the aforementioned launch party. Thanks also to Sylvia Campbell and Tony Anderson, for being gaffers with heart and letting me work a fifth less than I used to. Thanks to Special Agent Gerald of The Agency Group, for outstanding services to author neuroses. Also to 'Charlie's Angels' and Del for letting me use their names (can't sue me now . . .). Also, Sarah King at IPC Media for the Tom Waits quote and Kevin Burton Smith for reminding me of the joys of Cat.

Special thanks to those who bought, begged, borrowed or stole the previous books. I know who you are. In fact, I'm watching you right now.

Extra special thanks to Allan 'Old & Peculier' Guthrie for his eyes and ears. And extra, extra special thanks (bowing and scraping included) to my beloved missus, without whom none of this would be happening.

Indirect thanks: Mr Waits. Mr Cornwell. Mr Byrne. Mr Guthrie (Woody). Mr Islam. Mr Gano. And of course, The Diamond.